Biblioasis International Translation Series
General Editor: Stephen Henighan

Since 2007, the Biblioasis International Translation Series has been publishing exciting literature from Europe, Latin America, Africa and the minority languages of Canada. Committed to the idea that translations must come from the margins of linguistic cultures as well as from the power centres, the Biblioasis International Translation Series is dedicated to publishing world literature in English in Canada. The editors believe that translation is the lifeblood of literature, that a language that is not in touch with other linguistic traditions loses its creative vitality, and that the worldwide spread of English makes literary translation more urgent now than ever before.

1. *I Wrote Stone: The Selected Poetry of Ryszard Kapuściński* (Poland)
Translated by Diana Kuprel and Marek Kusiba

2. *Good Morning Comrades*
by Ondjaki (Angola)
Translated by Stephen Henighan

3. *Kahn & Engelmann*
by Hans Eichner (Austria-Canada)
Translated by Jean M. Snook

4. *Dance with Snakes*
by Horacio Castellanos Moya (El Salvador)
Translated by Lee Paula Springer

5. *Black Alley*
by Mauricio Segura (Quebec)
Translated by Dawn M. Cornelio

6. *The Accident*
by Mihail Sebastian (Romania)
Translated by Stephen Henighan

7. *Love Poems*
by Jaime Sabines (Mexico)
Translated by Colin Carberry

8. *The End of the Story*
by Liliana Heker (Argentina)
Translated by Andrea G. Labinger

9. *The Tuner of Silences*
by Mia Couto (Mozambique)
Translated by David Brookshaw

10. *For as Far as the Eye Can See*
by Robert Melançon (Quebec)
Translated by Judith Cowan

11. *Eucalyptus*
by Mauricio Segura (Quebec)
Translated by Donald Winkler

12. *Granma Nineteen and the Soviet's Secret*
by Ondjaki (Angola)
Translated by Stephen Henighan

13. *Montreal Before Spring*
by Robert Melançon (Quebec)
Translated by Donald McGrath

14. *Pensativities: Essays and Provocations*
by Mia Couto (Mozambique)
Translated by David Brookshaw

15. *Arvida*
by Samuel Archibald (Quebec)
Translated by Donald Winkler

16. *The Orange Grove*
by Larry Tremblay (Quebec)
Translated by Sheila Fischman

17. *The Party Wall*
by Catherine Leroux (Quebec)
Translated by Lazer Lederhendler

THE PARTY WALL

CATHERINE LEROUX

THE PARTY WALL

TRANSLATED FROM THE FRENCH BY
LAZER LEDERHENDLER

BIBLIOASIS
WINDSOR, ONTARIO

Originally published as *Le mur mitoyen*, Éditions Alto, Quebec City, Quebec, 2013.
Copyright © Catherine Leroux, 2013
Translation copyright © Lazer Lederhendler, 2016

FIRST EDITION
Second printing, September 2016

Library and Archives Canada Cataloguing in Publication

Leroux, Catherine, 1979-
[Mur mitoyen. English]
  The party wall / Catherine Leroux ; translated from the French by Lazer Leder-
hendler.

(Biblioasis international translation series)
Issued in print and electronic formats.
ISBN 978-1-77196-076-2 (paperback).--ISBN 978-1-77196-077-9 (ebook)

  I. Lederhendler, Lazer, 1950-, translator II. Title. III. Title: Mur mitoyen.
English. IV. Series: Biblioasis international translation series

PS8623.E685M8713 2016   C843'.6   C2015-907395-2
                C2015-907396-0

Published with the generous assistance of the Canada Council for the Arts and the
Ontario Arts Council. Biblioasis also acknowledges the support of the Government
of Canada through the Canada Book Fund and the Government of Ontario through
the Ontario Book Publishing Tax Credit. Biblioasis also acknowledges the financial
support of the Government of Canada through the National Translation Program for
Book Publishing, an initiative of the *Roadmap for Canada's Official Languages 2013–
2018: Education, Immigration, Communities*, for our translation activities.

Edited by Stephen Henighan
Copy-edited by Allana Amlin
Cover designed by Kate Hargreaves
Typeset by Chris Andrechek

PRINTED AND BOUND IN CANADA

MIX
Paper from
responsible sources
FSC® C004071

Contents

Weeds
(MONETTE AND ANGIE)

THE TWISTING wind wraps itself around Angie's ankles, a ground-level wave that takes her by surprise. The wind, as a rule, does not linger at people's feet. Except the strong, low wind produced by a passing train. As if to trip you up. She looks down to examine her shins, her knock-knees. The children she knows are simply thin, or else they are chubby, plump, fleshy. Angie is nine years old and as gnarled as a crone. She resembles the pine trees growing on mountaintops. The shape of her fingers and toes is complicated, and her elbows protrude from the middle of her spindly arms, two black pearls mounted on taut wires. She dreads the day her breasts will appear, convinced as she is that they will emerge, not like the pretty apples flaunted by the girls in junior high, but like two angular bumps, two angry fists pounding their way through her chest.

Inside, Monette is still negotiating with her sandals. Though perfectly capable of putting them on, she takes an inordinate amount of time to fasten the straps because even the slightest misalignment of the Velcro strips is intolerable to her. She attaches them, detaches them, repositions the hook side over the loop side with the concentration of a Tibetan monk, inspects her work, finds it wanting, and starts over. Under the silky rays of the sun, Angie does not lose patience. While waiting for her little sister, she contemplates the languid swaying of the willow, their tree, the biggest one on the street.

Mam told them, "It's nice out. Go for a walk!" She will use the time to swab down the house, a house so old and memory-laden that cleaning it is well-nigh impossible. Still, come May, Mam scrubs everything, including the wooden floors made porous by the floodwaters and the windows turned chalky from being permanently fogged-up.

Monette finally comes out into the bright daylight, blinks and wipes a tear from the corner of her eye. Though dazzled, she manages to find her sister's hand. As usual, she twitches at the touch of the callused palm, which reminds her of the rough side of Velcro, but the next instant her own skin nestles in it as if it were the comforting cloth of an old woollen blanket. Together, they walk down the four cracked concrete steps. The crack in the second-to-last stair looks like a dragon. She avoids treading on it. The pavement leading to the sidewalk is also broken and has weeds sprouting in the gaps. Mam does not pull them out and has taught her daughters to respect these humble shoots. "There's no such thing as weeds. That's just a name for some flowers thought up by racist gardeners." Monette ruffles their petals with a caress.

As always, the moment they reach the street they instantly leave behind the world of home. Yet no fence separates the front yard from the avenue. There is, however, an invisible barrier that makes it possible to be completely oblivious of what transpires on the other side and that hides the house from strangers, Angie hopes. Two boys go by dribbling a basketball. They wear loose-fitting t-shirts and their skin is coated with a fine mist. Their voices are loud and they spout obscenities. Angie covers her younger sister's ears. Monette has heard far worse, but Angie believes in the gesture of covering her ears, in the intention behind it. Once they've let the teenagers pass, Angie motions with her chin in the direction they're to walk: south. Before starting out, Monette looks down, examines her sandals, hesitating momentarily. Then she sets off, her pudgy little hand welded to her sister's.

The street is divided in such a lopsided way that it seems about to keel over, like a boat in which the passengers have all gathered on the same side. The houses on the eastern side are narrow and dilapidated, and the paint on most of them is peeling off in delicate white plumes; across the street, they are massive, stately, adorned with a complex arrangement of balconies and bay windows. Mam claims the railroad is the reason the east side of the block has such modest dwellings. No one well-off wants to move there, right beside the tracks. But surely, Angie says to herself, the residents across the way must also hear the whistle and the inhuman squealing of the train.

As usual, Monette pulls Angie by the hand to cross the road and walk past the luxurious homes, but her sister rarely gives in. The small houses remind Angie of her own; she seems to know them by name, and their windows, though cracked, watch the girls benevolently as they go by. By staying on this side, Angie feels she is restoring balance and keeping the neighbourhood from capsizing.

At the fifth intersection, the row of posh-looking residences tumbles over a wide cross street and gets dispersed in a middle-class district. The area, according to Mam, was developed years ago in the hope of attracting prosperous Black families. Today it's almost deserted. Monette and Angie continue along a sparsely populated stretch of road riddled with vacant lots where the grasses reach dizzying heights and hide the crouching cats and opossums gnawing at their meagre prey.

They walk past a wrecking yard; recognizing the place, Monette starts to hop up and down and sets the heavy braids Angie had plaited that very morning dancing around her head.

They come to a shack painted pink that exudes a warm odour of manure. Monette's hand grows damp with excitement; she gives her sister a pleading look that is answered with an approving nod, at which she loosens her grip. Monette dashes ahead.

The enclosure looks empty, and Angie is afraid the child will throw a fit, but for now she shows no signs of discouragement. Monette resolutely tears little fistfuls of grass and dandelions out of the ditch and comes back to jiggle them between the slats in the fence while emitting sharp, amazingly precise sounds through her clumsy lips. A shape stirs in the shadows, and Angie's heart inconspicuously leaps into her mouth. The swayback pony obediently steps forward. As always, Angie is overcome by a strange sensation at the sight of this horse, perpetually small, yet so old, so weary.

The animal chews tamely on the proffered snack, then Angie lifts up Monette so she can stroke—ever so lightly—its peeled muzzle, its scrawny croup, its ragged coat. From the back of the pink shed, a man wearing a flawless moustache appears and, beaming with pride, greets them. Old Craig is fond of his filly.

"What's the horse's name?"

"She's not a horse, she's a pony. Her name is Belle," Craig replies patiently.

"How old is she?"

"Thirty-nine years old."

Monette solemnly nods her head and stores the information in a place where it can slumber until something can make better sense of it. The old man enters the paddock and, pulling on the halter, leads the animal back toward the shed.

"She has to rest now. She's working this afternoon," Craig says, pointing to the junk wagon that he has been driving through the streets of Savannah for decades.

The little girl reluctantly lets the animal move away and returns to the sidewalk, where she once again takes her older sister's callused hand. Angie and Belle resemble each other, but Monette does not understand why. Overhead, a military jet cuts through the sky and the droning of the cicadas. Having taken off from the nearby base, it streaks toward an unintelligible country where death is not content merely to lurk in the tall grass of vacant lots.

Nothing but the Flesh
(MADELEINE AND MADELEINE)

THE WEEPING willow stands far from the house and that's good. Its long, groping roots are constantly hunting for water and digging down to icy depths in search of something to drink, tunnelling if need be through a house's plumbing and stone foundations. Madeleine generally avoids the willow, especially since her husband was buried at the foot of the tree. The daffodils blossomed early and she has cut nine of them, one for each year since Micha died. This is the first time she's thought fit to pick such cheerful flowers. Before, she would bring lilies and tulips. In their black hearts, tulips understand the gravity of grief, and the lilies' heady fragrance speaks the language of the dead. The daffodils, with their double petals, their frills and sparkling colours say something quite different: "I no longer mourn for you," and Madeleine confirms this out loud as she straddles the small springtime brook that splits the property in two. The truth is she stopped mourning years ago. But she has never dared to declare it to him so clearly.

It was Micha who asked that his ashes be interred by the willow tree. He liked to go there for a smoke and some tranquility. Her husband was neither a gambler nor a philanderer; he never lied and hardly ever drank. But he bore a burden that had to be laid down from time to time the way one lays down arms or a dead weight. He would take this break at the foot of the willow, a cigarette between his lips, his eyes searching through the vaulted branches. Madeleine comes up to the willow and enters the precinct of the boughs as though setting foot in a temple.

The stone that marks the place where the ashes are buried is as smooth as the day her son lifted it out of the sea. One of the last things they did together, as a family. That was before he became no more than a sail on the horizon. Madeleine mechanically runs her hand over the stone and places the daffodils beside it. For five minutes she remains silent with her eyes closed before heading back. She finds nothing to say to Micha on such occasions, which is odd because she talks to him constantly. People who hear her no doubt believe that Madeleine keeps up this conversation with the unseen to ward off her solitude. They are unaware that, even when her husband was alive, she never stopped speaking to him like this. From the very beginning of their marriage she had gotten into the habit of telling him certain things when he was not around.

Back in the house, she opens the windows wide. The smell of gasoline comes out of nowhere. Sniffing the air absentmindedly, she consults a blue notebook containing sixty or so phone numbers. Madeleine dials the last one on the list, the number of a farm in Mississippi. But the voice that answers is not her son's. "He left three days ago," the person at the other end informs her in the lilting English that is scorned in the US but that Madeleine has always been fond of. She hangs up and puts a pencil stroke through the number. He's moved again without warning. "Don't worry, you'll hear from him soon. It's always like this, you know that," she tells herself reassuringly.

The young man crosses the misty village. The scent of hay at this hour is stronger than anything, but it will soon be supplanted by the smell of hot asphalt. Out of the corner of his eye he catches sight of what he needs. What he's been looking for without knowing it, the thing that could save his life. His emaciated shadow leaves the road, followed by his tail, a slim braid almost a metre in length slipping out from his close-cropped hair. He's wearing a khaki jacket, worn out jeans, and a battered pair of sneakers; a bag like an empty stomach is slung over his shoulder. The outfit of someone who is just passing through. His face is gaunt and yellowish. His hands are empty but they could have been carrying a heavy rock. Or a bone.

He hunches his shoulders as he walks toward an old Chevrolet Monte Carlo. Squinting, he sees the car's interior is overrun with tall grass. Just when he is about to give up, he realizes his mistake: the relatively clean windows have created the illusion that the vegetation growing all around has invaded the inside of the car. He runs his fingers over the pitted body, where the rust has traced the map of an elusive territory, possibly the Everglades or Baffin Island. Near the house, the owner of the car looks up from the huge mower blade he's been polishing. One of those old men who stay strong as a draft horse to the very last, as anyone can tell just by looking at his hands laying the tools down on the porch like the fangs of an enormous dog letting go of its prey. He walks toward the visitor with a stooped yet steady gait. An honest man, the young man decides, true to his habit of sizing people up in a flash. He is rarely wrong.

The old hand settles on the chrome next to the young.

"How old is she?"

"Twenty-three. Runs like she was ten years less. I've pampered her her whole life. But since there's only me here now, I'm keeping just the other one," the old man says, pointing to a grey pickup farther up the driveway.

"How much are you asking?"

"Five hundred."

The visitor opens the door and grimaces as he sits down in the driver's seat. The old man hands him the key; the motor growls without putting up a fuss. The leather is torn here and there, the wing mirror is cracked and breaks up the sky on the passenger side. The young man pulls the hood release and steps out to inspect the motor. Then he shuts the massive lid, which drops down with a mighty thwack.

"Three hundred and I'll take it off your hands right away."

"Three fifty. The tank's full. That's worth almost fifty dollars."

The young man rummages in the back pocket of his jeans, pulls out a wad of bills and counts them while trying to keep his fingers from trembling. Along with the money, he gives the old man the sun-bleached For Sale sign. The old man pins it under his arm, counts the money and offers his hand, which the young man pumps with a show of energy before seating himself again behind the steering wheel.

"Come around this way. I've got my lettuce over there."

The young man gently eases himself out of the tall grass. The fragrance of spring rises together with the scent of leather and gasoline. The car responds smoothly, but the brake pedal's action is a little slow, something he'll have to remember. He touches the tip of his cap by way of goodbye, a salute he reserves exclusively for old people, for the witnesses to a disappearing world. Everything here seems to be on the point of dying. The village road is deserted, except for a cat, except for the fox keeping watch from a distance. The young man presses down on the accelerator and speeds eastward with the windows rolled down. The radio is dead. What a shame. What luck.

From the window of her office, Madeleine looks at the watchman doing his rounds. This is what she does when her eyes need a rest. There's the sea, of course, but it isn't at all restful. It's a struggle, a call, a mystery whispered with every rising tide. The watchman, on the other hand, is calm and predictable. Afflicted by gout, he limps but has never taken a day off. He circles around the lighthouse like a grey satellite; his hobbling in no way diminishes his reassuring presence.

Like everyone else, the watchman has a name, but Madeleine always calls him *monsieur le gardien*. He is a kind, quiet man who believes in angels and extraterrestrials. About once a year he uses his break time to tell her about an apparition, a glow glimpsed from the shore, a movement in the autumn sky. Madeleine is not put out by these strange beliefs. On the contrary, knowing her watchman is on the alert for all possible forms of intrusion gives her a sense of tranquility.

As for the students whose job it is to welcome the crowds of tourists during peak season, they are all called Sarah or Sandra. Madeleine did her best to hire a Megan this year, but the girl declined after the interview. So she will have to fall back on the same Sandra as last year, the one who fabricated historical facts rather than rely on the documented information about the lighthouse. For the time being, Madeleine and the watchman are the only ones welcoming the "regular" off-season visitors—groups of school children and elderly people.

A class of seventh graders is expected at ten o'clock, the youngsters of group twelve of the local high school. Kids who are struggling. Madeleine goes to meet them and their ripped jeans, their defiant way of chewing gum, their certainty that they're already losers. During the visit, a slender teenage girl dressed head to toe in black stares at her with burning intensity. Her gaze is so insistent that Madeleine is convinced the girl is about to speak to her, to confide in her, to share the secret that weighs on her soul, a secret that will free them both, the girl and Madeleine, at the same time, one of those revelations that add a layer of truth to the world. But at the end of the presentation the little black widow moves off with the others. The morning's fine weather gives way to a shower that sends up a salty mist. And each time this happens, the sound of the foghorn seems to be missing. The lighthouse has been voiceless for ten years yet its silence is as piercing as ever.

Night has come and she can't sleep. Once again, her son is the matter—either that or she ate too much chocolate before going to bed. Shabby, the cat, refused to come inside and the foot of the bed is abnormally cold. Toward midnight, Madeleine slips into the doorway and calls it once more. She smiles in the shadows when she discerns its little gallop in the distance. It arrives from where the willow stands, its tattered ears pointed in her direction, and rubs its patchy fur against her terrycloth robe. "Come on, in you go." A few hours later, the ring of the telephone wrenches her out of sleep. Madeleine grabs the receiver only to be met with silence yet again. These mute calls have been recurrent; she utters a few hoarse "hellos" as a matter of form and hangs up. Her ears are humming as though filled with a sudden gust of wind and she hears something creaking, apparently on the ground floor. "Is someone there?" No answer. The house breathes, and dreams come and go.

Despite the persistent pain, the first night in the Monte Carlo was far more comfortable than he had imagined. The back seat is wide and firm and still recalls the four or five kids who would pile in on Sunday with the scent of soil and rhubarb trailing behind them; it remembers the crates of okra hauled to the market and the honey seeping out of the jar on the bumpy roads. The young man woke at six, left the tree-lined backroad where he had pulled over to sleep, and found a truck stop where could clean up and order a coffee. A stupid idea given his condition, but there are only two more days to go.

In the late morning he stops for a hitchhiker and takes fifteen seconds to study the man's face. It's furrowed in the wrong places, but he has good eyes. The young man swings the car door open for him.

"Quite the boat, your car! Where are you headed?"

"North. Across the border. You?"

"I'm going home, near Memphis."

"That's on my way."

The passenger twiddles the radio dials but to no avail, and he clucks his tongue in frustration. Then he pulls a bottle of soda out of his backpack and offers some to the driver. After a few minutes he begins to hum a popular song, a bubble-gum tune that grows soulful and solemn between his lips. The temperature seems suddenly to rise three degrees and the pain in the driver's body recedes. Then the melody stops.

"What sort of guy are you? You give a Black man a ride a few miles from the federal prison without asking the slightest question—you some sort of psychopath? Going to chop me up into little pieces and eat my liver?"

The young man burst out laughing.

"I'm the sort of guy who doesn't let a man rot by the side of the road."

The passenger nods and takes another gulp.

"My name's Lloyd. I did seven years for theft and possession of stolen goods."

"What did you steal?"

"Cars. Don't worry, yours doesn't interest me. Anyway, I'm done with that foolishness. I'm keeping on the straight and narrow, with the help of God."

"In the eyes of God, no one deserves to go to jail. In the eyes of men, everyone's got a good reason to be locked up."

A bump jolts the car, and the pain returns like a needle burrowing into the muscles. The driver's fingers tighten on the steering wheel.

"It must be strange to be out, all at once."

"If it weren't so hot I'd swear it was a dream. At night, I constantly dreamed I was free. But if you want to know if it's real, there's a trick: you never sweat in dreams. Whereas today…"

"We're melting away."

"It's nicer than every second spent inside."

Late in the afternoon the young man insists on going out of his way and takes the exit pointed out by his passenger. He knows very well Lloyd is right: a Black man can wait with his thumb in the air for hours on the side of the road before someone stops to pick him up, if the police don't come along first. He drives Lloyd to his mother's place but doesn't turn around immediately. He waits to see the front door open, to see an arm reach out, to see Lloyd stepping toward the one who had waited steadfastly for seven years. The scene is both familiar and incomprehensible. He averts his eyes just as mother and son embrace each other and then continues on his way, clinging to Lloyd's last words, which still hover inside the car. God bless you.

Madeleine is especially pleased with the last set of photos. In the developer tray, a nascent storm emerges where the roiling of the clouds melds with that of the water so that the horizon can barely be made out and it is hard, amid the mirages and reflections, to separate what belongs to the sky from what belongs to the sea. This is the sole subject of Madeleine's work: the horizon, the boundary between the two worlds, and what manages, unbeknown to scientists and the gods, to travel from one to the other.

Her interest in photography began backwards: she learned to develop before ever touching a lens. Micha was the one who handled the camera. After he died she mastered the darkroom he had set up in the basement in order to find out what the kilometres of film that he'd left behind contained. What they contained for the most part were insects. Micha could spend hours photographing them with a macro lens that captured the minute details of a wing, an iridescent shell or a globular eye. He loathed those tiny creatures, all of which he identified as pillbugs, but season after season he forced himself to recognize them, to magnify them, to fix his eyes on them one by one without blinking. "I hate them because they will end up eating us. I study them for the same reason," he would say.

Once she had gone through the four hundred and thirty-two posthumous pictures, Madeleine turned her attention to the camera. Her first subject was travellers' faces, red-eyed and blurry-mouthed. As the months passed, she honed her technique and their features became more sharply defined, until they deserved to be framed. They multiplied: youths, unadorned, their gaze hard and dreamy, their bodies tattooed, glorious, or beaten, weary and suntanned, posing in front of the sea or the willow, their hair windblown. Madeleine hangs them on the corridor wall among the portraits of persecuted ancestors and pictures of her son as a child, never as an adult. Each time he passes through, Madeleine promises herself she will photograph him. He goes away without leaving a trace on the plastic film.

She gradually lost interest in people, perhaps because it is more acceptable to fail when tackling a landscape than when facing a human being. Or perhaps because she recognizes herself more readily in the unstable symmetry of the sky and the sea than in another's face.

Night comes on with a ruddy breath that gilds the road and lends an ochre tinge to the sign held up by the girl, which bears one word: FAR. The driver pulls over for the second time today. The girl hurries to the car towing a dust-covered trolley case utterly unsuited to her chosen mode of transportation.

With a superhuman effort, she hoists the beast onto the back seat before climbing into the front. Her name is Yun and her goal is to reach the extremities of the hemisphere: the Maritimes, Alaska, Tierra del Fuego. The young man tells her they can travel part of the way together. Delighted to hear this, she relaxes. Silence sets in, and she makes no attempt to switch on the radio. She leans her head out the window and breathes in the cool evening air. An hour later she asks:

"And you? What's your name?"

"Édouard."

"Édouard—that's a lovely name."

"It's because I was conceived on Prince Edward Island, l'Île-du-Prince-Édouard."

"No kidding?"

"That's what I was told. Yun—what kind of name is that?"

"Korean. It means 'melody.'"

"You're a musician?"

"Hardly. I'm a chemist."

They spend the night in a room with one bed. Yun doesn't like to French kiss; she says it's cannibalistic. But, supple as a bow, she enjoys running her lips along the spine, brushing the floating ribs, meandering over the inner thighs. They don't get much sleep before sunrise, then they drowse until the cleaning lady raps on the door. At eleven o'clock sharp they are sitting in the Monte Carlo once again.

The road turns dreary. The extravagance of the South, its incongruous vegetation, the madness of the religious billboards give way to the monotony of Yankee farmland. Édouard steps on the gas. There's no time to lose; the pain is gaining ground and he must get to Montreal post-haste. When he can't bear it any more, Yun takes the wheel. She strokes Édouard's forehead while steering the Monte Carlo with a lack of precision that, even so, doesn't frighten Édouard. They reach downtown Montreal at nightfall.

"I can't remember the last time I saw a skyscraper," Édouard remarks.

On a piece of hamburger wrapping, he scribbles an address and a few directions; then he hands Yun the car keys.

"You should arrive by midday tomorrow if you don't stop too often."

"You look weak. Are you sure you don't want me to stay with you?"

"Quite sure. I'll be in good hands. A friend of mine is driving down in a few days. I'll catch up with you as soon as I'm done here."

She gives him a tongueless kiss, which nevertheless thrills him to the marrow; then she strides away, her hair beating time on her perfect shoulders, and Édouard could swear there is a brass band marching somewhere among the glass towers.

Again, the telephone rings when Madeleine is in bed. This time it's for real: a girl with an indeterminate accent announces she'll be arriving the next day. This makes Madeleine smile. Such manners are a rarity among the guests, who, generally without warning, just show up as willowy silhouettes at the far end of the road. For years Madeleine has been putting up passing strangers, travellers, and drifters from all over the continent. When her son went looking for adventure at the age of seventeen, he began to give his mother's address to the people he met on the road. Some dream of exploring the Maritimes, others, of learning French. A few simply need a tranquil place to rest, regain their health, find some peace, sometimes their souls.

Reticent at first to open her door to strangers, Madeleine soon grew accustomed to their company, which in the end she came to genuinely appreciate. No one in Grande-Anse, her hometown, can surprise her anymore. Not one of its seven hundred and thirty-nine inhabitants has ever slept under the stars, stolen out of hunger, or hopped a freight train heading who-knows-where. None have awoken in an unidentified city. None have found true love on a godforsaken road only to lose it again a few hours later with nothing but a guitar tune, a hawk feather, and a hickey to remember it by.

So she fixed up a room for these unexpected guests and laid down some rules. Alcohol and drugs are not allowed in her house. Visitors must choose a task to be carried out during their stay, but the task need not be confined to the domestic sphere. Accordingly, a young man decided to carve a bas-relief on the trunk of the old elm tree behind the house. A girl gave a classical song recital in the village. A couple spent their whole time there hauling seawater to the garden as part of a (failed) saltwater pond experiment. The last rule—the most important one for Madeleine—is that every guest must write home before leaving.

The system works quite well, even though two or three objects disappeared from the house after some visitors had come and gone, and she had to accompany one of her lodgers to the psychiatric hospital after a disturbing episode involving a racoon and a blowtorch. But aside from those few complications, the presence of these travellers does her good. Through them she feels she has connected with Édouard. What's more, her guests' stories and eccentricities distracted her from grieving in the aftermath of Micha's death, which is when Édouard's wanderings began.

There was the thirty-year-old man with a quasi-aristocratic bearing and studied manners. His name was Frank but he insisted on being called François. He spoke French flawlessly and was helpful, courteous, and jovial. The only thing peculiar about him was this: a few days after arriving he announced to Madeleine that on this day of June 6, 1944 he was celebrating the great victory of the Normandy landings. Fifty years after the fact, François lived through the ensuing weeks as if they were the last days of the Second World

War; he kept Madeleine abreast of the slightest retreat of Axis troops, every Allied manoeuvre, and described for her the wild parties he claimed to go to at night in the basements of Saint-Germain-des-Près. Fearing at first that she might have to make another trip to the psychiatric ward, Madeleine soon put her mind at rest. Frank was neither unbalanced nor delirious. He had simply decided to recreate that year, so crucial for the history of the West, and to experience each moment with the same intensity that Europeans must have felt at the time. When the Third Reich finally collapsed, Frank dropped his Parisian accent, returned to the 1990s and picked up his backpack, telling Madeleine, "Thank you so much, Madame Sicotte, for welcoming me to Grande-Anse. I'm a new man." Then he turned around and she never heard from him again.

Madeleine was also visited by a woman with long grey hair—which always seemed to snare dead leaves or bits of wood—who said she was completely amnesiac. As a result, her stay at Madeleine's house was a total reconstruction, a project in which Madeleine immersed herself body and soul, trying by every possible means to help the woman find clues about her identity, making phone calls left and right, even hiring a hypnotherapist from Gaspésie in the hope of dislodging a few fragments of her history. The woman asked to be called Missy and favoured a different approach, whereby she reconstructed her past through suppositions. "My fingers are long and slender, so I'll bet I was a concert pianist," she proposed. Or: "I have the feeling I was surrounded by men my whole life, which no doubt means I was a prostitute or a madam in a brothel." After a few weeks Madeleine gave up the idea of discovering even a smidgen of information about the woman, who, in any case, preferred to speculate. Then Madeleine received a phone call from Édouard. She filled him in on the situation and asked him if he remembered Missy and how he'd met her. "A crone with witch's hair? Yes, her name is Cynthia," he answered. "I don't know if she's amnesiac but when I met her she remembered very clearly how her husband had left her for a Hooters waitress. She ended up on the streets because he refused to give her so much as a penny." Following that conversation, Madeleine approached Missy ever so gingerly and told her she'd found out that her real name was Cynthia and that she hailed from Colorado. Missy's eyes went blank. "Yes, my dear, it's true. I was trying to forget it," she answered before packing her suitcase.

Madeleine came to understand that these passing travellers are all to some extent liars, runaways, and crazy, and that her house matters for them in ways that are beyond her. So she welcomes them without judging or questioning; she receives these characters as if they were living postcards sent by her son, who never writes.

She is busy planting lettuce when Yun arrives after covering the last kilometre on foot; the Monte Carlo started to belch out smoke just past Bathurst. She is lugging her enormous suitcase, and the dust it churns up on the small road signals Yun's presence from afar. Madeleine straightens up and shields her eyes against the sun with a soil-encrusted hand. The travellers always arrive on foot. She drops her tools and goes to meet the new visitor. As soon as they shake hands Madeleine senses that her guest is no exception to the rule: she has come with a mystery in tow. Without knowing why, Madeleine has a feeling this girl's secret concerns her. Banishing the little voice in her throat that yearns to interrogate, she shows the young woman around her house.

"Your place so beautiful! Édouard is lucky to have grown up here."

"I'm not sure he sees things that way. Anyway, he's in no hurry to come back."

Madeleine instantly regrets saying this and bites her lip. Wide-eyed with astonishment, Yun stops midway up the stairs.

"He hasn't told you? He'll be here in a few days!"

"Here? In Grande-Anse?"

Yun nods yes. A hum fills Madeleine's chest. It's been a year since she last saw her son. She clears her throat.

"So, how is he?"

"He's in Montreal. There are a few small things he needs to do before heading out."

Yun puts her suitcase down at the foot of the guest bed and casts her gaze out the window. The enigma moves through the room, as dense and round as the full moon, which tugs at people's hearts and, month after month, ordains the Earth's moods.

For her chore Yun chooses to remove the dead wood from the copse at the edge of the property. Whatever is too far gone to be of any use she burns; the rest she proposes to turn into firewood, which she will stack in the shed. This initiative delights Madeleine, who fetches the axe in the workshop, believing the girl already knows how to use to it. But from the very first blow she realizes this is a training project. Yun's method is crude; it consists in lifting the axe as high as possible, swinging it down while bending forward with her eyes shut, and striking as hard as possible, usually off-target. After the blade lands a few centimetres from the girl's foot, Madeleine feels compelled to wrest the implement from her hands to show her how it's done.

It takes Yun two days to master the technique but from then on each of her moves is perfect. Madeleine is mesmerized by the girl's work, transfixed by the precise arc of the blade striking the log and splitting it into halves filled with signs, which she would like to read like the lines of a hand. At night, they settle in in front of the fire, toast marshmallows that they don't eat, chat and absorb a smoky scent that they bring back to their sheets to keep themselves warm when, toward four in the morning, the mercury drops below ten degrees.

Yun discovered North America at the age of six, when her parents left her little hometown in South Korea for Virginia. She grew up between soccer games and *Kumon*, "after-school school," where the children were subjected to endless math exercises. Inspired by the Huckleberry Finn story, Yun dreamed of building a raft and sailing down the rivers of the South. But it had been decided she would pursue a science career, and even when she ran away on a makeshift boat she was brought back to her allotted path by her chemistry teacher, who happened to be fishing in a cove.

So she reined in her rebellious urges and surrendered to her parents' vision of her future. By the age of eighteen she had carved out an enviable place for herself among the top candidates for admission to Emory University in Atlanta. During the summer holidays after her freshman year, rather than rushing into one of the unpaid internships her fellow students were vying for, she gathered her meagre savings and purchased a spluttering scooter, which she bravely drove to Key West. She explored the back roads of Florida, Louisiana, and Alabama, where she was treated to canned beer, stalked on moonless nights, seated before platefuls of scrambled eggs and grits, called "squinty," "slut," and "communist," and gallantly kissed on the hand. In September she returned to her residence with a sunburn of Biblical proportions and a lost cat under her arm. By Thanksgiving the creature had died of pneumonia, and her scooter did not make it through the winter. But the following summer Yun was back on the road again.

When Édouard met her she was on her third trip, determined this time to tour the Americas and not go back to school. Her training in chemistry had not yielded anything even remotely comparable to the bliss she felt while knocking around, so, drawing on all the wisdom of her twenty-one years, she concluded that if a career didn't afford her as much happiness as travelling it wasn't worth pursuing.

Night after night Madeleine follows the narrative of her adventures and smiles. Yun expresses herself with the objectivity and precision of someone trained in the sciences, but also with such gentleness that the listener feels she is sharing in a conversation rather than listening to a traveller's monologue. On their fourth night sitting by the campfire, Madeleine finally clears her throat and responds.

"You know, I have the feeling my son must be very fond of you."

The next day, Édouard's silhouette emerges from the dust on the gravel road.

Sitting on the veranda petting Shabby in a desultory way, Madeleine spots in the distance the peculiar, backlighted form of the constantly entwined bodies of her son and Yun. True to his habit, Édouard barely said hello to his mother when he arrived. This time, however, instead of raiding the refrigerator, he locked himself in his bedroom with his new girlfriend for two whole days. Watching the two of them, Madeleine suspects they share the secret that Yun brought with her, but she hasn't found a way of learning more about it from her son, who replies only in monosyllables. The willow sways in the rising wind and sends a message in a strange language, a message that Madeleine grasps but is unable to articulate. "If only I could be alone with him just for a minute," she says under her breath. The answer comes of its own accord: "What difference would that make?"

The afternoon sun moves in with the authority of a landlord. Madeleine's car plunges inland, where the properties appear sturdier and tidier than the jumbled dunes along the shore. When she reaches Paul's place, she finds him hammer in hand, in the middle of building a new beehive for his steadily growing colony.

"How are the bees?"

"Bursting with inspiration! Here, take a look at their latest masterpiece…"

Untroubled by the comings and goings of the stinging insects, he approaches one of the older hives and pulls out of its entrails a frame overflowing with heavy, coppery syrup. Whenever she visits, Madeleine admires the ease with which Paul moves through this miniature city, and at the same time she wonders if it isn't precisely his ability to so easily dominate this structured universe that pleases him. Here, Paul is great and all-powerful. And he takes what he wants.

He lifts the frame of honey to Madeleine's mouth, and she eats out of his hand like a trained animal. Paul kisses her; his beard chafes.

"Your son is back?" he asks, getting back to his work.

"Yes."

"Apparently there's a girl with him. They were seen on the beach."

"They're on the point of total fusion."

"So they're in love?"

"I don't know," Madeleine answers thoughtfully.

It seems to her that her son's adventures never follow this sort of arc. As far as she can tell, his love affairs are mainly about sex.

The bees trace complex diagrams in the air; Paul puts away his tools haphazardly, as if they have become useless junk now their job is done. He turns toward her again.

"You're looking out of sorts."

"Me? No, everything's fine."

"Mommy doesn't like to share her little boy?" he teases.

Madeleine's face grows hot and crimson. Inwardly, she

responds in the most scathing terms: "Mommy doesn't have a little boy to share anymore. He hasn't been hers for a very long time." But she clenches her jaws and waits for her flushed cheeks to cool down. Paul is one of those people who always think they know more about others than they do themselves. It makes him obnoxious but she wants him, which is no doubt why she continues to see him. And the annoyance he elicits heightens her desire for him. With her husband it was the opposite. Everything was a matter of tenderness and patience. And she marvelled at the fact Micha managed to draw all that gentleness out of her grouchy soul. Even after the desire had flown away, it was the kindness that won out and made her open her arms.

Paul keeps looking at her gleefully, like a mischievous uncle having fun making the little girls blush. He proffers a sticky jar.

"Here, take this back to him—to your son. If he's anything like his mother he's got a huge sweet tooth. Anyway, it's good for lovers."

Madeleine accepts the glistening honeypot. Paul points to the house with his chin.

"Are you coming in? Your sugar craving needs to be satisfied, too."

He takes her hand and they walk toward the house, which from afar looks as vacant as the new hive.

The rays of sunlight fall on the museum parking lot like pillars. Madeleine eats her snack while enjoying these first sensations of springtime warmth. An elderly group is waiting in the hall, and the thrumming of their mobility scooters can be heard outside. Just as Madeleine gets up to throw away her apple core, a huge, lumbering automobile pulls up alongside her with Yun aboard. She's come to say goodbye before heading off on a trip to Cape Breton.

"It seems I've got some distant relations out there."

"And you trust this car to get you there?"

"No way! I'm going to sing Patsy Cline to it the whole time. It's the only thing that stops it from acting up, apparently."

"Well, good luck! I hope you come back to see us again some day."

"Oh, I'm coming back very soon! I'll be gone for barely a week, just long enough to let Édouard touch down. He needs to get his bearings, you understand…"

Madeleine nods affirmatively, though she doesn't grasp the meaning of that puzzling statement, any more than she does the mutual allegiance that seems to exist between her son and this young woman too studious to be a true bohemian and too unpredictable to put down roots. But she feels a mute gratitude toward Yun. The two women kiss each other on the cheek, and Madeleine waves as if to encourage the Monte Carlo's grinding motor. The noise emanating from the colossal machine does nothing to reassure her, but Yun is unperturbed as she steers her white monster down the road. She drives off in a din of metal and country music, which is soon covered over by the roar of the ocean. Madeleine goes back to her mobile visitors, who are turning in circles like seagulls over an island.

It feels as though something is rumbling beneath her feet, as though the willow's roots are stirring beneath the house. Madeleine shudders. It's only the wind or perhaps the spring tides making their presence felt. Some waves remind her of sumo wrestlers before a fight, lifting their massive legs high in the air and then pounding the floor to make the ground tremble and chase away evil spirits. This is probably why Madeleine has always longed to be near the sea. Those repeated blows on the shoreline driving the demons away. It was the same for Micha. They had this in common: the need to feel the ocean's proximity, to feel in each of their cells the water's to-and-fro and the texture of salt. Micha had a legion of monsters to keep at bay.

The door slams. Shabby scampers in followed by Édouard looking exhausted after a hike.

"All hell's about to break loose!"

"What?"

"The storm! Didn't you hear the thunder?"

"Oh, yes. But I thought it was the sea."

"You always think it's the sea."

Édouard leans over the sink to wash his face, his long braid blending with the water flowing between his fingers. The chicken soup is still simmering on the stove. He serves himself a bowlful. Madeleine sits down at the table facing him and watches him eat. Her mind travels light-years back, and she finds herself stunned at the sight of those hands so tiny a short while ago clasping her finger, that mouth just moments before awkwardly suckling a single food, those limbs fashioned inside her now so large, magnified by time, out of her reach for good. She grabs a dishrag and wrings it underneath the table to push away the too-close image of the child who once was hers. The soup gradually disappears, then Édouard stretches a tired arm out toward Paul's honey-pot and plunges his index finger into it like a gold prospector. The storm is still rumbling on the horizon like a guest dithering on the doorstep.

"Mother, I'm sick. I need a kidney."

Madeleine is struck dumb, with the dishrag hanging from her fingertips. Édouard starts weeping over the honeypot.

"I'm sorry, Ma. There's no one else I can ask."

Madeleine steps toward him and, without giving it any thought, takes him in her arms. Édouard's body feels so big, so tangled, so hard to comprehend. It seems to her everything is coated with honey, that her hands are sticking to her son's skin, attaching themselves to it in a complicated, sweet and salty embrace, a bungled knot.

The storm gathers strength, flattening the dahlias and bell-flowers and whatever still strives to remain upright. As Madeleine watches the spectacle, she recalls how during her pregnancy she slept curled up, so distraught because of a previous miscarriage that even at night she sought to shield her child against the unseen blows that make babies disappear before their mothers can see their faces.

You spend your life fearing the worst. First, you're afraid of crib death and all the congenital diseases that can show up after birth. You wave your arms, snap your fingers to make sure his eyes can see, his ears can hear. You wait for the first steps, the first words. At every new stage you eliminate a set of handicaps you don't want to contemplate but that stay planted in your mind like stings.

He grows and you avert your eyes when the TV shows bald children asking for their last wish to be fulfilled. He learns to ride a bicycle, to climb trees, and you pray he won't fall. He dives into the waves and you keep your eyes glued to the big bubbles in his wake. He goes to play far from the house and you hope he'll remember not to speak to strangers, to never get into a van with tinted windows. Adolescence comes and you're afraid the lectures on drugs were inadequate; you'd like to secretly follow him to make sure he doesn't touch a drop of alcohol before getting behind the wheel, that he always carries condoms, that he doesn't dive off a high cliff to impress the girls. Then he becomes a man, and you're left with no choice. You have to let go. And now it happens. I shouldn't have let my guard down.

Madeleine interrupts her monologue on hearing her son step out of the shower. He slowly comes downstairs and settles in by the fire, which is sucking the dampness out of the air. He looks calmer, but a furrow has appeared on his forehead. It will never go away again. Years later a woman covered with the same sheet as him will run her finger over the little gap and say, "What about this one?" He will answer: "I don't recall anymore. It appeared in my late twenties." Madeleine pictures this with a desperate wishfulness. She too approaches the fireplace now, rests one foot on the hearthstone, and lets the heat climb up her leg. Outside, peals of distant thunder are still audible. The storm is heading toward Labrador.

"Explain to me what's going on."

Édouard clutches the corner of a cushion and squeezes it in his fist.

"There was an infection: fever, tiredness—the usual. I figured it was the flu. I let it drag on, didn't want to go to the hospital. It's expensive down there. Then I saw blood in my urine. I thought I'd caught—you know—one of those diseases."

Now Madeleine nods her head.

"It wasn't that. It kept getting worse. My stomach hurt, I lost weight. I was worn out. So I came back. Enough time had gone by for the bacteria to almost completely eat up my kidneys. They put me on dialysis right away. I went back today. That's what the hike was really about. I have to go there three times a week now. They told me my only way out is a transplant."

Madeleine puts a finger in her mouth and bites down. A small detonation goes off in the fireplace. She has always wondered why wood goes through this sort of blast as it burns. Exploding knots, perhaps. She thinks of the hard kernel in Édouard's abdomen. She'd like to blow it up, too. An anatomical big bang. Poof.

As the sun moves past the zenith, a hazy shape comes into view at the far end of the road and very quickly grows larger. Rubbing her eyes, bloodshot from lack of sleep, at first

Madeleine believes she is seeing a car, possibly Yun already returning from her trip. But the spot is too small, too light. Too red. Soon the slender outline of a bicycle appears and, perched on it, a stooped creature, bending over as though adapting to a frame that is too small, pedals that are too high, handlebars that are too narrow. A few moments later, an extraordinarily tall woman alights and greets Madeleine with a benevolent smile. Her hair is the red of clay cliffs; the blue of her gaze is barely visible through her nearly closed eyelids, which leave just a slit for her eyes fringed with starbursts of deep creases. The face of someone who has spent her life squinting into the sun.

"I'm Joanna," the woman declares with a thick accent. "You put people up?"

Madeleine contemplates the weary amazon's body. She must be over six foot three. She wears a man's shirt that flaps in the wind. Her fingers, partly sheathed in cycling gloves, seem as long as pencils. Her bike is full of nicks half-hidden by stickers from various countries. As she deciphers a Wall Drug logo that masks some Zapatista graffiti, Madeleine searches for the right words to explain to this woman who looks like she's just circumnavigated the globe that this is not the best time for her to take in visitors.

"The house is a bit upside down these days. My son is ill."

"If you like, I may be able to help. I'm a nurse. Trained at the best school in the Netherlands."

"I don't know. The situation is complicated."

"I work in refugee camps, in Africa. I'm used to complicated."

The lighthouse stands on the point like a reminder of humanity. It is often said that lighthouse keepers are solitary, sad, and reclusive. For Madeleine, this perception is too narrow; it obscures the lighthouse's primary function: to serve as a bridge of light between land dwellers and seafarers. It is, in reality, the building of the multitudes.

After the lighthouse watchman had detoured from his usual route to give Madeleine an awkward pat on the shoulder, she shut herself in her office to avoid visits. Like everyone else, he had heard the news of Édouard's illness. Madeleine realizes she ought to be touched by the man's solicitude, but she doesn't know how to receive all this sympathy, how to come up with a response that isn't a prolonged howl of despair. The compatibility tests were performed the day before and already she has the impression it's taking forever for the results to arrive. She would like to sleep until next week, until the moment they announce that Édouard is saved.

Sleep. Édouard does nothing else between his dialysis sessions, waking only to take a small sip of the herbal tea prepared by Joanna, before he sinks back to sleep. The Dutch woman has integrated into the household's difficult ecology with astonishing ease, asks no questions, offers her help only when she can be useful, and withdraws at just the right moment. Her waking hours coincide exactly with the sun's daily cycle. Most of her time is spent on her bicycle, and when she is in the house she seems to adapt to the moods and wishes of its inhabitants, cutting flowers when the atmosphere is too gloomy, opening a window when the weather is too hot, humming a Dutch song when the silence weighs too heavily. Joanna's only annoying habit is a baffling proclivity for being right behind Madeleine when she starts to talk to herself. If Madeleine says, *Now where in the world did I put the bread knife?* she hears behind her: "It's under the yellow cloth." When she whispers, *No point in watering the tomatoes—it's going to rain tonight*, a voice chimes in: "Yes, the oncoming clouds look very heavy indeed." When she complains, *It's taking far too much time—how much longer?* Joanna answers simply: "I don't know."

Madeleine deals with insomnia by drinking herbal tea all night while perusing medical dictionaries, fussing with Shabby's fur in the vain hope of removing the knots, and making lists. Lists of things to do, to clean, to throw out, but, especially, lists of close or distant relatives who might act as donors for her son should the test results disqualify her.

When she shows Édouard the list, he balks.

"Your sister Josette? Ma, we're not going to ask a woman who's been struggling her whole life with schizophrenia to donate a kidney! And Jan and Tomas? I don't even know who they are!"

"They're your father's brothers."

"I thought they all died during the war."

"Not all."

"So you're suggesting we cross the ocean to explain to some perfect strangers why they have to give me a kidney? It's out of the question!"

Resigned, Madeleine puts away her list of donors and pockets her shopping list. The moment she sets foot in the village grocery store she is swamped with stories.

"I have a diabetic uncle who never managed to find a donor, so he went to the Îles-de-la-Madeleine—the Magdalen Islands—to consult a healer. She prescribed edible seaweeds and ever since then it's as if he's got *four* kidneys!"

"My neighbour's sister-in-law found a donor in just a few weeks—a man who committed suicide by tying a plastic bag around his head. Now she's the picture of health! But she's stopped using plastic bags to wrap her orders at the supermarket."

Madeleine is left drained and exits the store without her groceries; she drives toward the lighthouse and parks her car on the side of the road to avoid going by the museum. Holding her arms open, she slowly makes her way to the old wooden tower painted white and, in the manner of those who hug trees, she embraces with all her might this misunderstood sentinel, this guide for lost souls.

After several days of persistent insomnia, Madeleine throws in the towel. The night is clear, the wind is fair, and the salt air seeks her out even in the depths of the basement, where she is making a half-hearted effort to classify the seeds scattered by the cat a few days before. Moving about on tiptoes, she takes some virgin rolls of film from the cabinet, grabs her camera, pulls on her rubber boots, and goes out. She walks amid the friendly silence, and the night seems to want to speak to her.

The spectacle at the seashore is arresting. The moon illuminates the pebble beach, which the spring tide has littered with debris. Madeleine realizes she has not been on the beach after nightfall since she was young. She and Micha would come to bathe here when the cool air made the water feel warm, like a kiss in the middle of winter. For a brief moment she inhales the rush of nostalgia, then she unpacks her equipment. Her camera starts to snap up all that's visible and invisible like a large, greedy hand. Using her tripod, Madeleine sets long exposures, barely peeking through the lens. A shot in the dark, the prey felled by chance. The light is incomprehensible; it seems to emanate not from the sky but from the sand, from the salt shimmering on the water's surface. As if the landscape were shown in negative.

Back home she finds the Monte Carlo parked in front. In the first rays of dawn, Yun is busy smoothing out her long hair, windblown and tangled from the drive.

"Well, it looks as though we've both spent a sleepless night," she says on seeing Madeleine approaching.

"Did you have a good trip?"

"Yes! I ate clams and swam with the seals. But I didn't come across a single Korean."

"That's odd."

"How is Édouard?"

"Okay. He told me everything after you'd left."

"Good. I warned him I wouldn't come back until he'd talked to you."

"How did you know that he had?"

"I didn't know. But I figured the threat would have an effect."

Madeleine smiles and invites Yun to come along to the kitchen. Her head is strangely clear after a night on the shore and she sets about making pancakes. While she watches the batter turn into golden parchment, Édouard comes downstairs bleary-eyed. When he catches sight of Yun he simply spreads his arms in a gesture of relief and surrender. She rushes toward him. Madeleine flips the pancake, which lands in the skillet with a slap. Shabby leaps onto the counter to get a better look at the lovers and her mistress lets him. Out of the corner of her eye she sees Yun's finger slide over the creases in her son's brow.

"Hey! This one is brand new."

The day before their appointment at the hospital, Madeleine arrives at dusk to find the house suffused with a peculiar halo. On coming closer she realizes there is steam dancing behind the window. Taken aback, she goes in to discover her son drowsing in the hammock that Yun set up in the living room a few days earlier so he might have "the feeling he was travelling while staying indoors." Tongues of yellow mist emanating from the kitchen and bearing a briny aroma brush against his motionless body. Through the mist she hears bursts of laughter.

"Watch out! There's one missing!" Yun's voice yells.

"Easy now, little guy. Easy now," Joanna's voice says reassuringly.

Madeleine treads cautiously and bumps into something hard. At her feet she discerns an armoured body moving unhurriedly and she lets out a scream.

"Madeleine, is that you?" Yun's voice asks.

"I'll open the windows. Make things easier," Joanna says.

Once the steam has lifted the scene is astonishing. A small inflatable wading pool placed in the centre of the kitchen is full of lobsters, seaweed, and, apparently, salt water. The creatures are piled on top of each other and move sluggishly as potfuls of boiling water continue to fog up the room. Yun bustles around the lobster while Joanna smiles serenely, as though watching over a well-behaved child at bath time.

"Aha! There's the runaway!" Yun shouts as she grabs the crustacean that was lurking near Madeleine's feet. "Sorry for the mess. We wanted to surprise you. A seafood banquet to boost your morale!"

"The scallops and mussels are almost ready, but there are no lobsters."

"Well, I wanted to give the poor things a last bath and now we've grown fond of them," Yun explains.

Studying the creatures, Madeleine is entranced by their sleepwalking slowness and their prehistoric appearance. Then she turns her eyes up toward the two red-faced, dishevelled women.

"It's true: lobsters are much more likeable than mussels."

They gently wake Édouard and tuck into a meal that to Madeleine's amazement actually succeeds in warming her heart. "There's something in seafood that makes one feel hopeful," she muses. The next day she and Édouard will be learning the results of the compatibility tests. Each hour is an endless crossing that this almost family dinner has managed to shorten somewhat.

Once the night has spread over the peninsula, Édouard goes upstairs to bed and Yun and Joanna clean up, singing softly as they work. Madeleine lingers quietly in front of her son's bedroom to listen to him breathing, as she did when he was small and his breath kept the house in a state of weightlessness. Toward midnight the three women make their way down to the seashore to release six completely bewildered lobsters.

Sitting side by side, Madeleine and Édouard wait in the over-lit but nonetheless grey hall of the Chaleur Hospital in Bathurst. This artificial lighting, Madeleine is thinking, obliterates any notion of seasons, of night and day, maybe to dilute the sensation of the passage of time. The endless waiting.

Some old women go by with the patience of those who can't ask much anymore of either their bodies or science. They slide with their walkers, hobble with their canes, or let themselves be pushed in a wheelchair. Others stoically shuffle along unaided. They're on the edge of the precipice.

As a rule, mother and son leave an empty seat between them, whether at the movies or the funeral parlour. This time, though, there's no gap, as if they wanted to improve the odds of compatibility by sitting closer together. When they are finally called, Madeleine immediately senses the news is bad. She guesses it from the sound of the nurse's voice; she perceives it in the stagnant air of the unadorned office they are ushered into. Without knowing what she is about to be told, from the moment the doctor sits down in front of them she understands that the verdict is far worse than the worst-case scenario she was prepared for. Édouard is oblivious; he did not hear the cannon's detonation a few seconds ago and he does not see the shell approaching. Madeleine nervously wrings her hands and her fingers feel like stranded squid.

She is not shocked when the doctor announces the test results, but Édouard's shoulders collapse. The doctor tries to reassure them: since he is young and does not smoke his case ranks as top priority for an organ donation. From the doctor's tone of voice, Madeleine can easily see he still has not told them everything, and a little voice inside her silently implores him to hurry up.

"Édouard, I'd like to speak with your mother in private, if you don't mind. You can wait outside and fill out the forms in the meantime."

Édouard does as he's asked. The doctor turns to Madeleine and his expression grows solemn.

"Madame Sicotte, the tests show something else I'd like to discuss with you. Frankly, I've never had to broach this sort of matter with a patient before."

Madeleine says nothing, does not tremble, stays dry-eyed. She waits for the blade to drop.

"The test failed to establish a genetic kinship between you and your son."

"Excuse me?"

"Based on your DNA, you are not Édouard's mother."

He continues. She hears him from a distance: "You see, my professional duty… social services… an investigation…" But a rumble within her muffles the words; it is overpowering, a cyclone, a landslide. She manages to stand up and go out without falling.

The road back runs alongside the sea and its unseen clamour; inside the car, Madeleine says nothing. Édouard doesn't ask her what the doctor had to say to her. He fidgets with his braid, probably imagining he's just been dealt a devastating diagnosis—devastating for her too—and that both of them will have to fritter away their days around the damned hospital until life has trickled out of them like water from a leaking cistern. But Madeleine's thoughts have taken her elsewhere. She finds herself twenty-seven years earlier, in a house on a cliff where a midwife has pulled out of her a small, viscous body. He was nestled in her arms even before he opened his eyes. She thinks of the placenta, the flood of fluids, the blood, the shit and the flesh, all that flesh, her flesh, battered and stretched, and the flesh that had come through her belly, the flesh she was holding in her hands, pressed against her breast so that it could live and grow. There ought to be nothing but the flesh, she tells herself. But no.

The Fox
(MONETTE AND ANGIE)

NO ONE reads the lines in a sidewalk like Monette. She interprets them like an archaeologist studying a wall of rock paintings. This crack represents a camel, and the adjacent crack, a cup of coffee. She generally avoids stepping on living things, while she mercilessly treads on electrical devices and guns, which are far more common than one might believe.

It takes her a few moments to realize that what is lying in front of her at the street corner where she is waiting for Angie does not belong to the concrete but to the earth and the beings moving over it. Once she has understood this, she stretches out her arm, automatically reaching for her older sister's reassuring grip and brief answers.

"What is it?"

"A dead fox. Don't touch."

"Why not?"

"Because it's dirty."

"Why is it dead?"

"It was hit by a car. Didn't look before crossing the street."

Amid the dense swarm of scavenger insects Monette meditates on the recklessness of animals and the cruelty of motorists, while Angie, unable to move away as quickly as she'd like, prods her half-heartedly. Angie is aware that the mere proximity of animal carcasses is noxious; she knows, though cannot name, the diseases and infections they spawn and the spirits that linger around them. Yet she is incapable of taking her eyes off the creature, whose upper body has been smashed. The head, seething with flies and parasites, is unrecognizable, but the slender, nimble gloved paws, seemingly still alive, are flexed as if about to leap—one can almost see it jumping, its magnificent orange tail held aloft like a pennant, its exploded skull guiding it into the shrubs in spite of everything. Angie is overcome by a sense of revolt at the sight of this creature, which could have been deprived of its tail rather than its head, the vain instead of the essential. She feels like crying, like finding a stick to flog the carcass; she wishes it would disappear.

Something stirs in the bushes along the road and the girls shudder. A hard beak emerges, followed by a dark, shiny, robust body. The crows had hidden when the two sisters arrived, some high up in the trees, others a few paces from the prey they were coveting. Having gotten used to the presence of these humans, they approach furtively; their breath is voracious, their appetite as sharp as an arrow. Without thinking, Angie charges at the scavengers, trying unsuccessfully to land a kick but still managing to chase them away. Then she raises her knotty arms skyward, waves them about wildly to scare off those circling from one branch to the next, and lets out raspy shrieks that shatter the calm of the vacant lots. At first Monette is taken aback by her sister's antics, but then she too bears down on the black birds, yelling, growling, laughing at the top of her small voice.

Once the crows have scattered, Angie completes her intervention by haphazardly pulling up clumps of vegetation and throwing them on the animal's body in the hope this seasoning will spoil the meal of scavengers, that the thin leaves will conceal the carcass from profiteers or any heartless creatures who feed on the misfortune of the foolhardy, and accompany the deceased to the far shore of the river that separates the

living from the immortals. Trying unenthusiastically to imitate her older sister, Monette complains:

"It smells bad."

While she pulls away the fingers her little sister was
attempting to force up her own nostrils, Angie closes her eyes
and concentrates. She is familiar with the stench of death. A
shadowy, ancient part of her brain has learned it by heart, and
at times she recognizes it drifting on the wind as it sweeps
over the neighbourhood, around certain shuttered houses
and under the nails of certain passersby. But today, on this
street corner, the odour that has caught in their throats is not
quite the same. She clasps Monette's hand again to cross the
deserted street.

"It doesn't smell bad. It smells of fox."

The Same Wish
(ARIEL AND MARIE)

THE CAMERAS are broadcasting real-time shots of the house, their house, with the blue paint that appears to be taking flight in the chilly air, the second-floor shutters, arms spread wide, the yellow bicycle with a flat tire chained to the balustrade, and the swing pushed by the August wind as if a ghost were seated on it. The reporters seem especially fond of this last object, and they take countless close-ups of it, hoping perhaps to raise a deceased ancestor bearing a secret, a message that would explode like a soon forgotten fireworks display.

Marie, mesmerized by the images streaming across the screen, wrestles with the urge to open a window and extend her arm in a gentle wave, the way children passing in front of an electronics store verify that it is indeed they who are pictured on the screen in the shop window, confirming their unimaginable profile, their peculiar gait snatched on the sidewalk. Ariel comes over and delicately ushers his wife away as if to prevent her from being struck down by an enraged beast. He whispers a few words in her ear, and the light coming through the curtains seems to grow more intense. Then he steps toward the windows and in his turn glances at the grey mass of people in front of his home.

"What do they want now? Didn't they get their fill at Lambert's place?" he asks, turning to Marc.

"That's it exactly. They camped out in front of his house for almost a month," his right-hand man answers. "It whetted their appetite. Better get used to it. This won't be the last time you'll see them keeping watch at your house. You had a public life. From now on it'll be transparent."

Grumbling, Ariel goes back to pacing up and down so quickly that one can almost see a golden streak in his wake. He sees himself three nights ago face to face with the suddenly distorted features of the party veterans, the ones known as "the cops" precisely because of their role in constructing that unavoidable transparency. For many hours they confronted Ariel with his past, looking for hypothetical skeletons in his hotly indignant breathing, scrutinizing the film of sweat glistening on his brow for a hint of an admission of guilt. After the double life of Daniel Lambert, the former opposition leader, got splashed across the front page of a tabloid amid a slew of public statements by barely pubescent male prostitutes, the party could hardly afford another blunder. The brutality of the cops' questions was in proportion to the magnitude of their mismanagement.

Humiliated, Ariel gave the veterans the information they sought; the tone of his voice was a blend of gall and satisfaction, because he knew his track record was beyond reproach and also that he would demolish the careers of the three men once he became head of the Labour Party.

Now, the official verdict is about to be pronounced and he is jubilant. The closeness of power is such that the texture of things and the composition of his own cells seem to have changed. Only a few minutes stand between him and what he has been preparing to become since the end of his adolescence: a leader.

Spurred on by this prospect, he goes back to the speech he has been working on with Marc since the day before, ejects a comma, inserts an exclamation mark, and then resumes his rounds, striding like a conqueror. As for Marie, she is still glued to the screen but has changed channels. Disturbing pictures of yet another storm on the coast give way to two or three preachers in quick succession. The last one is the host of a talk show where a facial composite melding the Devil's features with those of Daniel Lambert says it all. Marie shuts off the TV and moves closer to Ariel, steps through the feverish aura surrounding him, and places her hand on the back of his neck.

"And you? Will they put a halo on you, Golden Boy?"

Ariel smiles, kisses his wife's pale forehead perpetually aflutter with nervous little wings. Just then, the telephone rings. The committee has ended its deliberations. As though sensing the momentous news has arrived, the cameras move in closer, like jaws tightening around the house, still slightly parted before biting into the apple.

Marie is choking. She feels as though she's been plunged into water, as though she is watching the celebrations going on around her through a crude glass jar. She leans against a pillar and focuses on her breathing; her lungs don't fill up with water, and the smells of victory are enough to subdue the muddy vortex whistling in her chest. Groping in her handbag, she finds a small candy box. She swallows a tablet that leaves a bitter trail as it slides down her throat. Then she waits a moment and from another container pulls out a menthol lozenge. A wholesome chill inundates her mouth. She is ready to go back and mingle with the crowd, in the middle of which Ariel stands beaming.

He grabs his wife's cool hand and squeezes it. Her bony fist seems to shrink inside his palm and grow hard and dense, a hidden gemstone granting him access to a silent, unaltered region of his being in which he left behind everything he had to give up to get where he is. Marie, with her

pure heart, her unshakable integrity, her undisguised idealism. If it is true these qualities are at odds with political
life, then to have such an open-hearted woman at his side
convinces Ariel he has not abandoned what led him to take
up this profession. He notices her arm is trembling. She
isn't feeling well. He turns toward her, but her eyes reassure him. It will soon pass.

The air in the two-hundred-year-old house where Ariel
grew up is tinged with the fragrance of jonquils. Some people, when holding a party, make it a point of honour to ensure
there is enough alcohol for the guests to drink themselves
into oblivion. Ariel's parents stake their reputation on flower
arrangements. Bouquets the size of Cadillacs have pride
of place in every corner, nearly overshadowing the platters
stacked high with petits fours and sweets. Never before have
the Goldsteins had such an extraordinary opportunity to fête
their only son and show him how immensely proud they are
of him. From the moment he entered their lives they knew he
was destined for great things. Granted, the road has been full
of twists and turns—the underground art scene where Ariel
performed as a slammer, his unpalatable girlfriends and his
even more dubious hairstyles—but as soon as he entered law
school they were reassured. His adolescence was simply the
forge in which their son's talents were tempered.

Amid the toasts of uncles, aunts, and old friends, Ariel
receives the praise with the same magnanimous pride he dis-
played at his bar mitzvah. His old high school buddies taunt
him with teasing grins.

"Real politics will get the better of you, Goldstein the
Good. You'll crack as soon as you're offered your first bribe!"

"Come now, my son is above all that!" Mrs. Goldstein
protests.

"No need to cheat when you're the best," his father adds,
giving Ariel an affectionate pat on the back.

Marie smiles. Goldstein family gatherings invariably throw her into a state of melancholic delight. Her husband grew up surrounded by a munificence of finer feelings. No wonder he's endowed with an unshakable confidence in the future and in himself. There's no comparison with her own childhood, which was spent under the yoke of powerful clan where she was so glaringly out of place. In many ways it was her meeting with Ariel that drew her out of her acute shyness and her vocational dithering. If he hadn't been there to encourage her, she would never have dared to found a humanitarian organization, nor would she have had the strength to deal with powerful men, of which her husband, ironically, was now one.

A strong hand has just settled on her shoulder. Even before Marie turns around, she senses that the hand belongs to Rachel, her sister. From atop her warrior-like stature, Rachel rattles off her congratulations and then laconically apologizes for their parents' absence. Marie cuts her short. She knows perfectly well why they haven't come. It's already hard enough for her father to have a confirmed federalist for a son-in-law; to be seen at a Labour celebration would finish him off. Marie kisses her sister, her ruddy cheeks and the powerful muscles of her canine jaws. Rachel is half a head taller than most of the guests.

Circulating among his own people, Ariel continues to shake hands. Ordinarily, the well-honed gesture is an automatic reflex, but this morning, after officially addressing the party membership, he finds the handshaking intensely satisfying. At last, he's no longer the one who's striving, trying his luck, begging for trust, working behind the scenes. He has fulfilled the hopes his parents had placed in him; he has proven his pre-eminence beyond the shadow of a doubt, and everyone—including the husky guys who, fifteen years ago, demolished him on the ice rink—has to acknowledge this. Savouring the moment, he forces himself not to think of the colossal task that awaits him. He will get to work tomorrow. Right now he ad-libs a little speech reminding his familiars of the days when, with the help of an out-of-tune guitar, he made up lines and rhymes for an intoxicated audience.

When he thanks Marie, she lifts her hand to her chest. Her head is spinning, perhaps from exhaustion or because of the pills; she feels the ground giving way beneath her feet. Or maybe it's the smell of the jonquils going to her head. She hears the sap rumbling in their stems, their stamens launching vague messages into the air. For a fraction of a second she is convinced she understands them. Then, like everything else, the sensation passes.

The first thing to do. Given the widespread public cynicism, given the five wars the country is mired in, given the shantytowns burgeoning on the outskirts of Canada's largest cities and the epidemic of environmental cancers, the first thing to do is neither to consider withdrawing the military nor to discuss social programs and air pollution. The dossiers that Ariel has prepared in recent months are put on the back burner by his director of public relations.

"The first thing to do," she announces, "is to establish you as a normal person. Faithful husband. Good son. Amiable neighbour. Future father. In a word, the antithesis of Lambert. We must offset your predecessor's indiscretions—and your young age—with an image of integrity."

"An image? So what's the current perception? That I'm a corrupt old satrap?"

"No, but the public has no idea. You need to show people who you are."

"Am I going to wear a badge: Good Boy Goldstein?"

Ariel taps on his desk impatiently. He knew very well that once he became leader he would have to submit to some window dressing, but he dislikes it. For years now, he has attended to his image. He yearns to move on to issues of substance, to plunge his hands into the inaccessible matter that he has wanted to mould ever since he took his first steps inside the party. Unaffected by her leader's mood, the publicist continues to lay out her ideas.

"Everything centres on you and Marie. Over the coming weeks we'll need to follow you as much as possible, so people can see you at the restaurant or catch you off guard when you're shopping. In interviews, you'll joke about your domesticity. You have to be approachable and look like Mr. Average."

"In any event," Marc adds, "you'll be under constant scrutiny from now on. Every Tom, Dick, and Jane will take your picture and broadcast everything you say and do on the social networks. That's why Prime Minister Milton avoids being seen in public. You, however, will take the opposite tack. Once you've become a friendly, familiar face for Canadians, we'll address the other issues. Just in time for the elections."

Ariel grudgingly opens the folder his publicist has given him, but he is unable to concentrate. The little MP's office where he grew accustomed to working alone now seems far away. His new quarters bustle day and night; pressing yet altogether insignificant issues arise at all hours. He thinks about his parents, who picture him toiling over the fate of the nation, and feels somewhat ashamed as he turns a page filled with the twelve prescribed shirt styles, arranged in a gamut from "impromptu stroll," to "formal ceremony." Then his thoughts turn to Marie.

When he describes how he spent his day, she of course will refrain from criticizing, but her silence is what will hurt him the most. Without saying a word, she has witnessed each of his compromises since he was first elected, and her extraordinary rectitude has hovered over the hard decisions to which Ariel gave his consent. He must win this election. A single action on his part, the slightest correction of the country's ruinous trajectory would be enough for him to win the wager he made.

Keeping the tumult that surrounds him at bay, Ariel hangs on for an instant to the bright, hazy image of his wife and lets it dance momentarily above the Ottawa skyline before he opens his eyes again, signs an official letter, forwards an email message, clears his throat, replies to a counterpart, straightens his tie, shakes a hand, finds the right tone, refines an argument, improves his standing in the polls, defends his position, aims higher, qualifies without lying, drives his point home without shouting, bends without breaking.

"There's always something blinking," Marie grumbles as she slips a shawl over her eyes in a vain attempt to shut out the icy glow given off by the computer, the mobile phone, the router, the satellite radio, the alarm clock that in less than three hours will start screaming to wrench them out of sleep. Only three hours of sleep left. The thought is enough to rouse the little beasts running through the most rebellious parts of her body: her hands so sensitive to the cold, her hair poking around in the orifices of her face, her feet rippling with tiny spasms. The ticking of her watch on the dresser punctuates the twitching of her extremities. She clenches her jaw.

When you're trying hard to sleep, the slightest rustle, the tiniest tremor in the air becomes unbearable. Marie has been awake for four hours on this her third day battling insomnia. But she forces herself to stay still. She knows that even in the deepest recesses of a dream, Ariel manages to distinguish the sinuous movements of sleep from the firm, sharp ones of wakefulness; in a few seconds, he would be sitting up in the bed asking her what's the matter.

And there would be so much to say in answer to that question. From the moment Ariel's position as party leader was confirmed, Marie has been worrying herself sick. This was unexpected. She had believed she would experience nothing but joy on seeing her husband's unflagging efforts finally rewarded. And yet, the phone call that decided their future filled her straightaway with a sense of foreboding. She has the feeling they will never again be alone and that the lack of privacy will destroy them. Even now in their bedroom, where no one else sets foot, it's as though they were here: the advisers, the delegates, the spokespeople—a shadow cabinet surrounding their bed, together with reporters behaving like Dobermans, and, in the closets or under the box-spring, hordes of lobbyists also waiting for a bone. And this is just the start.

She does not relish the thought of the entire nation knowing her name from now on. She does not relish the prospect of being held up to scrutiny, of people detecting the weariness underneath her foundation, the blood rushing to her cheeks, the nervousness gathering in the hollow of her fist; she, who has no secrets, all at once feels she has so much to hide when it comes to her tastes, her failings and rare moments of cowardice, her family, her background, her youthful peccadilloes. She would never dare to voice this malaise to Ariel, who is more inured to public life. He would not understand why things now appear so burdensome to her. He would not acknowledge that their lives no longer belong to them, that they no longer constitute a closed unit, let alone a family in the making. The house's framework lets out a creak, and she starts in spite of herself.

On the east side of the bed, Ariel is dreaming of a gigantic hedge, a row of trees so dense one cannot see through it. But on the other side he hears the roar of an approaching storm, a ravenous ogre on the march. Suddenly the trees all come crashing down together. He opens his eyes, turns westward and, stretching his arm, strokes his wife's back.

"What's the matter, my love?"

Before she has time to respond, he sits up, and turns on the bedside lamp, instantly killing the constellation of blinking lights. Marie's rumpled face comes into view. Ariel gets up, takes his wife by the hand and leads her downstairs. In the kitchen, he boils some whole milk, to which he adds a drop of rum. Then he opens the door onto the night as vast as the sea. Marie steps out onto the porch, straightens the plush blanket on the swing, and sits down next to Ariel. They let the tenderness of late August rock them, with its headwinds unsure of which season to usher in. Behind a thin layer of clouds, the Perseids are on the wane. The silence is absolute.

"You see," Ariel says, "there's no one. No reporters, no staff. Nights still belong to us."

Marie nods in agreement, warmed by the delicate puffs of vapour rising from her cup.

"Our core hasn't moved, my love. It's smaller but denser. What we put into it doesn't change. And it doesn't concern anyone but us."

"A child?"

"Secrets. New honeymoons, getaways to inns that the satellites can't see. A child—yes, of course. As many children as you wish. You don't believe me?"

Marie purses her lips. So Ariel gently gets to his feet, removes the cup from her hand, and kneels down in front of her to split open her nightgown one button at a time. After the twelfth, he'll plunge into the narrow precinct of his wife's breasts, where her scent is sweetest, and he will make love to her with a kind of intensity that arises just once a year, when the seasons waver between hot and cold, baffled by incomprehensible climate cycles, by ocean currents that have become strangers to themselves.

The first time they met, they fainted. Ariel approached her with a leaflet put out by the student association, Marie extended her fingers toward the hand that he held out to her insistently, and as soon as their palms touched they both collapsed in perfect synchronicity on the parched campus lawn. When they regained consciousness they had no recollection of falling down, only the feeling that a warm wave had swept over their bodies and lingered like the pleasant burning sensation one gets after a day in the sun. Some students who were reading nearby told them they had lain there inert for more than three minutes. No one ventured to revive them because they were thought to be actors rehearsing a scene.

This peculiar prelude did not keep them from agreeing to meet three days later in a draughty café on the McGill University campus. Ariel came up behind her, laid his hand on Marie's shoulder, but before she could even turn around and recognize him they both crumpled to the floor in a peaceful, almost graceful fall. This time an attempt was made to rouse them, but to no avail. Their immobility, though harmless, was persistent.

Their third blackout occurred when they tried to kiss each other on the cheek in a university hallway. After waiting for them to come around, a medical student who had witnessed the scene checked their vital signs and advised them to consult a specialist, which they did the following week. The doctors were hard put to offer an explanation other than a mysterious form of simultaneous epilepsy, a hypothesis that none of the test results supported. On paper they appeared to be absolutely normal.

The fainting spells grew less frequent and less intense only when they began to make love. When they moved in together a few months after the first episode the manifestations of their amorous epilepsy entirely vanished. But traces of it remained each time they touched, however slightly. A sort of quivering that stirred their cells like a tiny, invisible earthquake.

"The strong showing early on in the campaign makes it hard not to see Ariel Goldstein as the Labour Party's long-awaited saviour," the radio voice murmurs from the four cardinal points. "Will this be enough for the party to take back the reins of government, which have eluded it for twenty years? Canadians have three more weeks to decide."

Marc turns the receiver off with a wave of his hand and silence descends like a curtain all around them. He raises his glass:

"To our saviour!"

The gathering erupts in laughter and then follows his lead. Seeing the former military man make such a lighthearted toast has lifted everyone's spirits. For the small team that has been working without letup since the election was called, this friendly brunch is like a break in the clouds. Ariel looks proudly at each one of them and, though he would never admit it, feels relieved to have them by his side. Thanks to them the beginner's blunders that the National Party was counting on never occurred. During his first weeks in the House of Commons he was able to consolidate his reputation and increase his support among voters. After the election campaign was launched his confidence grew. Working a crowd, mixing with "ordinary folks"—that is what he does best, and he knows it.

To his right, Marie's head is spinning and her thoughts are buoyant. She is not in the habit of drinking wine before noon, but something in the room's geometry, in the colour of the walls and the perfectly cooked pumpkin soufflé prompts her to overdo it. Marc and Emmanuelle's home is the picture of perfection. The house, standing on the slopes of Mount Royal, the minimalist furniture, their hi-tech sound system, and the organic champagne are at once extravagant and sublimely necessary.

"Shit!" the publicist blurts out, disrupting the tranquil mood of the meal. "The evangelist media have fished out some Biblical passages warning against the arrival of an ungodly prophet. It's all over the blogs."

"Because Ariel is Jewish? That's ridiculous! No one's going to take it seriously!" Emmanuelle exclaims.

"Not in your progressive bubble, no. But in the rest of the world, absolutely," Marc snaps back.

Marie gets up and steps toward the window. Their hosts' altercations weary her. She knows how fond Ariel is of Marc, but Emmanuelle, the fiery artist, makes her uncomfortable. She can't understand their way of behaving more like adversaries than lovers or their tendency to lock horns in public. Whenever the subject is politics, Marc attacks Emmanuelle; she, on the other hand, takes pains to appear utterly ingenuous, as if she were honour-bound to remain ignorant of the world her husband is part of.

Evidently delighted at finding an excuse to leave the table, Emmanuelle goes to join Marie at the window.

"Election campaigns—they're such a nuisance, don't you think? You must miss Ariel…"

Marie, her thoughts scattered around her, agrees. She desperately misses Ariel. But what she hasn't the strength to explain to Emmanuelle is that she misses him even when she accompanies him to party events, even when she appears beside him as they climb down from the campaign bus, when she hands him a pastry offered by a pro-Labour shop owner, or when she listens to him rehearsing a new speech. To find herself alone with him, by the sea or at a lake, far from everything—that is what she'd like. Nighttime, of course, is still theirs, the opaque cloth where they nestle for a few hours before going out into the world again, but it's not enough. Marie would like to dig wells, tunnels, underground warrens, to dive down into the depths of their love and resurface, breathless, holding in their hands a treasure or an unknown animal. But the campaign monopolizes everything.

After standing next to Marie for a while munching on grapes, Emmanuelle goes away, no doubt vexed by the other's silence. Marie contemplates the landscape spread out below the house. Seen from this angle, the city always makes her feel slightly dizzy. Thousands of dogs and their owners stroll along the paths of Mount Royal, carving ruts into the mountain's back. Canada geese execute Pythagorean manoeuvres in preparation for their departure. The St. Lawrence rumbles like an ogre. Centimetre by centimetre it eats away at the banks. Soon the city will be nothing but a vast bed for a sterile river. Each time she thinks about the rising waters, Marie wants to cry. Ariel comes over and wraps her in his arms.

"We'll learn to breathe under water," he whispers.

Nothing in Canada is colder than a Northern Ontario highway in the middle of the night. It's already winter here. A thin, chalky sheet covers the roadway, where the wind is etching scraggly arabesques. With rhythmic regularity, the icy brightness from the lampposts bleaches the interior of the election campaign bus, a light so harsh it seems audible to Ariel, a caustic whistle close to his ear.

The convoy has already been travelling for six hours. The team is scheduled to reach Kapuskasing at dawn for a tour of a former mine that has been converted into a movie theatre. Because many towns in the region have been closed down over the past few decades, Ariel must reassure the residents, although the bulky folder he is studying provides no reason to be hopeful. He sighs. Around him, Marc and the other advisers are drowsing, their bodies bent in ridiculous postures. Sitting in his huge velvet seat at the front of the vehicle, the driver is invisible. The bus might as well be driving itself.

Through the window, a few moribund hamlets can be seen flashing by with a feeble glow and some wisps of smoke. Misery has nowhere to hide here, nor do Ariel's thoughts. It is far easier to be persuaded one can change things when sitting in Ottawa or Montreal or Toronto. But in the light of these areas left behind by progress and stripped of the amenities they were promised, their decline appears to be unstoppable. Ariel searches almost haphazardly through the database prepared by his team. Despite all the serious research that has been done on poverty-related issues, nothing has gotten to the heart of the matter; no term, no definition is close enough, straightforward enough, incisive enough.

He stands up and shakes out his stiff limbs. The convoy enters an unlit stretch of road, and it's as if the bus had plunged into deep water and were diving toward an abyss where heavy, fearful fossils lie sleeping. As slowly as a mime, Ariel passes his hand in front of his colleagues' faces to verify that they are indeed asleep. He smiles at the childhood trick. Then he tiptoes to the back of the vehicle, where a private nook has been set up for him. His personal effects are there: the old Andreï Markov sweater, his lucky charm, a biography of Pierre Elliott Trudeau that his father gave him a few days ago, and a slim, triangular case. Smiling, he pops open the clasps, which crack like two tiny whips. Nestled inside the padded box is a miniature guitar. A gift received from Marie at the start of the tour. *To stave off boredom while you're on the road. So you don't lose your way*, the card said.

Ariel lovingly lifts the delicate instrument out of its case and presses his tired lips against the neck of the guitar. The kiss leaves a taste of varnish that pricks his tongue. Then, ensconced in his seat, he strokes the strings, muting the sound so as not to wake anyone. A melody rises in a minor key, the scale that never finds happiness yet does not despair.

Marie shuts the door of her childhood room, which has become the realm of Frère Jacques, her parents' malamute. She flops down beside the animal, which is sleeping on the rug, stroking its fur as thick as stalks of strong, nourishing grain, inhaling its rich scent. As far back as she can recall, her family has always had malamutes. A hardy, loyal, dignified breed, embodying all that the Leclercs value. Marie buries her nose in the salt-and-pepper pelt; the dog moans blissfully. She has an urge to whisper one or two secrets into the dog's dense coat, or even to shout, but she contents herself with kissing it.

The little room with a sloping ceiling has remained untouched since she left some fifteen years ago. Whenever she visits it, Marie relives her childhood in reverse, starting with the morning she packed her bags, at once terrified and euphoric at the thought of leaving her home town for McGill University, where her life would finally take flight. Then her adolescence streams by, dreary and terrible; she sees herself bent over her schoolbooks, cloistered in the school environment, the one sphere in which she allowed herself a certain lack of moderation, the one place where she could excel without drawing attention to herself. She contemplates the spectral presence of the Lego cities she built with Rachel, and that of the dolls she would create on Sunday afternoons, little papier-mâché figurines to which she poured out her heart when it was brimming over. She stretches out on the bed, wrapped in the particular atmosphere of a room where one has lived long enough to experience boredom, that blend of living dust and dead time.

The walk from the car to her parents' front door tired her out. There were reporters waiting for them, Ariel and her, in front of the house. It took her father's stentorian voice to open a path through the throng clustered under the large maples in the front yard. Martial greeted his daughter with a hug. Ever since she was a child, it's in moments like this that their relationship has acquired a little substance: Marie having a difficult time, Martial protecting her. Otherwise the fragile little girl and the larger-than-life man repel each other like inverted magnets, she, frightened by him, he, too clumsy to reassure her.

"Are they ever going to leave us alone, those people?" Hortense shouted from the kitchen. "We already had it up to here with our computer being repeatedly broken into! Sixteen hours it took for your father's geeks to get the company's network up and running again."

From the back of the dining room Rachel stood up to speak, her silhouette rearing up as if a Greek column had suddenly been planted in the room.

"Mother, I'll say it again: the hacking has nothing to do with Ariel's new position. It happened before and will happen again."

Rachel is in charge of operations in the family business and has kept an eye on all the hacking incidents; she had already confided to Marie that the frequency of these intrusions had doubled since the beginning of the election campaign. Thankful for this little lie, Marie abandoned herself to the smothering embraces of her sister and mother amid the boisterous barking of Frère Jacques.

As is always the case at the Leclerc residence, the meal was an expeditious affair carried out in a series of quasi-military stages. As soon as Martial had blown out the sixty-one candles on his colossal chocolate cake, Ariel excused himself. Although she was sad to see him head off to a rally at the far end of the country, Marie was relieved. Throughout the meal, her parents constantly badgered him with questions and innuendos. In such moments, which have multiplied in recent months, even Marie is unable to ascertain whether the Leclercs' intention is to punish Ariel for his federalist convictions or rather to influence his decisions regarding Quebec. Either way, their efforts have been unavailing. Regardless of how he feels about their arguments, Ariel inwardly seethes at being lectured to by his in-laws.

Late in the evening, Marie muses on her childhood woes, which roll across the wooden floor of her room like faded marbles. To return to Saint-Roch is to once again drink a concentrated dose of the painful loneliness that for Marie is at the root of everything. She swallows a sleeping pill; Frère Jacques twitches his paws, chasing in a dream a prey that outruns him. The sound of resonant snoring reaches her upstairs room and prickles her skin like the kiss of an incipient beard.

With her head buried in a flattened pillow, she takes a deep breath and wedges her hand between the box spring and the small, sagging mattress. She finds her stuffed monkey stuck to the warped spring box. Endlessly petted, clutched, kissed, soaked with tears, and dressed in useless clothes meant to shield it against bad weather, its synthetic fur is as rough as an old woollen sock. Marie strokes the squashed toy, which has lain hidden under the mattress for nearly two decades, but she does not extract it from its hiding place. When, half-asleep, she finally lets go, she has the fleeting impression of hearing a cloth heart beating through her pillow.

Oddly enough, it was a long time before they realized they had both been adopted. Marie, haunted by her origins, preferred to wait before broaching the subject and kept the truth sealed inside her chest. As for Ariel, his sense of belonging to the Goldstein family was so powerful that he rarely gave any thought to the fact he had been born elsewhere, welcomed into the world by unknown hands, which had passed him on to someone else like a baton in a relay race that was to lead to as-yet-unseen heights.

It was when they first ran off together to the country, to the crude cabin that had belonged to the Leclercs for generations, that they became aware of how similar their paths were. The coincidence did not entirely surprise them. It explained the extraordinary understanding they shared from the very first moment. Marie, who had read extensively on the topic, knew that adopted children often befriend each other spontaneously, sometimes without having the slightest idea of their own origins. Their fractured beginnings lead them to one another, as though guided by a melancholy horse.

"How old were you when you found out?"

"I was eight, I believe. A boy in my class had asked me why my parents had red hair, while mine was brown. When I asked my father, he told me everything."

"You've never wondered who your real parents were?"

"No. I have no memories that don't involve the Goldsteins. I was only a few days old when they took me home. I may as well have been born there. What about you?"

"It's a blur. The things I remember, I probably imagined them. I was four when my parents told me where I came from. The next day the planes crashed into the World Trade Center. For a long time I believed there was a connection between the two events."

"Were you upset?"

"Not at first. They told me my mother was a teenager when she gave birth, and too poor to take care of an infant. The explanation seemed to make sense. But growing up I began to question it. And I envied Rachel for being a biological child."

"Do you still envy her?"

"No. But I wish I looked like her. I've always felt I was the one blot on the illusion of the perfect family."

"Well, I'm very glad you don't look like a field marshal."

Marie smiles at her lover's teasing play on her father's name. Something tells her her father would appreciate it.

"And you? Do you know who your birth mother was?"

"No. I only know she was Jewish, because it was important to my parents to maintain the heritage."

"And here you are with a shiksa, threatening to break the lineage."

"My darling, I'm afraid both of us are disrupting the purity of our lineages."

They laughed as they embraced inside the quilted sleeping bag that the mosquitoes still managed to get through, their skin damp and their limbs welded together. In the mossy woods, among fallen trees, they were a nest of warmth and desire. At some point the moon dropped its chiselled reflection onto the perfectly smooth lake, and all at once Marie rose and dived in, her white body summoning the nocturnal fish and making the luminescent algae dance from the surface all the way down to their hidden roots.

For days he has been gripped by a wild urge to work in the garden. The rain comes down like shards of glass, the ground shrivels up from the cold, November has injected a sterile venom into the air, nothing could grow or even take root in the ground, but Ariel is obsessed with the idea of plunging his hands into the soil, of turning it over and planting rows of lettuce and tufts of chives. This is the incongruous image that emerges on the screen each time he places his fingers on the keyboard to edit a watered-down speech.

His body feels stiff as he stands up and walks over to the rain-streaked window. The outside world is blurred, unintelligible. Cancelled. Ariel starts to weep. A first since the campaign was launched. Until now he has suffered from searing headaches, been assailed by frightful cramps and plagued by bouts of sweating that seemed to sheathe his skin in molten metal, but despite all the stress and frustration, he kept the tears at bay. Tonight, however, with election day looming and the final push just a few hours away, the inner anger that has spurred him on gives way to something new. Disappointment. A gust of wind lashes the window with a spray of rain and Ariel recoils.

A muffled noise ripples down from the second floor. Among other fabulous qualities, Marie's feet, when moving over a wooden floor, have the ability to produce the sound of a brush on raw canvas. The note whispered at the beginning of the world. He listens to the delicate rhythm approaching until it sweeps down on him. She wraps her arms around him and he feels somewhat ashamed. She is the one who for weeks has endured his campaign. Through no choice of her own, she has been photographed, shouted at, caricatured; reporters have analyzed her hairdo, her outfits, her way of smiling at the elderly; they have dissected her elocution, her education, her family. She is the one who can't sleep, who gorges herself on tranquilizers and stands around next to him during public appearances. And now he's the one crying.

"You'd think we were about to be drowned."

"No, no. The rain will stop. And this time tomorrow we'll be celebrating your victory."

Ariel lowers his eyes in the direction of his wife.

"What victory? I wanted to win this election on my terms. And I haven't stopped compromising. It's not my program I'm defending but the packaging.

"To reach your goals compromises are unavoidable—you know that."

"But *you* don't make compromises."

"And I never reach my goals."

Ariel smiles wanly. Marie is mistaken, he thinks. Working daily for a cause you yourself have defined, under conditions you have chosen, constitutes a kind of victory that he is more and more convinced will always elude him. As if she has heard her husband's thoughts, Marie grasps his face between her hands and tightens her grip.

"Your campaign has been extraordinary. No matter what you think, you defended your values and some crucial ideas. Your objectives are so high that you're always sure you've failed. But you succeeded where people had already given up hope of seeing someone even try. And I'm very, very proud of you."

Ariel, his cheeks aflame, leans down to kiss his wife. In her legs she senses a faint echo of their bygone blackouts, and she smiles.

"Now, leave your speech alone and come along. I'll uncork the bottle of cognac my uncle gave us at our wedding. Unless you'd prefer to keep it for your birthday?"

Ariel shrugs.

"I'm not having a birthday this year."

"Oh, yes you are. You have no choice. I'm preparing a surprise! Thirty-five—that's something to celebrate!"

Ariel brightens up. Year after year, his birthday, which falls on December 24, in the shadow of both the Jewish and Christian holidays, is eclipsed by the profusion of garlands and dreidels. Still, Marie insists on throwing a party for him, knowing that her husband can't resist the childish enjoyment of presents and surprises, of holding something shiny in his hands. At the mere mention of it he forgets the rain, the speech, and his horticultural cravings. He is seven years old again and the world has recovered its magical glow. The one thing Marie knows for certain is that this part of him must stay alive if he is to win the election.

Ariel presses down on his computer, which folds onto his draft like a large, tired hand. Outside, the wind has become a wail, a high-pitched whistle, almost a call for help.

"Do you hear something?" Ariel asks.

They stare at each other. Marie runs to the door and—it seems to her—barely grazes the handle, yet already the door has swung open, letting in the water, the fury, and the madness of the weather. The storm goes quiet just long enough for a misshapen creature to dash across the threshold and plant itself on the makeshift promontory of the coffee table, from which it surveys the premises. Once it stops moving, Marie and Ariel finally manage to examine it and recognize a shape under the layer of mud puddling at its feet. A cat.

"And where have you come from, little fellow?"

It opens wide its huge golden eyes and lets out a meow that says it all. It has come out of nowhere. It has never known a litter box, a home, or the teats of a female cat. It rose out of the mud on a stormy evening and ran toward the light, toward the promise of warmth, and will never leave it.

Canada's new prime minister. He's young. He brings people together. Has ideas. Energy. Charm. A knack for the quick rejoinder. John F. Kennedy. He speaks four languages, including Hebrew and Inuktitut. He knows how to mollify the Québécois. He is the youngest person ever to have held this position, and the first Jew, though not a practising Jew. But neither is he an atheist. He plays the guitar. He loves brioches and had one in every city during his election tour because everywhere he stopped he was treated to them. He is good at hockey, even better at tennis. He knows his classics. Neil Young, Cronenberg, Atwood, Terry Fox. Canadiana. According to his medical records he is epileptic. He does not smoke. Drinks in moderation. Jogs. Won't decline a motorcycle ride when a helmet is available. He rode one four times over the course of the campaign. He voted in his Montreal West riding, a stone's throw away from where he grew up. Where the old-timers know him. Call him Golden Boy, like everyone else. He's going to change the face of the country. Give the silent majority a voice. The frustrated, overburdened, cynical, apathetic majority. Ariel Goldstein is going to clean things up. Fire corrupt civil servants. Invest in schools. Bring back women's right to abortion. Take our children out of prison. Kick the media's ass. Hold out a friendly hand to dissenters, outsmart the terrorists, rein in the militias. Put an end to racism. Transform every single slum into a palace. Reverse climate change. Establish universal peace.

Ariel Goldstein, the thirty-sixth prime minister of Canada. Golden Boy.

The camera flashes turn the crowd into something sparkling and, what's more, indistinct. The mass of supporters parts like the waters of the Dead Sea to let the couple pass, and, borne along by a groundswell, they are up on the stage in no time. They approach the podium together. Marie plants an appropriate kiss on her husband's feverish cheek, then steps back. Ariel is left alone at the mic. Unbeknown to the audience, he wrings his hands a little. All that is visible is Ariel's winning smile. Even without seeing his face, Marie senses the smile and the deep breath that comes next. "This country has been turned into a place that is not in our image."

Ariel waits for the renewed surge of applause to abate. Though he cannot see them, he can guess where his crew of strategists is standing. Their hands clap with metronomic regularity and self-congratulatory strength, with the satisfaction of a job well done and the smugness of victory. Deep in his heart Ariel is jubilant. He is no longer working for them. His address continues, full of promises and acknowledgements. He had the feeling he had not properly rehearsed his speech, but now that he is on stage, looking out at this sea seething with such a wild, collective joy, the words come to him so naturally he could just as well be extemporizing. Last night's anxiety has given way to that almost unseemly euphoria that grabs hold of him whenever he addresses a crowd. Years ago, a comrade asked him where he drew his confidence when speaking in public. "I always have the feeling I'm speaking to just one person," Ariel had replied. It was true before he met Marie. Ever since, he knows he was always speaking to her.

The celebration explodes into a strange blend of dignity and excess, in which the desire to project the right image is at odds with the heady sensation of seeing the horizon open up before one's very eyes and with the need to dance at the prospect of all the new possibilities. Once the evening is over, only Marie, Ariel, Marc, and Emmanuelle stay behind, drinking spring water in the hope of recovering a semblance of respectability before dawn. Jubilation gives way to the contemplation of the months ahead, the anticipation of the time of major reorganization that awaits them.

"It's strange," Marie says. "It's as though everything has just shifted. And it took just one day."

"And 11,558 votes," Ariel adds.

"That's politics for you," Marc observes. "There are two possible worlds, and in a few brief moments everything gets decided, we're thrust into one or the other and our lives are transformed."

"It's like falling in love!" Emmanuelle exclaims, her cheeks gone crimson.

"I don't agree," Marie retorts. "Love isn't a momentary thing. It's something that has always existed deep inside us and that rises to the surface when we summon it. Like a permanence of being."

The four comrades fall silent, but then Marc lets out a dry little laugh, which is immediately cut short by Emmanuelle, whose gaze is fixed on Marie.

"Shush. It's important, what she just said."

Cursing the Ontario wine that loosens her tongue like this, Marie tugs discreetly at Ariel's sleeve. His voice exhausted by the evening's speeches and endless conversations, Ariel announces they are leaving. Hand in hand, Mr. Prime Minister and his wife go out into the bracing air and take their seats in the car that is now theirs, with two bodyguards sitting up front. Marie shivers. They've become bodies that must be guarded. From now on something vague and evil lies lurking and must be fended off.

The cat did not enjoy the trip to the capital. As soon as the car set out, he began to snarl in his cage and scratch at invisible adversaries. Since arriving at the official residence two weeks ago, it has lost none of its rancour; it hisses whenever anyone approaches and leaves puddles of urine in different corners, forcing the residents to spend hours sniffing out the exact spot like clumsy creatures. Neither Marie nor Ariel understands exactly why the animal—which they've named Wretch—has adopted them. It does not seek their care or affection and turns its nose up at most of the meals they serve it, insisting instead on rustling up its provender outdoors. They are even more at a loss to explain the docile attachment they feel toward it.

The official residence is inhabited by shadows, by ossified, impassive mirages, the legacy of generations of people who lived there knowing they were only passing through, dreading they would be driven out too soon or sometimes horrified at feeling imprisoned there. A long line of prime ministers' spouses has repainted, changed the wallpaper, and refurnished in the hope of making the premises their own, but without ever managing to feel at home inside these walls, which close in imperceptibly from year to year, thickened by the layers of colour added over and over.

Marie was not planning to redecorate. For her, this dwelling is just a pied-à-terre. Her home is still Montreal, the little house where she and Ariel have lived since their wedding, with its cracked walls, creaking beams, unkempt yard, and misty windows. But Ariel, in a surprising display of superstitious inclinations, got very worked up. Living amid the decor of the previous government would surely bring bad luck, politically speaking. So Marie has hired a marvellously authoritarian designer and bows unquestioningly to his directives. Yes, acid green in the kitchen. Very well, a mauve wall in the living room. Oversized light fixtures. And a giant steel egg in the hall—why not?

Reassured by the makeover of his new house, Ariel tackles the transition process with renewed vitality. He has put the ups and downs of the election campaign behind him and is prepared to wipe the slate clean; between meetings, he repeats ready-made phrases that bolster his morale. In the morning, Marie hears him mumbling words that sound like "first day of the rest of my career" while he knots his tie. The reins of the nation weigh a ton and the team under harness is made up of dogs who ignore each other. He needs such maxims to convince himself that he will be able to lead them in the right direction.

As for Marie, she tries to adjust to the numbing pace of working at home. She is unused to the fuzzy boundaries between work and private life, and the borderline seems to be disappearing in every area of her life. She wanders around in pyjamas and wastes hours viewing rubbish instead of organizing her symposium on the death penalty. The cat claws at her ankles when they cross paths, believing that there are enemies hiding under the long panels of her dressing gown. This is the state that Ariel's parents surprise her in when they show up unannounced.

"Are you ailing, dear?" her mother-in-law immediately inquires as she presses the backs of her thin fingers against her daughter-in-law's cheek.

"No, no, I'm simply a little slow today," Marie replies, aware that her dazed appearance is only fuelling the Goldsteins' conjectures as to her first pregnancy, which they anticipate nearly more impatiently than she does.

Under their inquisitive gaze, she shows them around the house while attempting to collect the scraps of herself adrift on the floor. The Goldsteins fan out like a flock of birds, their frenetic presence fills the sealed up boudoirs, and their flapping wings upset the silence in which Marie has wrapped herself. After taking the kitchen, the television stations, and the arrangement of the closets by storm, they direct their efforts to training the cat. Marie takes refuge in the bathroom and gulps down some pills that dampen the invasive commotion going on around her. In the evening, her guests refuse to go to bed and stay up until midnight waiting to welcome Ariel home. When he arrives, they ignore his tiredness and bombard him with a jumble of high-handed questions and advice. The Goldsteins have never been able to share their son, but this is the first time it has made Marie feel sick. After a few days, she announces she has to go to Quebec City to take care of some urgent matters. She boards the train and watches the kilometres between her new and old lives slip past like prayer beads. Back in his office, Ariel experiences a swaying sensation. He misses his wife already.

The winter holiday festivities have gotten under way weeks ahead of time. Labour's Christmas party. The donors' cocktail party. The media gala. The cabinet dinner. But the event that does Ariel the most good is the private meal with Marc and Emmanuelle. Alongside the mass of adversaries and false allies that have been crowding him for months, his right-hand man has stood out as a true friend, one who does not indulge in whispered slander and backstabbing. In their beloved old house in Notre-Dame-de-Grâce, flanked by Marie's boreal beauty and Marc's solid, upright presence, Ariel finds that all's well in his world. Emmanuelle, with her perennially sullen air, is the only one out of tune. She chafes at Marc's new schedule and constantly insinuates he is unfaithful to her. Evidently, spending Christmas Eve in the prime minister's company was not part of her vacation plans. Ariel tries to ignore the sour mood radiating from Emmanuelle by stroking his wife's knee. Marie clutches his fingers with an almost animal violence, which each of her gestures has evinced since the evening began. He could make love to her right here and now.

As soon as the guests have left, Ariel grabs Marie by the hips. He feels the words rising, ready to materialize in his mouth laced with the sugary flavour of Port. He wants them to have a child. Tonight. He does not want to wait for the right strategic moment, for his power to be consolidated, for the winning conditions. He wants to give his wife everything she desires, right now.

His impulse is curbed by the sound of the telephone. Marie seizes the chance to tiptoe away. In her bedroom she finds the two envelopes that she prepared. Her heart is pounding so hard it makes her reel. She hasn't taken any medication since the beginning of the week. She wanted to be clear-headed for this moment, which she has been planning in absolute secrecy for months. She goes down the stairs gripping the handrail, as if on a ship in the middle of a storm. Through the buzzing that fills her head she hears Ariel scolding a political aide.

"Don't you have a father, an aunt, a neighbour, Odile? A Madagascan roommate? So now you're going to hang up, put on a clean sweater and leave the office to go wish him Merry Christmas, and if you can manage that, then have a glass of some alcoholic beverage. Anything will do. Mouthwash if need be. And don't call me anymore because of what some asinine amateur blogger has to say. For the next twenty-four hours, I don't exist."

When he hangs up, Marie is standing in front of him; her complexion is opalescent, her gaze poignant.

"Happy birthday!"

Ariel smiles and moves closer, ready to dive under his wife's skirt. She checks him with a trembling hand that proffers an envelope decorated with a gold ribbon. Her other hand holds a second envelope just as bulky as the first.

"You've brought me work? A case that needs to be dealt with during the holidays? You're too kind!" he scoffs, snatching up his gift with a wink.

Marie does not laugh. She solemnly places her hand on her husband's to stop him from opening the envelope too soon.

79

"Inside, there's a surprise for both of us. I wanted for us to have a chance to get to know ourselves better, to understand ourselves better. These papers…"

She pauses, muzzled by an invisible filter. Ariel pulls her over to the loveseat, to the gentle warmth of the hearth.

"These documents contain the identities of our birth mothers."

Ariel stops. Each of his movements—of his guiding arms, of his coiling spinal column, of his faithfully returning breath—hovers in mid-air.

"I know you would have preferred to wait, but… if we're thinking of having kids, I feel it's important to know where we come from. I don't expect the contents of these envelopes to go beyond the walls of this house. We can throw them in the fire afterwards, if you like. Your parents won't know. This is for us. For the nucleus. It belongs to us."

Ariel plops down on a cushion and takes a gulp of Port as he contemplates the golden ribbon and the secrets wrapped within it.

"You have no idea what we'll find in there?"

"No. I did whatever it took to wait until we could open them together."

"Well, okay then, let's do it."

There are moments that nothing can prepare you for. Such as fainting on shaking hands with a stranger. Or reading your mother's name for the first time. You don't know what to do, how to behave. You forget how to breathe, blink your eyes, swallow the stones building up in your mouth. Ariel unties the ribbon, slips the set of papers out of the envelope, skims through them. Barely moving his lips he murmurs a woman's name while Marie, sitting beside him, performs the same gestures, and in her turn utters a name. Like an echo. A poisoned refrain.

For many minutes, they remain frozen next to each other, unable to speak, unable to cry, paralyzed in a moment like the one experienced by suicides, the deafening minutes that elapse before they decide to pull the trigger. Finally, Marie holds out her hand. Ariel passes her his papers, and she gives him hers. There's no mistake. There it is in black and white. Eva Volant. The same name twice. Two parallel lines that nevertheless meet at the source. A geometrical aberration. Thirty-three years earlier, Eva Volant, fifteen years old, gives birth to two premature babies. She gives up the girl for adoption, but wants to keep the boy. A month later, the boy is placed in the care of a private agency. Their three paths should never have crossed again.

After the vomiting, the screaming, the blows against the wall and the convulsions, it takes hours for them to start speaking again. "I love you," they say in the same flat voice. Then Ariel pulls on his coat and goes out into the winter that crunches like a thousand bones.

They had wanted a small, private wedding, but, of course, the proprieties, etiquette, and the countless relations of their respective families forced them to revise their invitation list. All told, two hundred and ten people gathered together to watch them exchange their promises in the most beautiful garden of La Belle Province, at the foot of a weeping willow ringed around by wild roses. Everything went wrong, from the storm that broke a few minutes before the ceremony began, to the indigestion that Ariel miraculously contained when he made his vows, not to mention the door that had slammed shut on Marie's hand that same morning. By the time he put the wedding band on her ring finger, the nail had turned completely black. And yet they took none of these unfortunate incidents to be a bad omen. They were so elated at getting married that on seeing the wedding pictures later on they would have to look closely to recall that it had rained, that they had been ill and injured, that the train of Marie's gown had caught fire during the first dance, that a stray dog had burst in and stolen the spit-roasted lamb shank. The mishaps made them laugh. The more disastrous the wedding, the happier the marriage, they kept repeating.

In the small hours, they slipped away from the tent where some drunken dancers kept on swaying. The sky had cleared and was now suffused with an unreal moonlight. They followed a little winding path to the lake. They joked about the monster inhabiting its waters and commanded it to show itself. They lay down on the wharf, and the love they made was so exquisitely joyous they thought they heard music, an untuned guitar. The morning found them sleeping on the old, furry wood, both of them swathed in the myriad folds of her layer-cake wedding gown. It was, they believed, the start of an eternity.

"Who else knows?"

"No one."

"The people you contacted? To find the paper trails?"

"Two different agencies. Yours, as you know, exclusively handled adoptions of Jewish—or supposedly Jewish—children. Mine was run by reformist Christians and covered the entire continent. No one will make the connection."

"And the government? They have files, archives…"

"Of course. But someone would have to do some very specific research to be able to discover the link."

"Which is certainly likely to happen over the four years of my mandate."

"I don't know what to say. I…"

"Don't apologize, Marie. It would have come out sooner or later."

Their conversation dissolves into nothing but sobs. In any case, words have become worthless. Expressing their love for each other is forbidden now, and pretending to feel nothing, impossible. Voicing their disgust is unthinkable. They have called each other every day since the night of December 24, at first to say nothing, to hear the other breathing, to get used to what this dizzying symmetry involves. Then they tried— though not in so many words—to consider what to do next. De facto separation; a semblance of marriage. Later, the public announcement. They'll wait a few months for that. First they must succeed in grasping it themselves. Until then, whenever they find themselves overwhelmed by panic, they can still hang on to a tissue of illusion. Nothing has happened. They are still married.

Marie asks for sick leave. For weeks she trails after Wretch, who, even in January, finds a way to bring back bloody carcasses she does not have the strength to dispose of. She sleeps, cries, grows thinner, prostrated in front of a screen that, like the cat, manages to deliver the daily carnage of the outside world. The southwest of the country is buried in snow; in Toronto, it reaches to the second floor of build-ings. Eight people die of asphyxiation. Army helicopters hover continuously, on the lookout for residents in distress, yet every day two or three victims vanish, swallowed up by the winter. In the West, the cities are paralyzed by protest-ing Christian fundamentalists. Using burnished crosses, the Protestants smash store windows and car windshields. They are opposed to the reintroduction of biology courses in the high-school curriculum, an election promise that Ariel has just fulfilled. It seems to Marie that she sees him in every thirty-second clip. She imagines the decisions he must make, his hesitations, his sweaty hands at 11 p.m. and the magnifi-cent lines that crease his forehead in moments of conflict. At times she goes so far as to offer advice, as if he were there, sharing his concerns. They are not made to be apart. That is the frightening conclusion she has drawn from the disclo-sure of their origins.

Ariel, meanwhile, can't sleep. His nights are populated by monsters, prehistoric birds that devour his liver. To escape them he throws himself into his work, keeping tabs on the rescue operations in Toronto. He addresses the evangelist protestors on a daily basis. He feverishly prepares for the new parliamentary session and insists on tracking the progress of every ministerial issue. He overdoes it, but this is ascribed to beginner's zeal. No one suspects that a head of state's workaholism conceals a personal calamity.

A week before the opening of Parliament, an outburst of violence in Quebec makes it imperative to hold an emergency meeting. In Montreal, automobiles are being blown up. The pattern is always the same: unemployed youths from regions outside the big city target non-francophone institutions. In reaction to these attacks, neo-Loyalist organizations issue countervailing threats. Street fighting proliferates. Within the Labour cabinet there is no lack of good ideas to calm things down.

"Goldstein, I think a tour of Quebec is needed."

"It's time for you and your lovely wife to launch a charm offensive to douse the torches of our perennial angry hicks."

"With language like that, we're sure to charm them," Ariel snaps back.

"You may want to start in Marie's native region. To show that you're a local boy by marriage. What do you think?"

"A few photos with the in-laws would be even better! Nothing beats a schmooze with separatists when it comes to outsmarting the mad dogs."

"I'm sure the Leclercs will be delighted."

Ariel's half-hearted sarcasm is lost on his advisers, who go away pleased with their leader's cooperation. As soon as his office door closes behind them, Ariel collapses. Marc is completely taken aback.

"Come on! You knew very well things would be dicey in Quebec!"

Ariel shakes his head.

"There's something I have to tell you. I need your help and your absolute discretion. We could lose everything."

Marie is distressed by the explosions. At this rate, politicians will be targeted next. A few days after the second bombing of the new year, her sister shows up, intending to take her out of the big city and harm's way.

"You're on sick leave? Come to Saint-Roch to recuperate. You're not going to get better with all the bombs going off. What's the matter, anyway?"

Marie sighs. She hasn't the slightest wish to leave her home, whose every corner reminds her of Ariel. She can spend hours stretched out in a closet, sniffing the clothes he'll no longer wear, brushing against the walls he's leaned on and through which their love came to life. Dusting is out of the question. Every particle contains a little of him, of his DNA, so close to her own. If she can't see him, she wants at least to wallow in his dust, to coat herself with what's left of him.

Rachel frowns as she contemplates Marie's pallor. She is aware of just three remedies for existential woes: exercise, a T-bone steak, and good night's sleep. This is the treatment she sets out to inflict, in that order, on her neurasthenic sister over the six days she has decided to spend in the chaos of the city. Marie wobbles when they take a walk, vomits at the mere sight of red meat, and paces back and forth at night, but Rachel remains unfazed. Until the morning she finds her sister unconscious on the bathroom floor, with an empty bottle of pills beside her.

In her imagination, the colour of death's door was white; what she discovers is just the opposite. For forty-eight hours, she feels as though she's being attacked by a Jackson Pollock painting. A network of agitated veins tightens around her, torments her arms and legs as if to drown her, as if to smother the part of her that still wants to live and damn the part trying to die. That is why she decides to fight. She would like to end it all, but not like this, not like the last beluga caught in a filthy net.

She wakes up in her bed, with Rachel to her right and a doctor to her left. Their first words amount to amorphous mumbling. Her answers are hardly any clearer. Words and ambient sounds come to her like gently lapping water, as though her head were submerged. The doctor stammers a few words of advice before giving her an injection. This time she plunges into a sea of molten gold. For hours, it seems to her she's swimming in honey, waving her limbs about with a heavy, delicious slowness and finding comfort in that movement. She will not die. Her life does not end here.

When she resurfaces the morning light is like a benevolent blanket that someone has thrown over the house, as when a piece of furniture needs to be protected during a long period of disuse. Rachel, her face twitching, is asleep beside her, deep in conversation with someone in her dream.

"Where is Ariel?" Marie manages to utter.

Her sister rouses and, true to her habit, is instantly awake, clear-minded and ready for action.

"I haven't called him. He's not aware of what happened. I haven't told anyone, actually, except the doctor."

Dismayed, Marie turns her head away. Her tongue feels coated. She reaches for a glass of water standing on the night table, but her arms flop down like a sail gone slack. Rachel helps her take a sip, then she stands up and pulls a sheaf of papers from the drawer. The documents, the damned files. Eva Volant. A surge of blood revives Marie's limbs and she straightens up.

"While you were unconscious, I found this. I've decided to keep your suicide attempt under wraps for the time being. So as not to bring all the journalists running. Ariel's family. Our family."

There is no way of telling whether her tone of voice is disgusted, accusatory, or indulgent. Or none of the above. When confronted with tragedies or moral dilemmas, Rachel generally stays neutral. Cool headed. Torn between resentment at her sister's prying and gratitude for her presence of mind, Marie says nothing. Except:

"I think I'd like some red meat now."

In February, a man sneaks onto the grounds of the official residence in the middle of the night and starts firing bullets at the windows. The bodyguards shoot him down just as the fifth windowpane shatters. Ariel, who was taking a shower, is not even aware of the attack. The assailant is identified as Rachad Maliki, a man beset with psychiatric problems. Security at 24 Sussex Drive is tightened as well as the surveillance of white supremacist militias, which see the incident as additional justification for stalking any man whose face is darker than theirs. But the episode acts as a spur on Ariel, just as Marie's suicide attempt brings her back to the world of the living. She resumes her impassioned advocacy of intergenerational justice; Ariel is able to sleep, eat, and function like a man and not just a statesman. They manage to appear together at official events. To look at them, there is nothing amiss. The tremor inside them is undetectable. They say very little to each other, do not touch, hardly look at each other. Too dangerous. Like Tristan and Iseult, they need a sword, a blade to keep them from falling on one another like the particles of a collapsing star.

Early one Sunday morning, a neighbour comes knocking at the door of their Montreal home looking ill at ease.

"I'm sorry, Marie, but have you been out of the house today?"

Marie shakes her head and steps out onto the porch, her feet clad in no more than a pair of pilled socks. Someone has written on the wall in green letters: *Marie Leclerc, chienne de Goldstein. Rase-toi la tête, pute des Juifs.* In short: Shave your head, bitch. Whore to the Jews.

The neighbour scarcely has time to offer a hand in repainting the wall. She shuts and locks the door, paces around the telephone, and finally dials Ariel's number. They stopped communicating directly in January. Any contact between them goes through Marc, who efficiently and discreetly arranges their public appearances. Marie has written a thousand letters to Ariel but never sent them. She stores them in the sleeves of her husband's bathrobe, which otherwise is a flat and mournful article of clothing, an empty skin. Over time, it has filled out thanks to the accumulated layers of paper.

"Is that you?" Ariel answers after one ring.

"It's me. I don't know what to do."

She relays the message tattooed on the house. Of course, she knows what should be done: take pictures and then cover the writing while waiting for the police. That is not the reason she hesitates. What's gnawing at her is the urge to climb a skyscraper, a mountain, or some other promontory and kiss her husband with the whole country looking on, to respond to the attack by causing a sensation. This affront, more than anything else, has eroded the wall so painfully erected between them. But she doesn't know how to say this to Ariel. In any case, it would do no good.

"Don't worry. I'll handle it."

She hangs up, shaken by the few sentences they exchanged. It takes so little. She sinks to the floor like a puddle of water. Planted in front of her, Wretch the cat looks at her with contempt. If he had opposable thumbs, she could swear he was to blame.

She waits all day for the government people to arrive, the ones that Ariel presumably will have sent to take care of the situation before the media arrive. To no avail. Around eight p.m., she hears a commotion outside. Believing the vandals have returned, she grabs her can of pepper spray, the holy water of solitary, nervous women. But a few seconds before opening the door, she drops her weapon. The person on the other side is Ariel; of this she is suddenly and absolutely certain.

She finds him in a ski jacket, gloveless, and shivering as he tries to pop open a container of paint with a dry branch while his two bodyguards prowl around the house.

"'Spiced azure,' wasn't that it, the colour?"

Unable to do otherwise, Marie opens her arms to him.

After disclosing the terrible secret to Marc, Ariel had to solemnly swear to never again find himself alone with Marie. On that condition, his right-hand man succeeded in erasing all bureaucratic traces of the blood ties between the prime minister and his wife. As for Marie, she made the same promise to Rachel. Still, they do not feel they are cheating. They are the real victims, duped by reality, destined since birth to be ambushed, an unavoidable trap they did not deserve.

They make love all night, transported by a flood tide that lifts them above shame and biology; they climax each in turn, oblivious, their bodies nimble, their skins washed. They reiterate the only possible mode of existence for them—being together. Ariel traces with his finger the features of his wife's face etched beneath the damp sheet.

"I never found that we looked alike," he declares sadly.

"Yet that's what others told us."

"They say that about all lovers. When two people love each other they end up sharing a family likeness."

"Lovers are all twins at the outset. Parts of a being believed to have been split in two. Plato described it as a body with four legs and four arms that Zeus is said to have sliced in two, fearing its power. The halves are condemned to search each other out."

A blast of wind shakes the frame of the house, which sends a torrent of words of love spilling into the room. The language of wood. This house understands them.

They are awoken by repeated calls. It takes them a moment to untangle their naked limbs. The ringing of the telephone is a jarring din around their nucleus, where nothing retains its meaning, a magnetic field that overturns the laws of physics. They rise, neither happy nor sad but simply sated, filled with the same certainty that sustains migratory birds. After a few teetering paces in the cottony morning, Ariel finds his bathrobe stuffed with letters, which pour out of the sleeves when he steps into it. Marie floats down to the ground floor, hunts up a bag of frozen bagels and lights the oven. The heat spreads quickly. Ariel dawdles amid the familiar scents, calling the cat, which did not come home the night before.

"You have to go back to Ottawa right away?"

"Depends on the news," Ariel answers as he switches on the TV.

A bizarre déjà vu takes shape on the screen. Their house. The empty swing pinned down by the weight of the snow. On the porch, the can of paint left behind the day before, the coat of blue half-concealing the green insults. At the bottom of the frame, a headline scrolls past. *Another scandal for the Labour Party of Canada*. The words trickle out with agonizing slowness. Marie gently parts the curtains and then turns around looking drained.

"They're here," she confirms.

The news ticker unfurls implacably. *The Prime Minister…* Ariel reads. The camera lens scans the grounds. Branches brought down by the ice appear on the screen… *married…* the text continues. The camera sweeps over the official car, where the bodyguards stand waiting impassively… *to his sister*, the TV concludes. At exactly that instant, Ariel and Marie simultaneously make the same unspoken wish: to never again leave this house.

The Stairway
(MONETTE AND ANGIE)

ANGIE HAS regained her composure. The calming effect that walking has on her—something she can't explain—rises from her legs to her head in the same way the cold does when she goes out barefoot in the evening. She is a little ashamed now of having lost her temper, of letting Monette witness her anger against the birds, her useless, sentimental actions. Animals die every day in the wild, Mam says, and one ought not grieve over it any more than one rejoices at the birth of their offspring. Monette turns around a few times trying to spot the crows. Angie doesn't ask her if they've returned.

The little girls leave the string of vacant lots and come back to the more populated section of the street, where the buildings are taller and much older. For the umpteenth time, Angie fingers the change nestled in the pocket of her shorts. It's all there; everything is fine. They reach the bridge that crosses one of the countless rivers and streams running through the city—greenish, foul-smelling, yet teeming with the prodigious activity of sub-species of fish, salamanders, and tadpoles mired in a translucent mud through which their smooth or sudden movements can be discerned.

Monette stops halfway across the bridge, bends her head forward, and then looks imploringly at Angie, who signals her consent with a nod. The delighted younger sister diligently puffs her cheeks and lets fly a wad of spit that hits the surface of the river with a noticeable splash. Satisfied, she resumes her walk. When Angie crosses here alone, she takes the liberty of dropping something she's found into the water, usually a piece of wood that will drift down to the sea. But not today.

Gradually, the street comes alive. Old ladies sweep their porches with unexpected energy; kids throw basketballs through hoops with gaping nets. Passersby go in and out of nameless stores that have mysteriously survived the arrival of large malls on the outskirts of Savannah. The coins in Angie's pocket jingle. Out of the corner of her eye, she recognizes a few girls from her school but pretends not the see them.

A ball rolls up to Monette's feet, and she immediately bends down to pick it up but is checked at the very last moment by her sister, who senses a trap. Behind a hedge two boys are stifling their giggles. With the tip of her sole Angie kicks back the ball covered with dog shit and nudges her little sister toward the other side of the street. They'll be there soon.

Half a dozen teenage boys are lolling on the grocery stair-way; it's an old building, which from a distance appears for all the world to be resting on piles—not such an absurd idea, given the climate along the Georgia coast. The youngsters chew on jujubes and peppered beef jerky and swap slaps in a furtive exchange of invisible objects, practising the covert moves that all too soon will be their bread and butter. When the two young girls arrive, the boys give them the sideways look that manages to stare without ever meeting the other's gaze, the intent look whose weight Monette does not yet grasp and Angie has already learned to evade.

Intimidated by the group, who leave little room for them to climb the stairs, Monette stops, but Angie prods her, know-ing how important it is not to slow down, not to leave an opening for the pack. The little girl is uneasy and stumbles as she makes her way up the stairs; the boys snicker. Seeing her sister's tiny shoulders sag, Angie deftly lifts her up and sets her back on her feet. As she does when walking in the woods, Angie has the feeling snakes could slither out from any direction and coil themselves around her feet; she would like to run inside the store but holds back and straightens her angular body in order to appear strong and proud. Finally, Monette reaches the door, stretches her arm out to open it but doesn't manage to turn the knob. Angie comes to her rescue and soon they hear the familiar tinkling of the rusted bell. The street disappears; the numbing tenderness of the air-conditioning takes hold of them.

The Cat's Tail
(SIMON AND CARMEN)

THE RAIN is so heavy that neither the bay nor the end of the bridge can be made out. Only the lights along the shore, the harbour lights and those on the poor boats steaming out to sea pierce the darkness. Yet it is still early. Carmen cranes her neck in an attempt to glimpse Alcatraz through the storm. She always looks for the island when crossing the bay. That she's unable to see it now annoys her.

"Look straight ahead," Simon grumbles in the passenger seat. "If only they would keep the lighthouse working."

She rummages through her handbag, pulls out her mobile phone, and reads a message while her brother sighs impatiently beside her.

"Do you know how many people die each year fiddling with their phones while driving?"

Carmen shrugs. Deep down she's convinced of having more than two eyes. When she looks at the landscape she still manages to watch the road ahead. When she sends an SMS she has no trouble seeing Simon's frown of exasperation. Running races has nurtured this ability. A sort of double vision or, rather, double consciousness. The ability to be simultaneously in one's body and elsewhere. Though unaware of it, Simon shares this gift. He is too focused on the straight and narrow to let himself be diverted like this.

Simon is yoked to his chosen course, and he follows it like a soldier on the march.

"Have you heard about this re-enactment business at Alcatraz? It happened a few months ago, in the fall, I believe. A bunch of youths took advantage of the island being closed on a holiday and landed there at night. They occupied the cells, the guardrooms, and recreated penitentiary life as it was in the fifties. They left a long rope made of sheets knotted together hanging from a window. Ring a bell? Surely you must have investigated."

After muttering a few words that sound like "coast guard jurisdiction," Simon leans forward to switch on the radio. Barack Obama's voice rings out, broadcasting a message to the nation that the brother and sister only half listen to. The bridge makes landfall. To their right the dinosaurs of the port of Oakland keep on unloading cargo with sweeping elliptical movements, their rasping machinery not the least bit bothered by the rain. As they drive past the high-rise apartment buildings of Emeryville, Carmen tries to pick out her mother's window. Just like Alcatraz Island, the apartment is empty, dark, and impossible to distinguish in the grey light. She turns onto a wide street washed by the downpour. In the distance the neon sign of the hospital shows the way. All the windows there are lit up.

The instant he sets foot outside the car Simon feels the tremor. Instinctively, he looks around him. It's a vast parking lot and nothing can fall on them, except a lamppost. But that would require some bad luck. He waits, his hand pressed against the dripping roof of the car. On the opposite side of the car Carmen does the same, alive to the seismic waves rumbling beneath their feet. Residents of the area have a contradictory attitude toward earthquakes. On one hand they are so inured to them that nighttime tremors don't even wake them up anymore. Yet they remain keenly aware that any quake could be "the big one," the one that will plunge the coast into the Pacific Ocean, submerging centuries of history, and flood the rest of the region with an unprecedented tsunami. Simon checks his watch. Over a minute. Nothing collapses; the hospital looks completely undisturbed. At last, the rumbling subsides and recedes into the boiling entrails out of which it came, and the ground grows still. Carmen locks the doors and heads toward the visitors' entrance.

"Francisca Lopez," Simon asks the receptionist tersely.

"224," she snaps right back.

The corridors are strewn with miscellaneous objects. Evidently the tremor did shake the hospital. Some of the staff are busy cleaning up while others go in and out of the rooms where terrified voices can be heard wailing. From the far end of the corridor a gravelly voice reaches them above the clamour. The call grows more distinct as they approach.

"Help! I need help!"

A red-faced nurse steps out of room 224 just when Carmen and Simon arrive.

"Are you her children? That's good—you'll be able to calm her down. She just tossed her bedpan against the wall."

"Empty, I hope?"

"You figure?" the nurse replies, holding up a urine-soaked rag in her gloved hand.

Carmen goes in first. The lights are dimmed, the bedclothes in disarray. Under the sheets is a tiny woman, whose brittle bones seem to be enveloped not in flesh but fine, crumpled paper. She is howling at the top of her lungs.

"Help! Don't leave me here!"

Carmen places her hand on her mother's scrawny arm.

"We're here, mother. Everything's all right."

Frannie turns toward her and opens her enormous black eyes, whose pupils can't be distinguished from the rest.

"Simon? Carmen? God in heaven, you're going to get me out of here. This shitty building is going to collapse, and these dickwad quacks are going to let me croak alone."

Simon steps closer. He knows he ought to touch his mother to reassure her, kiss her on the forehead, but he can't bring himself to do it. Years ago, the lukewarm disdain he had felt for Frannie's body transformed into an aversion. He can't bear her emaciation and her hollow gaze. He comes nearer and strokes the pillow a few centimetres from her cheek.

"The earthquake is over, mother," Carmen says. "It wasn't very strong. Nothing is in danger of collapsing."

"Liar!" Frannie shouts at her daughter.

Simon steps in.

"Look, we're here with you. You know very well we wouldn't stay here if it was dangerous."

Frannie gives him a mollified look.

"If you say so, my boy."

Reaching her hands out, she demands her sheets. Carmen covers her, and her body vanishes under the greenish cotton. The hospital colours clash with the patient's feverish energy. Hard to believe she had a heart attack just earlier today. Simon thinks of his wife. When he suggested she come with them to the hospital, this was precisely the prediction that served to justify her refusal. "I bet you'll find your mother in top shape. It's not worth the trip." Then she dove back into her countless urgent cases, and Simon slammed the door in a rage. Realizing she was right infuriates him even more.

He surfaces from his thoughts and notes that Frannie has been chattering on for several minutes. Nothing of her monologue has stayed with him; fortunately, Carmen is paying attention. She nods and punctuates the narrative with timely "uh-huhs," summoning up the remarkable endurance that Simon has never been able to explain to himself. As a child he would enjoy challenging her to put this phenomenal aptitude to the test. He would ask her to stay balanced on her head or to keep a jalapeño in her mouth for as long as possible. If ever she cut short the experiment, it was always because of external factors—Frannie's intervention, for instance. Usually, though, it was Simon himself, after what seemed to him an eternity, who would beg her to stop, cursing himself for having subjected his sister to such torture.

The nurse they'd met earlier comes back with a clean bedpan. Her brusque manner bespeaks her contempt for the patient, but she says nothing. As she is about to go out, Frannie calls out to her:

"Next time, don't leave me marinating in my piss for an hour. That way, I won't make a mess for you."

Carmen rolls her eyes and wonders if there is some way to leave a tip for hospital workers. She notices out of the corner of her eye that Simon is rocking from one foot to the other. Something is bothering him. Carmen takes him into the corridor.

"What's the matter?"

"The matter is I'd really like to see her medical report. She looks healthier than a quarterback at the start of the season. I don't want to have her mouldering away here for no good reason."

"You mean *you* don't feel like mouldering here."

Simon half smiles at her sheepishly.

"Okay, keep her company while I go find out how things stand."

She sets off down the corridor, which is gradually returning to some semblance of order. The moaning has stopped and the shattered bottles of medicine have disappeared from the floor. The geriatric department has recovered its padded atmosphere punctuated by the beeps and buzzes that chart the path of the dying. The nurses' station appears at the intersection of three long corridors; Carmen would have preferred to walk another kilometre to find it. She does a better job than her brother of putting up with their mother, but it must come in small doses. In fact, that is what motivated her to start running. As a teenager, she needed an excuse to leave the house, and acceptable excuses were rare as far as Frannie was concerned. Long-distance running naturally arose as the next step: to go farther away and for longer periods of time. The army cadets saved Simon; for Carmen it was marathons.

An overweight staff member makes a note of her request, assuring her that a doctor will soon come to see them. Carmen slowly returns to room 224. A few doors away, an old man calls out to her.

"*Hija! Hija mia!*"

Carmen stops in her tracks and stares at the haggard eyes, the tortured eyebrows, the twisted lower lip.

"I'm not your daughter, sir. Sorry."

Back in the room, Simon is standing guard with his arms folded at the foot of the bed, while Frannie offers advice on what Alan and Jessica, Simon's children, should choose as academic majors. Each day since they were born she has found something to say about their education, their nutrition, their leisure activities, and their clothes. Simon endures these interventions while inwardly railing against them. As for Carmen, she has been spared this litany ever since she informed her mother that her future included neither husband nor progeny.

When she catches sight of her daughter, Frannie waves for her to come closer and whispers: "The bag! The bag!" Underneath a table, Carmen fishes out a large plastic shopping bag. In a conspiratorial tone of voice, Frannie orders Simon to shut the door.

"What's inside the bag?"

"Nothing. Just Bastard."

Carmen and Simon look at each other in alarm. Bastard is the tabby cat Frannie adopted thirty years ago. Her love for him (which, in her case, involved shouting at him most of the time) was such that when he died she could not bring herself to part with him.

Frannie gently opens the bag, revealing the animal's stiff carcass, stripes intact, ears pricked up for all eternity.

"Mother!" Simon exclaims. "Put that away immediately. Do you realize what would happen if someone were to see that?"

"That, that,… It's not a 'that'; it's a cat. An adorable pussycat!" Frannie shoots back, tenderly stroking the creature's dry fur.

Carmen can't help smiling. In the past, the moments when her mother petted her cat were the only intervals of calm in the house, rare interludes that she hung on to to remind herself that Frannie had a heart. Because of allergies, Simon could never tolerate the animal, which, unfortunately for him, enjoyed an exceptionally long life. As luck would have it, however, the cat's stuffed version is non-allergenic.

"Simon's right, mother. You have to put it back in the bag. If they find it, they'll confiscate it."

Outraged, Frannie grabs Bastard by the neck and waves him high in the air.

"I'd like to see them try! No one is going to come between me and my pussycat!"

Brother and sister manage willy-nilly to take the animal and hide it just as someone knocks on the door.

The doctor is a man with dishevelled hair—not a good sign for Simon. Certain professions, including his own and the doctor's, demand good grooming. A police officer or a doctor with shaggy hair give the people they are supposed to serve and protect a chaotic impression, a feeling of uncertainty just when everything is shifting.

Outside the door he summarizes an evidently voluminous medical report. Contrary to Simon's suspicions their mother is indeed unwell. She suffered a serious heart attack that very morning. The tests indicate that her heart is working at a fraction of its normal capacity and that her blood is too thick, putting her at risk of a fatal stroke or thrombosis. On hearing this, Simon probes his own heart for sadness or fear. But it's as if its volume has suddenly shrunk to the point where nothing is left but a grain of salt, a breadcrumb.

"We're giving her anticoagulants and hope that her blood will thin. In a day or two she'll be able to go home, provided a family member or close friend is there to look after her."

Carmen fights back a sigh.

"And her heart—can it be fixed?" she inquires.

"At her age, no. All we can do is to help her live with what's left of it."

Having said this, the doctor goes quiet and stares at the sister and brother in turn, waiting for comments or questions. But there is nothing to be said. Living with what's left of their mother's heart is what they've been doing for years.

"So, am I dying?" Frannie snaps when they come back into the room.

"No, mother, but you'll have to be careful with your heart."

"Oh! My heart! You know very well that my heart stopped years ago. When I lost your father."

Simon freezes. His wife tells him that when he does this he looks like a dog. When he pricks up his ears he stops moving altogether. He waits to catch sight of the game. But Frannie changes the subject. For a hundredth, a thousandth time, the answer eludes him; the hare dashes off into the tall grass, where Simon never ventures to go. The truth about their father is a wily, agile prey despite its weight. His and Carmen's personal Moby Dick. One of Frannie's lifetime exploits will have been to mention their father almost every day without ever revealing his identity. Still today, at forty-three and forty-five years of age, brother and sister regularly call each other in the middle of the day or night to share a new, occasionally credible clue but more often than not a piece of science fiction. A man on the bus who looks like them. A torn letter found in Frannie's things. A sibylline remark made by an old friend of their mother's.

Claire finds these inquiries and late-night phone calls hard to bear. She is a down-to-earth woman and believes that people who reach middle age without knowing their father can very well go on living in the state of ignorance around which their lives have been built. "Get over it, for goodness sake!" What she is more loath to express is her exasperation at how much room this quest takes up and at the exclusive bond it nurtures between her husband and sister-in-law. A shared struggle she can neither take part in nor understand.

As Simon looks at his mother, he suddenly feels he can see it, the poor organ ravaged by the years, a heart glowing wanly through her chest, asking for attention, for Frannie's acts of meanness to finally be overlooked so that this rusted muscle, at once guilty and innocent, may be touched. He averts his eyes.

Frannie has retrieved her stuffed cat, which this time she has entirely removed from its wrapping, thereby disclosing that half its tail is missing.

"What in the world happened to it?" Carmen asks.

"I don't know. The girl is coming by soon to bring me the missing part. I'm sure she tore it off to take revenge. She must be jealous."

"Right," Carmen sighs, trying to imagine the adorable student who minds her mother three days a week tearing off Bastard's tail while Frannie was napping.

"I should always check what's in her bag when she's leaving," Frannie adds. "They're all thieves, those black women."

"Mother!"

Carmen refrains from reminding her mother how much she herself was the victim of prejudice, and especially how she hated being subjected to those humiliating searches when she worked as a cleaning lady for the rich folks living in the hills. That was how she came to relieve her employers of their possessions. "They already take me for a thief, so what's the point of being honest?" She was crafty and took only small objects, which she hid where she was sure not to be inspected: in her bra, between her then ample breasts. Simon tearfully rejected the toys she brought them, and Carmen ended up returning them to their owners on the sly. The story of her childhood: tacking between her mother's misdemeanours and her brother's inflexibility. She herself is amazed at having grown so upright. It seems to her she should have developed like those twisted trees that climb toward the sun while trying to escape from the insects.

Frannie is talking to the cat and the tension eases in the room; even the medical devices appear to be less fussy. Simon taps on his telephone, the nurses go by the room without stopping, and Carmen thinks she can hear the muscles of her mother's heart contracting, stubborn and resistant. Unless it's her own heart she hears.

Then the beating becomes more distinct and rapid, like an underground drumroll. For the second time this evening, Simon and Carmen exchange a tectonic look and, in unison, position themselves on either side of their mother, their bodies arched above her brittle limbs, praying for the ground not to open up beneath her bed. Frannie starts yelping, hugging Bastard tightly against her stomach, as the tremor seizes the entire building. The aftershock is more powerful than the initial earthquake—that, at least, is the impression conveyed by the vibrations rippling through the hospital. "There it is! This is it! The big one!" Frannie screams, before choking with a harrowing groan. Carmen grips the sides of the bed and tries to locate something stable, but her gaze registers nothing but movement. Even Simon appears blurred. She shuts her eyes.

When the tremor finally ends she is astonished to find the room practically intact. Then she straightens up and realizes she is mistaken. Eyes staring blankly, mouth agape, skin gone grey—Frannie is not intact. In a flash, Simon hits the emergency button and leans over her.

"She's not breathing."

He confidently begins to give her a heart massage. Moments later, a nurse arrives, exchanges a few words with Simon and immediately heads off to find a doctor. Carmen steps back with her thumb stuck between her teeth. The California coast has undoubtedly not sunk into the Pacific, but Frannie was right: this was indeed her big one.

When the doctor leaves the room, Frannie is still unconscious but under the sway now of a new cocktail of intravenous drugs. Her face is unrecognizable. Simon remembers when Claire's father died a few years earlier. His features metamorphosed in the same way. It was as if some crucial chunk of the person had broken off, like the collapse of part of an ice field that leaves the whole disfigured. That's what this heart attack was. The massive blow, the point of no return. From out of nowhere the tears well up and he turns away to hide them from Carmen. But she steps closer to him all the same and takes him by the shoulders.

"You saved her, Simon."

"I don't know."

Is it really saving someone when she is very old, disease-ridden, filled with gall and bad blood to the point of paralysis? He did nothing but what he is conditioned to do: sustain life, maintain the order of things. Not let his mother die, no matter what. He curses his reflexes and curses himself for being unable to prevent the tremor, for not having foreseen the aftershock.

"If she had been sedated she wouldn't have felt the earthquake. Her heart wouldn't have given out."

"It would have given out sooner or later. The doctor said so. It's an old, worn-out muscle."

A new medical team takes over the room to carry out further tests, and Carmen suggests they go have a bite in the cafeteria. Frannie's condition is stable and, in any case, they're obliged to leave the room. Simon realizes he's famished and accepts. They find themselves once again walking along corridors cluttered with debris though looking less devastated than Frannie. When they reach their destination the door is locked. They're told the tremor set off a small fire. The kitchen is closed until further notice.

They fall back on one of the many all-night *taquerias* near the Berkeley campus. Carmen takes the wheel and slaloms in and out of the branches and empty trashcans littering the streets, amid clusters of excited, zigzagging students. "You'd think it was Halloween," she remarks as they enter the restaurant.

During the meal not a single word passes between them. Simon has an idea of what is going through his sister's head. He remembers all too well Carmen's Berkeley years. He would come to visit her, sleep on the floor of her co-op room, a squalid cubbyhole she shared with a corpulent girl whose snoring was horrendous; he woke up every hour, afraid of being attacked by a rat. At the outset, Carmen had planned to devote herself to mathematics, but after the first year she opted instead for Women's Studies. She shaved her head and joined the row of activists who lined the campus's main road and handed out radical leaflets to passersby on behalf of a small circle that published a monthly titled *Queen Sappho*.

During that same period, Simon enrolled in the police academy and looked on his sister's new interests with suspicion, especially after she was arrested while taking part in a rally. But he never stopped visiting her, and Carmen never once trotted out for him her anti-patriarchy spiel. Their relationship steered clear of the gender war.

A vagrant with a limp barges into the restaurant waving a battered Bible. Immediately, the kitchen staff arrive to usher him back out.

"The Last Judgment! It's all written here! The earth has shaken; the time of reckoning has come for the wicked; the righteous shall be rewarded. The earth calls out for the truth!"

A few moments later, he is marshalled out into the shifting darkness of the street.

There is something rank about Carmen's memories of her university years. Those were heady days, of course, and it was there she understood who she was. But when she thinks about the physical and ideological excesses she committed there, she feels nauseous. Looking at the students around them, she's no longer able to feel the pulse of their wonderful naiveté and the enthusiasm of their first steps in the world; all she sees is their obnoxious smugness and radicalism.

Her best memories are of running in the Berkeley Hills. Each morning, no matter what had happened the night before, she would plunge into the fickle fragrances of the woods and climb to the highest point in the city, where she could plant her feet in the damp earth and contemplate the San Pablo reservoir on one side, San Francisco Bay on the other and, on clear days, picture the soft roof of San José to the southwest, under which her younger brother still lived.

Thinking back, she realizes the seeds of her future life lay in what she then considered secondary. It wasn't the group that prevailed but her individuality; she was sustained not by her studies but by her passion for running—the abstract no longer dominated her existence. When her Olympic career ended the jobs she sought were exclusively down-to-earth, as she was incapable of re-immersing herself in the dialectics that she had donned out of the need to define her identity.

She manages to gobble down the last mouthful of her burrito, slightly ashamed of being so hungry while her mother is fighting for her life a few blocks away. The fact is, Frannie long ago imposed this detachment on her children. It would have been impossible for them to survive, to become full-fledged adults, had they let each of her mood swings affect them. Except that by protecting yourself from the bad, you also shield yourself from the good, from what's essential. Her mother's condition leaves Carmen in the grip of a strange to-and-fro between compassion and sadness, but she does not feel anxious. Does Simon feel the same detachment? Fidgeting with his empty Styrofoam coffee cup, he looks rather restless.

"Do you think that was the last time we could talk to her?" he asks.

Carmen gives him an I-don't-know shrug.

"That would be a pity," Simon continues. "She has things to tell us."

Suddenly she understands the source of Simon's agitation.

"That's true," she replies, "but even if she rallies, there's no guarantee she'll choose to tell us…"

Simon lowers his head. He's thinking of their father, of course. After all these years, the questions, the investigations, the furtive searches through Frannie's belongings, the contacts with other relations, this is their last hope. The possibility that at the eleventh hour their mother will finally remove the steel clamp that she's kept on this secret.

Because of Frannie's unflagging stubbornness, for a long time Simon held on to the idea that their father was a criminal. Soon after he'd earned his police badge, he began to nose around the prisons in search of a Hispanic who may have lived at one of their mother's many former addresses. Carmen patiently followed him to the penitentiaries, where they met a dozen inmates with their chin, their eyebrows, a vague family likeness. None of them remembered Francisca Lopez, except one who no doubt was hoping this would get him paroled. That was a few months before Simon's wedding. He would have liked to invite his father to the ceremony. Had he found him, Carmen tells herself, Simon might have made completely different choices. Perhaps he would not be married to Claire but to a generous woman who would respect him and not cheat on him with low-level management consultants. Perhaps if Simon found the answer to the oldest question of their existence, he would finally put an end to his rotten marriage.

As is always the case when Carmen thinks about her brother's wife, she gets angry.

"How's your new girlfriend doing?" Simon asks, as though he were reading her mind.

"It's over."

"Already?"

"It wasn't working."

"Come on!"

"I'm telling you, we were incompatible! And, just imagine, some people believe that being in an unhappy relationship is actually a legitimate reason to break up!"

"Stop. You don't have children, so you can't put yourself in my position."

"Exactly."

"What?"

Carmen looks away.

"She wanted a child? You refused? Carmen, how many lovers will you have to lose like this before you change your mind?"

"You know my views on the subject."

"But you're wrong! It's not because we had Frannie for a mother that we're doomed to repeat her mistakes. I'm very far from being the kind of parent she was for us."

"Maybe. But you found yourself a woman who's not so very far."

"That's not true. Claire may be cold, but she's not crazy."

"She's incapable of loving."

"Well, it appears that neither are you! You're doing everything you can to remain alone."

The brother gives the sister a foxlike stare, grabs his cup and goes for a refill. Carmen mulls over their conversation. He's right, of course; her brother is always right, and at the same time always wrong. Because the love she has felt for him, ever since she stood at his side when he took his first steps, proves that she has won out. Children abandoned for days at a time, deprived of food by way of punishment or hit with vinyl records don't all turn into monsters. Some become long-distance runners.

Outside, the rain is coming down again, blanketing the night in desolation. Couples in a hurry to lose their virginity run from one awning to the next to quickly reach the dormitories, miraculously deserted on this Sunday night. The coffee becomes more acid with every sip, and Simon drinks with no compassion for his stomach, which is about to cry out for mercy. He can't help admitting his sister is partly right. What does he really know about children, about the science of transforming babies into happy adults? At thirteen, his son Alan never seems to aspire to be anything but a blob addicted to anime and Cheezies. As for his daughter, every inch of freedom she gains serves only to distance her from the values Simon is trying to instill in her, and to drive her ever farther into the fringes. When he decided to marry and start a family, Simon never would have believed you could feel so far removed from those to whom you were supposed to be closest.

"You know, I think it would do Jessica good to spend some time with you."

"What makes you say that?"

"I don't know. She's changing."

"Is she gay?"

"I don't think so. She's just… different. And the people she hangs out with… Maybe it's a phase like the one you went through."

"It's not always merely a phase."

Simon lets out a sigh. The coffee has already begun to stir up a revolt in his esophagus. He thinks of Jessica coming home the previous night at eleven and then stealing down the fire escape at one in the morning only to come back the same way at five a.m. by resorting to circus animal stunts. He thinks of the cans of spray paint, the crowbar, and the other tools he found stashed away in her closet. He sees the crumpled leaflet in her wastepaper basket, full of coded directions, and the photos of an old military bunker hidden under her mattress. Whenever he rummages through his daughter's things, it's in search of drugs, condoms—the usual smoking guns of adolescent girls. But what he finds is far more troubling and enigmatic.

It was much easier to confirm that Claire was cheating on him. All he needed was to rifle through her sports bag, in which some perfectly clean clothes concealed a set of black lace underwear. Oddly enough, he admires the complexity of his daughter's secret. She, at least, doesn't reduce Simon to a pathetic cliché. He has never spoken to Claire about his discoveries—the ones concerning her infidelities aren't worth the trouble and those about Jessica are too bizarre. He refuses to submit them to his wife's insipid reactions.

"Do you remember Marcus Wilson?" Carmen asks, rousing him from his musings.

She, too, can't help thinking about their father tonight. Simon nods, his thoughts flooded with memories. They were fourteen and sixteen years old. Frannie, exasperated by their relentless questions about their background, had ordered them to take a large umbrella and wait for her in the car. They drove for an hour through a downpour to a rain-soaked cemetery on a hillside. There, Frannie furiously led them to the modest tombstone of one Marcus Wilson, then twelve years dead.

"That's him, your father. He was a boozer and he killed himself driving home from a bar when you were little. Now don't bother me about this again!"

She turned on her heel as furiously as she had come, leaving her son and daughter alone at the graveside. Carmen cried, and Simon followed suit, not so much out of sadness as the wish to behave appropriately. Actually, it took him several weeks to digest this revelation and incorporate it into his personal history. He had a father, the father had a name, an age that would never change, a final abode.

For almost a year Carmen and he paid regular visits to Marcus Wilson's grave, timidly at first and then unabashedly, leaving flowers and candies, stretching out to finally be able to speak to their father. Carmen asked him to help her get a high score on her SAT. Simon sometimes went there alone to confide his anxieties about girls, about Frannie's fits of rage. He could sit there for hours leaning his back against the granite headstone.

They might have kept up this routine their whole lives, if only Frannie had chosen a more remote, more anonymous monument of someone the world had forgotten. But when Simon and Carmen arrived at the cemetery to picnic, in June of the year following their first meeting with Marcus Wilson, they found three people gathered at the gravestone, an old woman and two young men in their early twenties, all of them African American.

Simon wanted to turn back immediately, but Carmen couldn't help approaching the family, so he kept his distance while she interrupted their prayers. She came back a few minutes later looking crushed. The two boys were Marcus Wilson's sons and the old woman, his mother. Wilson had died after a five-year battle with cancer.

"He was buried here because this was his home town, but he died in Chicago. He was living there with his family. He couldn't have known mother, much less have two children—two Latino children—by her."

It took them months to tell Frannie they had discovered the truth. When they finally dared to do so, she had no idea what they were talking about. The cemetery, the rain, Marcus Wilson—all forgotten.

A lull in the downpour allows them to return to the car without being swallowed whole. Carmen's Jeep is covered with white disks; some youngsters have been playing Frisbee with paper plates from the nearby pizzeria. Simon is itching to have a few words with some of them, but Carmen manages to distract him by asking him to check the oil. While he is busy under the hood, an elderly woman stops beside her.

"Excuse me, I think I recognize you from somewhere… Aren't you an athlete?"

"Runner. Carmen Lopez."

"That's it! At the Barcelona Games… You were fantastic! And then Atlanta! But what happened…"

"Thank you!" Carmen cuts her off and jumps in the car. Simon barely has time to sit down beside her before she pulls away.

The hospital parking lot is almost deserted. There are seven cars there. Seven families keeping deathwatch or awaiting the birth of a child. So few. Carmen looks at her brother with the choking sensation that they are alone in the world.

The hospital is still swarming with staff who are busy clearing away the traces of the second quake in the geriatric department, as if the absence of debris could banish all thought of the tremors that will cast these old people out of existence one by one, one piece at a time. A team is at work in room 224, and Carmen and Simon are asked to wait outside. They are getting Frannie ready for the night, a nurse explains. Simon has no idea what this means. Are they putting on her pyjamas? Brushing her teeth? Maybe their mother is naked, her numberless wounds and protrusions, her manifold ugliness starkly exposed; maybe he and Carmen are being spared a sight that would change them forever.

While they are waiting, a doctor arrives and introduces himself; his hair is neatly combed but there are unsightly patches of perspiration under the sleeves of his smock. Simon is willing to forgive this sort of impropriety. Sweat is the sign of vital effort, of one's commitment to something. A symptom that he values in his own person, the recurring confirmation he is not a bad policeman, but one who truly cares about his fellow human beings.

The doctor bluntly informs that Frannie had another heart failure while they were out.

"If I were you I would stay by her side tonight."

The nurses file out with the guilty expression of people who have presided over the end of an empire without attempting the impossible, and Simon forgives every one of them.

Frannie's body lies in the half-light, just a grim collection of bones and flesh that nothing holds together anymore; her face is distorted by the tubes serving as lifelines. Carmen and Simon pull up chairs on either side of their mother, ready for a sleepless night, white as a flag and long as a mast.

They have stopped speaking. Sometimes they stroke an arm, a cheek, terrified by the tentative gestures that were never possible before. Simon repeatedly places his hand on his burning chest; he needs some milk, and Carmen considers getting up to find some for him but she does not budge. She must stay there. The whole world is concentrated here now.

The hours go by. Carmen has the sensation there have been gaps in time, a sign that she has slept. At one point she realizes that Bastard has reappeared, nestled against his mistress's shoulder. It's an almost pretty picture, a strange quasi-still life. This is surely Simon's doing. Simon and his big heart under all those layers of rules and restrictions.

Later, she catches herself singing. This must have begun while she was sleeping because she can't remember starting into this old, approximate and cheerless Mexican serenade; nor does she even know where she could have learnt it. Frannie never sang them lullabies. And yet a fragment of childhood slips out between her lips to caress the dying woman, to draw her into her rare regions of happiness and lay her down there as one would a child, in the safety of warm blankets and the scent of milk.

First the hand comes to life, followed by the eyelids, fighting to open, and then the quivering arm rising toward the chin. Frannie tries to pull the tubes out of her nostrils. Simon does his best to stop her, but, as always, in vain; his mother knows what she wants. A great groan goes up from her throat. She's back.

Her breathing is a bow sliding over a cordless violin. Her chest pushes as hard as possible to draw the air inside, to enable one more breath. Her feet are completely frozen; the blood has already given up—there's no point in doing the full circuit. It nourishes whatever is indispensable: the fluttering nest of the abdomen, the commanding tower of the brain. But the extremities are left to fend for themselves. The throat stays sufficiently irrigated, because it must be. A few words still need to be uttered. But which? Nothing at all can be seen; before her eyes there is only turbulence, as when one tries to penetrate the sunrays dancing on the ocean's surface to plumb the depths. The spinal column saws away at the trunk, where the muscles no longer hold down the sides of the big tent. The ribs alone keep on working. It's enough. Enough to finish what needs to be finished. Francisca Lopez shall not die in silence.

"I want…"

Every atom in the room draws closer to her, as though the energy of the world were concentrating around her mouth to help her continue. The universe is all ears.

"I want…"

The waiting turns into a hum, the darkness grows luminous; something is still missing—one more try.

"I want some peanut butter."

There, it's said. Now the inner commotion can quiet down. One more gust of wind and it's over. Through the long exhalation that carries her off, Francisca can hardly hear a voice murmuring, "Mother, you're allergic to peanuts." She is far away now.

Brother and sister stare at each other, incredulous, dishevelled, demoralized. The electrocardiogram sends out a long beep, which Carmen kills by pressing a chrome-plated button. Simon stands up, walks around the room four times, seizes the cat and hurls it against the wall with all his might.

"Peanut butter?!"

Carmen picks up the animal's head, which has rolled to the foot of the bed.

"She was delirious, Simon."

He sinks into his chair and buries his forehead in his fingers.

Carmen comes over and places her hand on his shoulder. Frannie's body seems to be slowly vanishing, dissolving amid the urine-soaked sheets. The smell does not bother them; it dissipates in the room, where the walls have retained the effluvia of a thousand deaths, the miasma of bile, fear, sweat, damned breath, and swollen lips, which, at the very end speak nonsense, because the end of a life is never a redemption, because we die as we have lived. Absurdly and untruthfully.

Someone knocks softly on the door three times before opening. Simon gets up, Carmen steps toward the doorway, both of them dazzled by the chemical light flooding in from the corridor. A young woman stands unsteadily in front of them. She looks in the direction of the bed, and her eyes well up with water.

"I've come too late," she mutters.

She reaches into her bag and proffers two scraps of paper to the orphans along with a muddled clump of fur. Bastard the cat's tail.

Gold Mines in Russia
(MONETTE AND ANGIE)

TO ANYONE who shops in supermarkets, the shelves in Mr. Dodge's little grocery store seem to have undergone rationing befitting the era of world wars. But for Monette, what they hold is nothing short of princely. She shuttles between two aisles: confectionery, sprinkled with lollypops, liquorice, chewing gum, and jujubes that gleam with the magnetism of precious stones; and pastry, less appealing to the eye but with possibilities far beyond those of mere candies—chocolate, vanilla, the lightness of sponge cake, and the fabulous density of brownies.

Looking up from an inventory sheet, Mr. Dodge makes a show of coming to the little girl's assistance.

"Can I make some suggestions, miss? I notice that you have your eye on the soap chewing gum. A wise choice, if I may say so. It will last much longer than a jujube, which gets swallowed in no time. What's more, it wards off dirty words."

Monette gives the grocer a look of suspicion, but he is not in the least put off and points to another counter.

"Then again, we're offering excellent value for your money this week with our sugar-coated donuts. But be careful: the icing sugar leaves traces on your clothing that your mother can easily notice!"

Completely ignoring these recommendations, Monette continues to make her way down the pastry aisle, satisfied that she has shaken off the pattering salesman. While she grasps mouth-watering packages one by one to get a closer look, Angie leafs through magazines. On the first page of one periodical is a picture of a huge herd of dead cows. Another shows a woman in a race moving away from a tightly packed group of runners. In the middle of the last magazine, Angie gets lost in some dizzying photos of a Russian gold mine. Once she has gone through the series of photos, she realizes she must come to the aid of her younger sister, who is having as much trouble choosing a treat as she has tying her shoe-laces. When she comes alongside the little body hopping left and right, Angie gently takes hold of the coveted packages and reads aloud:

"Sugar, enriched flour, hydrogenated canola oil…"

Monette listens attentively to the litany her sister recites for three different products and finally settles on a molasses cookie, seduced no doubt by the terms *niacin* and *brown no. 28*. Mr. Dodge gives her a connoisseur's nod of approval, and the little girl, now free of the burden of decision, responds with a good-humoured greeting. Angie takes a few more moments to bask in the coolness of the shop before she opens the door and confronts the swelter of the morning and the stifling fabric knitted by the boys, who—maybe in expectation of the two girls exiting the shop—have tightened their ranks so that it is virtually impossible to go down the stairway.

Clutching her cookie, Monette looks up in despair at her sister. Angie instantly gives in to the mute appeal and lifts up the child, who twists her chubby limbs around her sister. Angie's voice is unwavering:

"Make way," she commands.

As if by magic, the boys part and open a path where Angie can gingerly set down one foot after the other, somehow managing to keep her balance under the weight of her precious cargo. She knows that Monette, facing backward, has closed her eyes; Angie can also smell the molasses cookie tucked securely between her shoulder and her sister's chest, safely out of sight. When she reaches the sidewalk, a voice rings out behind her, an arrogant organ just recently broken.

"Too bad; next time, wear a skirt. Not much to look at on the outside but maybe there's something worth seeing under your shorts."

Without flinching, Angie puts down Monette, who sprints across the street as if to lay down a definite boundary between them and the teenagers. With her head held high, Angie goes to join her. Behind her she senses the pack slowly moving off. One at a time, the boys get off their numb backsides, stand up on their lazy legs, and amble down the street, making sure to be noticed. Pretending to arrange one of her sister's braids, Angie waits. It's imperative for her to know which direction they will take. Praying that they continue southward, she prolongs the adjustments while Monette, already indifferent to the goings on across the road, fusses with the wrapping of her treat.

They seem to dither endlessly before heading off. They go north, toward the pony and their house, where Mam is scrubbing away at the floor with that old, animal-like brush that has always been there. Without further ado, Angie leads her sister to one of the many trails that cut through the woods.

"Where are we going?" Monette inquires.

"We'll walk along the train tracks to get home."

The little girl frowns. She's not fond of detours.

"Maybe we'll see a train!" the older sister coaxes.

Monette calms down. It's true, there's always the train.

To Be but One
(MADELEINE AND MADELEINE)

ALTHOUGH SHE has yanked out dozens of grey hairs—a losing battle, now given up—this one hurts a little more than the others. She begins three times, curling her index finger around a hair at the top of her skull, without daring to pull. In the end, a creaking sound upstairs prompts her to deliver the *coup de grâce*. She hastily slips the faded thread into a plastic bag identical to the one containing a lock stolen from Édouard's comb and hides the documents under a crumpled tablecloth. A few seconds later Joanna appears, already dressed in her cycling shorts, prepared to tackle the eighty-odd kilometres she covers each day "to stay in shape." She flashes her widest grin and goes out noiselessly, leaving Madeleine to marvel at how someone that big can be so unobtrusive.

Alone again, she completes the questionnaire and inserts everything in an envelope addressed to a private laboratory that usually receives the hairs of unlucky, cuckolded, or exceedingly suspicious men. "It's probably the first time they'll have tested a mother's hair," Madeleine mutters as she licks the flap. She has not spoken to anyone about her new course of action, fearing this would complicate things even further.

To eliminate the possibility of an error, the blood tests were repeated at the hospital, but the results came back with the same absurd degree of accuracy. The social worker assigned to the case already seems to regard Madeleine as a guilty party, a monster who may have stolen someone else's baby. The fact she is a widow with no other children doesn't help. A husband may have testified on her behalf; a second child would have put the incomprehensible revelations of her DNA into perspective. A living, rational blood relation might have bolstered the defence that she is timidly trying to marshal. But she is alone.

Having sealed the envelope, Madeleine collects her photographic equipment and goes out. The light outside has grown majestic after hours of false modesty. Spring has begun to crackle and sends up fragrances that astonish Madeleine every year as if she had never encountered them before. The mud warming in the artificial pond. The verdigris on the bronze sculpture near the day lilies. Her own sweat, which sends out a new note when the mercury ventures beyond a certain threshold.

She cautiously attaches a macro lens to the camera, which she mounts on a small tripod. Then she positions her arm in front of the lens. For days the only subject that has really interested her is her skin; her shots run the gamut from goose bumps to the crinkles on her water-soaked fingers, as she avidly seeks to penetrate the pores, to pierce the layers of skin as though they are walls keeping her from the truth. She has come to understand what her deceased husband was looking for with his close-ups of insect legs and antennae. The truth in the tiny. The devil in the details.

By the time Édouard wakes up, Madeleine is already on the road. She would rather not bump into her son, and apparently the feeling is mutual. When she arrives at Paul's place the house is silent and gaping on all sides, with the windows and shutters wide open. Paul is absent. Madeleine calls out a few times but there is no answer. Taken aback, she heads for the beehives. She has always kept her distance from the bee colony, not so much out of fear as incomprehension. Today, however, something impels her there. She wants to feel the swarm swirling around her, allow the more curious worker bees to land on her hair, to forage on her clothes, on the sparkle of her rings; she wants to let the buzzing whisper a message that she alone can grasp.

But instead of the perpetual vibration that ought to prevail there, she finds nothing but silence. Intrigued, she steps closer to examine the wooden frames that the owner so carefully maintains. They are deserted. Not a bee in sight.

"Paul?" Madeleine shouts again.

All at once, she slumps down amid the hives and bursts into tears. For the first time since Édouard told her about his disease, she lets herself sink into the heart of pain, to plunge where nothing holds up anymore, where the ground gives way with every step. She digs her fingers into the loose earth and watches her limbs writhe with distress. She wants to tear herself in two.

After a long while, a heavy pair of hands alights on her shoulders. Paul sits down behind her and hugs her with the strength of a sea monster. The kind of embrace that puts an end to sobbing and lifts the head. Here and there, puddles of honey ooze from the ground.

"It's hard when someone close falls ill. It's natural to be upset."

Madeleine doesn't answer. How can she explain to a man accustomed to the smallness of the peninsula and the Cartesian world of bees that she must fight to prove the obvious? How can she tell him she has just dropped two strands of hair into an envelope in the hope of demonstrating that she is indeed the mother of the boy she gave birth to? Most of all, how can she tell him there is nothing, absolutely nothing natural about this? She wipes away her tears and looks around her. The beehives are as quiet as they were before.

"The bees—where have they gone?"

Paul shrugs: "Vanished."

"How so?"

"I don't know. I'd heard about such occurrences, but to be honest, I didn't believe it. I didn't think it could happen here."

He steps up to his hives, brushes his hand over them. Without the colony, they seem smaller, a dolls' village that Paul moves through like a sad giant. Overhead, large birds sweep across the sky on the lookout, spot the lagoons, and fly back toward the shore like arrows. Madeleine stands up, shakes the dirt out of her clothes, and walks toward the car. She never says good-bye when she leaves. Paul watches her drive away, then turns around and enters the untamed fields where insects shrewdly assemble and where his bees may have gone to hide out.

When Joanna isn't riding her bike she's in the kitchen. Basil-stuffed eggplant lasagna, tagines so spicy they make your head spin, breads that sigh coming out of the oven, vegetable *feuilletés* that rustle like dried leaves lifted from between the pages of an old dictionary. All this, too, she does without making noise or small talk, thus surrounding herself with an impenetrable wall that no one dares go through to offer a hand or steal a piece of carrot. But Madeleine can't help watching from the next room. When their gazes meet, Joanna, sounding like a sorceress, says:

"I'm making tea. Want some?"

Madeleine does and sits down opposite her guest as though she, Madeleine, were the visitor. Smiling, Joanna speaks to her as if the conversation has been going on since daybreak:

"So you're all right?"

It's hard to complain in the presence of someone whose every wrinkle suggests the pain she has had to confront, undergo, and overcome to lead a life like hers. Madeleine wags her head hesitantly; she's unable to fish out a clear answer from the troubled waters of her situation.

"Your son is sick. But his chances of recovering are excellent. Why is the atmosphere so heavy in your house?" Joanna asks.

To lie to a woman like her is impossible. Madeleine sighs and lets the truth rise to her lips.

"It's me. When the test results came back, my blood didn't say what it was supposed to. It wasn't just a matter of being incompatible for an organ donation; the doctors don't believe that Édouard is my son."

"And you, are you certain that he is? It's a rarity, but sadly, you know, mistakes have been known to happen in nurseries. Could you inquire at the hospital where you gave birth?"

"I was with a midwife. I was her only patient that day."

"Hmmm. In that case, it is very strange."

She gets up and leans over a cooking pot to check on her stew.

"Well, I'm sure it will be cleared up very soon and the explanation will be far less terrifying that what you imagine. I can assure you," she insists, given Madeleine's sombre mood.

On the other side of the open window, Shabby pops up as though summoned by the Dutch woman's prediction. Its fur is haunted by nettles, thorns, and other small, almost living things. It gazes at the two women with pleading eyes, and Joanna compassionately slips it a piece of Gruyère, which it bolts down immediately.

As a little girl Madeleine would have given anything for someone to inform her she was not her parents' daughter. She dreamed that one day a man in a suit would show up at their house and announce an unfortunate error had been made years ago and she had been interchanged with a neighbour's child or, better yet, that she was the daughter of foreign travellers, who would come to retrieve her with tears of joy and take her back to Bavaria or Castile or another place full of castles and ghosts of headless horsemen.

Given her parents' lack of caution, such a blunder might not have been so preposterous were it not for the striking resemblance between them and their offspring. Of course, Madeleine did not see the resemblance. Among members of the same family the common traits are often lost in the sea of differences one tries so hard to underscore, especially when the idea of being the parents' "spitting image" falls under the heading of an insult or a curse.

The genetic lab's brochure specifies a waiting period of five business days for the results to be delivered. Five days that Madeleine spends without food or sleep, reeling between the museum and the lighthouse, where she leans her back against the wall at day's end. One night, she dozes off there and is found after closing hours by the watchman, who insists on seeing her home. She has told him nothing about her worries, but they are old acquaintances and each of them can easily sense the other's frame of mind.

He takes her back to her garden teeming with mosquitoes, and, lost in her questions, she neglects to thank him. Does her son resemble her? She always saw much more of Micha than of herself in both his physique and demeanour. Hasn't Édouard inherited his father's need for space, freedom, and travel? "Except that Micha never travelled, he expatriated himself," she inwardly replies. But he is detached and withdrawn, just like his father. "His mother is hardly any different," the inner voice responds again.

"It's not the same thing," she retorts crossly, startling Yun—Madeleine had not seen her perched on a tree branch.

"Sorry," she says to the young woman, who continues to climb toward the top of the beech tree as if hoping to discover coconuts up there.

"That's okay. I completely agree. Things are never the same."

When someone is on the road for months at a time it doesn't take much for him to feel at home. During his years of roving

Édouard found shelter in abandoned buses, hollows below train tracks, deserted sheds where three people took turns sleeping on a dilapidated mattress, and he learned to cherish these places with the kind of affection others reserve for the houses where they were born. But nothing could ever match Nora's cabin.

It was built out of a hodgepodge of plywood sheets and corrugated tin and might have brought to mind a shantytown hovel were it not for its weirdly artistic aspect. In spite of its less-than-modest dimensions, the shack had a dozen windows located at different heights, which overlaid the floor with geometric figures that changed according to the time of day. Nora kept the place clean, and whoever crossed the threshold had to respect the nearly fanatical order that she imposed on her environment.

Markedly older than most of the people who passed through her house, Nora was not altogether old. The criterion on which Édouard—he was twenty-two at the time—based himself in arriving at this conclusion was that he still found her desirable. She never explained where she was from or what had prompted her to build such a remote a dwelling, tucked away a kilometre inside a tract of government land in Oregon. It appears she had gone through a period of wandering before landing there, because she knew the US railroad network by heart as well as the way to cross the Canadian border into Alberta. She always had some advice for her visitors, whom she treated with a blend of kindness and sullen paternalism, but she never dwelled on her own travels. People arrived at her house in the company of one of her regular guests and loaded down with supplies; she would seize the provisions, which she transformed into phenomenal meals seasoned with nameless spices that she identified by their aromas. Sometimes without asking for permission she would confiscate an article of clothing or an object that might help to improve her cabin, and no one dared object to this arbitrary taxation. Life was good at Nora's place and whatever payment she deemed appropriate was the accepted price.

Édouard spent an entire month at her house. He let his travelling companions continue on without him, as he preferred to be of service to Nora, who needed help to prepare for winter. There were holes in the roof that needed patching, and enough wood had to be gathered for the little rusted stove to maintain a semblance of heat when the frost came scratching at the door. Aware of his amorous feelings, which Édouard was certain he had kept well hidden, Nora consented to share her bed with him and allowed him to nuzzle up against her but without letting the contact go any further. While Édouard detailed the deepest secrets of his young life, Nora listened but never disclosed the least bit of information about herself.

On the first cold day, she filled a bag with edibles and handed him a voucher for a Greyhound bus ticket.

"Go see your mother."

It hurt Édouard to be turned out of a place where he would have liked to stay forever, but he did his best to hide his disappointment.

"Why? You think she's worried?"

"You miss her. And you won't find her here."

The following summer, Édouard tried to go back to see her. Although he stayed in the area nearly two months, every hour of which would remain etched in his mind, he never managed to find Nora's cabin again, not even the ruins, not even her footprint on the ground.

The mailman came by almost two hours ago, and Madeleine has been on the verge of opening the letter a dozen times. She inserts the pewter letter opener in the corner of the flap, and just when she is about to slash the envelope open, she freezes.

As if she needed a much sharper instrument, a saw or an axe or maybe crab pincers instead of fingers.

Finally, at dusk, she decides on a new strategy. She boils some water and patiently holds the envelope over the jet of steam. It reminds her of Yellowstone Park, where the ground fumes, spews boiling water and sulphurous vapours whose mysteries the tourists come to ponder. That is what Madeleine would need far more than a form containing the numerical sequence of her DNA: a seer whom she could ask to enlighten her. The letters of her name warp on the envelope, which finally opens.

Twenty-three out of forty-six, the sheet announces. In her haste, Madeleine ignores the more discursive explanations; all she manages to read is the little box disclosing the identity of twenty-three out of the forty-six chromosomes that make up Édouard's DNA. A perfect correspondence. Only a minute later does she decipher the sober but glorious conclusion of the lab technicians who examined the strand of her hair: "You are the child's biological mother."

"Édouard!!!"

Madeleine bursts out of the house, body aflame, hand still clutching the letter, calling her son at the top of her lungs. But he is nowhere to be found. She continues running toward the sea and onto the deserted beach, where she strips naked and throws herself into the waves to lose herself in the seaweeds, the iodine, and the fish eggs.

She arrives at Paul's house at twilight. Frail yet imposing on the crooked veranda, he opens the door holding a table napkin.

"You were eating?"

"Are you hungry?"

Madeleine removes her clothes heavy with seawater and for the second time today stands naked in the open air. Unsurprised, Paul wraps his arms around her, softly lays her down on the worn wooden porch and embraces her, licks the salt, and kneads her skin with his large, scalding hands. His caresses burn right through his lover's body. Swept up by an uncommonly powerful swell, Madeleine distends, splits in two, divides and multiplies.

When they come ashore, night has fallen. Paul brings a blanket so they can enjoy the spectacle of his vast lands made purple by the star-studded sky. In the distance, animals run without harming themselves, the horses send out their neighs, and some owls flutter their wings in unseen nests. Paul gently strokes Madeleine's tousled hair.

"Things are looking up for your son?"

"Yes. Sort of. But they still haven't found a donor. And you? Your bees?"

"Can't find them anywhere. Luckily I still have the horses."

He lights a cigarette, not so much for him as for Madeleine, who likes to snatch a few puffs from him.

"I've heard you've been taking naps at the foot of the light-house these days."

"Occasionally," Madeleine answers, irked by how swiftly rumours travel on the peninsula.

"You know, if you're having trouble sleeping, you should spend the night here. I can rub your back."

In response to this recurring offer, Madeleine bites her lip. Groping about in the dark, she finds her clothes and gets dressed.

"Not tonight. I have to see my son."

Paul hugs her without a hint of resentment. The reasons she comes back to his house are the same as those that keep her from staying. She walks to her car in the beam of his flash-light and drives away without turning on her headlamps.

On arriving home, she finds the household asleep. From the corridor she can distinguish Édouard's hurried breathing alternating with Yun's, which is slower. Joanna's dry snoring on the ground floor adds to these sounds, to all this disparate humanity woven together by breath.

Carrying the letter from the laboratory, Madeleine tip-toes into the room and kneels down by her son's bed. She is reminded of Micha, an atheist through and through, but who persisted in bowing down at the foot of the bed each night, lowering his head, pressing his hands together, and silently formulating requests he shared with no one. Madeleine liked to believe that in doing so he was wrapping a sort of magical armour around his little family. After he died she realized he had excluded himself from his petitions.

In the half-light, the two bodies turn around in perfect sym-metry. Madeleine leans toward Édouard and murmurs a few barely audible words into his ear. Then she places the letter on the nightstand and cautiously straightens up. She has already gone out by the time Édouard's fingers stir and flit toward the sheet of paper left next to him. He heaves a sigh that releases what looks like blue smoke into the room. But no one can see it.

The toaster ejects the browned slices of bread. On either side of the table, Madeleine and Édouard sip the contents of a seemingly bottomless teapot. Now that the turmoil whipped up by the DNA question has passed, they are once again mother and son sharing breakfast with their noses buried in newspapers, moving silently through the morning, living without looking at each other. Yet Madeleine feels something ought to be said now, and she searches through the inept arti-cles and ads of the dailies to find words that may help her to speak about pain, tiredness, kidneys, and death. But such things are not to be found in Section B of the weekend edi-tion. She rises, picks up her son's empty plate, and, in passing, gently strokes the endless braid floating down along a spindle of his chair. He starts and pulls his braid onto his chest:

"Stop that, Ma."

Madeleine hurries over to the sink. She tries to set the dishes down softly but the cutlery drops with a clatter. Why is something supposedly easy so complicated with Édouard? He stands up waving the newspaper as if he wanted to change the subject even though nothing has been said.

"The inauguration of the Confederation Bridge takes place in a few days. I can't believe I'm going to miss it. I promised myself I'd be the first to walk across."

"I don't think they'll allow pedestrians across. And this is a bad time to wear yourself out."

"It makes me sick."

Madeleine squirts some detergent into the rising water of the sink. She dips her hand in to fish out a spoon. The water is too hot.

"Yes, I know. Me too."

A quarter of an hour later, the newspaper pages are still turning lazily when Yun bursts breathlessly into the room, her body peppered with white paint. Her gaze shifts from mother to son and her face becomes a mask of perplexity.

"What's the matter? You both look paralyzed!"

Édouard gets up and ushers his lover into the living room, leaving Madeleine alone with her fingers soaking in soapy water. From the next room, Yun's voice chimes out as if it were passing through Édouard's hand.

"You are so weird, the two of you!"

Some conspiracy theorists had crammed his head full of stories about extraterrestrials, so he decided to follow a small group of unemployed circus performers to Nevada. After setting his tent up on a makeshift campsite alongside some twenty other people, he spent the week a few kilometres from Area 51, scanning the sky in search of confirmation. But the power of desert legends resides in their never being proved. They hover at ground level to throttle the ankles of hikers, who lose their appetites and their sleep until they go insane.

One night a purple-haired girl pulled out of her gear an enormous bag of mushrooms that she had personally gathered in the Rockies. Édouard swallowed three disgusting, still-moist boletuses. After a few hours of seeing stars dance and his friends' limbs get twisted out of shape, he made up his mind to go strolling by himself in the surrounding moonscape. Wonderment soon turned into terror. Every glimmer, every rustle became a monster skulking in the Mojave night, ready to abduct him, to dissect him, to probe the stillness of his human body and of his brain harnessed to desperately futile goals.

Curled up against a porous rock in the foetal position, for many hours he begged to be spared and left in peace on his stunted planet. But the terror persisted. So he resolved to make his way back to the campsite, where he hoped to find solace in the arms of a girl with, or without, purple hair. For a long time he walked in concentric circles, unable to get back to his starting point. It was then he spotted, right there in the middle of nowhere, a phone booth that appeared to be waiting for him alone. Instinctively and with underwater slowness, he dialled the one number he knew by heart: his mother's. She was the only one who could comfort him at that instant, the only one whom he could tell that he was more than ever lost and ask how to find his way again.

The telephone rang for a long time, and Édouard sank into the recurrent dream he had had since leaving home, in which he would call there but was unable to open his mouth, so that when he heard his mother saying "Hello? Hello?" he couldn't manage even the slightest response. This time, though, the opposite happened. Someone picked up the receiver but did not speak. From the calm breathing at the other end Édouard guessed it was Madeleine. He began to recount his night, the bonfire, the mushrooms, his walk and his going astray, until he eventually broke into tears, overwhelmed by memories—his father's face, the garden when he was a child, the air along the Acadian Shore, and the time when it was so easy to be someone's son.

When he had finished his monologue he waited for an answer that never came. But just before hanging up, he thought he heard the faint vibrations of a foghorn. When he stepped out of the booth dawn was breaking with lavish gestures, stretching its pink, blue, and orangey fingers over the desert. In the distance he could make out the campsite. Madeleine never mentioned that call. A few years later, the Mojave phone booth would be disconnected for good.

Nothing has been neglected. Her hair and blood, again, but also cells from her mouth and skin, not to mention biopsies of her uterus and thyroid gland. She even noticed that one of the three doctors studying her case was gazing covetously at her teeth. With her jaws resolutely shut, she let them take whatever was necessary to solve the enigma of her body. Madeleine leaves the hospital feeling like a fruit that has been pressed dry.

The trip back is unusually quick. It's the kind of day when the clouds blot out the light an hour earlier than the normal twilight time. She parks in front of the house, and it seems to her that space has been hemmed in and the sky has shrunk. Everything is closer, everything is within reach. Once inside the entrance hall she finds Yun waiting for her in the rigid pose of a pointer.

"Édouard took a spill. He felt faint riding his bicycle."

"What do you mean, on his bicycle? Where is he?"

"They took him to Caraquet. They said not to worry—just a few cuts and bruises."

"Let's go."

As they are leaving, she glances at Shabby curled up in the armchair, deaf to the fuss, one paw resting nonchalantly on a geology textbook that once belonged to Micha. "You watch over him," she silently orders the hundred-year-old walls that for generations have supported and guarded, divided and kept watch.

On one level, the paramedics were right. Édouard's wounds are only superficial. But the consequences turn out to be disastrous for him. The fact he is no longer allowed to leave the house makes him even sicker than do his damaged kidneys. Constantly in a foul mood, he spins his wheels and kicks at Shabby, refuses to shave, and never opens his mouth except to whine. Only Yun succeeds in cheering him up. They spend long hours sprawled on lounge chairs looking at atlases, maps, and out-of-date travel guides, plotting like conquistadores about to take over a continent. Madeleine watches them from a distance, praying for something to happen: a phone call, an earthquake, a stray musical note that would stave off the immobility, the black prism through which the nascent summer is being tarnished.

A warm front arrives, in no way intimidated by the icy currents of the Atlantic. Madeleine finds nothing better than to try to keep the heat at bay with the help of a fan whose red paint chips with every stroke. The cat seems shabbier than usual, its fur weighed down and left misshapen by the humidity. All its pleas to be petted are ignored. In any case, its mistress feels completely incapable of doing anything. The heat wave has taken upon itself to stupefy everything still moving.

Still, she leaps to her feet when the telephone rings. It may be the kidney. It may be Paul, who's recovered his bees. It may be a foghorn. She answers. Her doctor's voice sounds different. She has known it to be cold, firm, tinged with a hint of accusation, then contrite, inquisitive, buoyed by scientific curiosity. This time it is gentle, incredibly gentle and friendly. When he suggests they meet on the beach instead of in the hospital she knows that what he needs to tell her is something he has never had to tell anyone before. She takes the road to the village, on foot, like a vagabond. She walks all the way to the sea.

The doctor is barefoot.

"It's incredible," he says. "I came to practise in Bathurst because I love the sea, yet in five years I've come down to the shore just two or three times."

"Too busy?"

"I forget. The beach is never too far away, but it doesn't occur to me anymore. It's silly."

The waves envelop his feet in seaweed. He shakes it off, steps closer to Madeleine, and leads her to a sea-washed tree trunk, where he invites her to sit down.

"As you know, Madeleine, we've been trying for weeks to understand your situation, which is quite particular, not to say extraordinary. The team at the Chaleur Hospital was struggling to find an explanation, so I paid a visit to some colleagues in New York State who specialize in genetic research. They're the ones who helped me find answers to our questions. I've just come back from that little trip and I called you right away."

Madeleine notices the clean, undamaged suitcase sitting on the sand. Nothing like the luggage of her son and people of his ilk. The doctor takes a deep breath, as if about to dive into deep water.

"You are two people."

His tone is meant to be solemn, but the statement is too preposterous.

"What do you mean by that?"

"I mean there are two distinct DNA's inside you because your body contains two human beings."

Madeleine opens her mouth and the offshore wind rushes into too quickly, making her cough.

"How's that possible?"

The doctor opens his briefcase, rummages through papers that apparently have nothing to do with Madeleine's case specifically, but this sort of diagnosis must be supported by documentation, any documentation.

"It appears you have a twin sister with whom you merged *in utero*. Actually, it's inexact to say 'you had a twin sister.' It would be more accurate to say, you are twins. Because one did not invade the other. You are two equal and indissociable parts of a whole."

Madeleine stands up, unable to utter another word. Her heels dig into the sand, and she has the sensation of being aware of them for the first time in her life. She starts weeping.

"You're not the only one," the doctor adds by way of consolation. "There are a few, very rare but very real, documented cases. Patients who are in this situation are referred to as chimeras."

"A chimera," Madeleine mumbles. "Science was obliged to draw on mythology to describe what I am."

"One of the twins took over the circulatory system, the other the skin and hair, and so on. You might say that you divided up between you the different zones of the same body."

"Mine or hers?"

"Yours. Both bodies. Let me try to explain it this way: if the merger process had not been completed, you would have become Siamese twins. You see? Inside you, there's the same separation that exists between two individuals, two twins. The partition is simply imperceptible, because there's just a single body. And a single brain, of course."

Stunned, Madeleine opens her hand and runs her fingers over her belly, her arms, her legs, endeavouring to distinguish two women where there is only one. It seems to her that by playing the arbiter of her own body she has just added a third term to the equation. The truth that she is doing her best to grasp explodes in her mind. Stepping into the water, she looks down at her distorted toes. "A foot for one, a foot for the other," she murmurs, knowing this to be inaccurate. "The skin of one, the blood of the other. Bones versus hair. The nails but not the muscles." The doctor comes next to her, briefcase hanging from his hand, trousers rolled up to the knees.

"Do you have any questions?" he asks softly.

"Hundreds!" Madeleine shouts through her tears. "At least tell me this: who is Édouard's mother?"

"Well, I guess it's the one who took possession of the reproductive system. The same one who's in your hair. But not in your blood."

"So you weren't entirely wrong. I'm not quite his mother."

"Which 'I' are you referring to? Your 'I' includes Édouard's mother, Madeleine. In any case, I think such distinctions fade away once you get past yourself."

The tide has risen at least a metre. When the doctor leaves, Madeleine slumps down in the water. Her skirt forms a shifting corolla around her and she could swear her ribs are dancing on either side of her spine and her limbs are out of joint. As if her body must deconstruct itself for her to be able to grasp it, compute it anew.

"I am two, I am two, I am two," she repeats, knotting her fingers together in a frenzied prayer in order to decipher in that entwinement the shadow of something manifest. "I am twins," she adds, disconcerted by the realization that the only way to speak the truth about herself is to defy grammar.

After an hour, maybe two, the words get lost. She lets herself flow in the back and forth of the water; she wraps her arms around herself and tries to hug her trunk, to embrace all of herself. In the distance, the shape of a boat emerges from the waves. A small isosceles sail and at the foot of the mast a creature whose black hair slants in the wind. The silhouette waves her hand, a greeting that Madeleine readily answers, knowing for certain it is Yun.

Édouard spent two days with the truck driver. He was not like the others; to start with, he was not fat. After only a few years on the road, most of his fellow truckers had put on excess weight and as a result were beset by a host of problems and illnesses that would eventually finish them off. But Joe had stayed slim and Édouard could not say if he was thirty or fifty years old. His moustache—so blond it was almost white—did not help. Although he did not seem to be especially conceited, he had stuck a photograph of himself on the rear-view mirror and never stepped off the truck without flicking his thumb over the picture.

Joe was a quiet man. He was heading to Oklahoma over the arrow-straight roads that blazed across the plains, but he never spoke the state's name, preferring the term "Dust Bowl" as if he'd been born in 1929 into a family of destitute farmers. Most truckers like to talk about the places they had grown up in; this one said very little about his hometown. He smoked cigarillos—their cherry aroma streaming out the half-open window—and scrupulously avoided religious radio stations as well as country music channels, favouring instead the rare classical music shows. He never used his CB radio to speak to the other truckers and did not wave to them when they passed. Whenever he drove past a dead deer or coyote on the side of the road, he would cross himself.

The one night Édouard spent in Joe's company, Joe insisted on giving up his bunk and chose to sleep under the stars. Young and incorrigible, Édouard used the opportunity to invite the truck stop waitress to join him in the cab when her shift ended. She was barely four feet eleven and had breasts like birthday balloons. When they slipped outside in the wee hours for one last kiss, Édouard saw Joe lying with his arms spread wide on the roof of the trailer, crucified between sleeplessness and dreams, between the Milky Way and the blacktop.

They reached Oklahoma in the late afternoon. Joe then left the interstate and took a backroad riddled with potholes. Édouard, who was going nowhere in particular, silently let himself be transported. Behind them, the trailer clanged like a cracked cymbal. It sounded as if the truck was empty. Joe finally stopped on the outskirts of a town, near a cemetery. Without saying a word, he alighted, walked over to the graves, where he quickly found the one he was searching for and knelt down in front of it.

Édouard waited two hours for the trucker to get up and take his seat again behind the wheel; it was then he realized that Joe had reached his destination. Determined to head out again in the first car that pulled over, Édouard stepped closer to say good-bye to Joe. On the grave where Joe was immersed in prayer were a few wildflowers, several stones of various shapes and colours arranged in a small mound, and a photograph that Joe apparently had just placed there. In the picture were two Joes, the first with his arm draped across the shoulders of the second Joe, who was also wearing a jean jacket and holding a bottle of beer. Only one of them was wearing a Chiefs cap.

Édouard cleared his throat to draw the trucker's attention. To no avail. The traveller timidly uttered some simple words of thanks but was cut short by the trucker's arm, which abruptly shot up to hush the voice that was disrupting his meditation.

Joe did not turn around for another hour and remained completely silent, as if petrified beside the grave of his double. A car stopped and took Édouard eastward, and the twins remained alone in their intangible communion. Now, every time Édouard recalls that episode, he is stricken with shame.

No matter how often Madeleine repeats to herself she is two, the news has left her prostrate with a feeling of overpowering solitude. She can't help harking back to a period of her child-hood when she would spend her days playing in a closet with faceless figurines. She might have shared all those terrible, gloomy hours giggling and exchanging secrets with another little girl. "Maybe that is what allowed us to survive," she tells herself by way of encouragement. "If we had not merged, we may not have had the strength."

The heat wave has grown too heavy for human restless-ness. Madeleine succumbs to it and scans the sky desper-ately hoping to glimpse a cloud or a passing iceberg. Inside the house muffled by the heat, the cat, dragging an invisible weight, laboriously grooms itself, while Édouard rests. Day by day his health is deteriorating despite the dialysis and the host of drugs he swallows each morning. His reaction on learn-ing of Madeleine's chimeric nature was rather indifferent. Whereas Joanna rushed to wrap her arms around Madeleine and Yun plunged into some books to find out more about the phenomenon, Édouard simply nodded:

"I'm not all that surprised. It explains why you're con-stantly talking to yourself."

Madeleine bit her thumb. A few days later she found a drawing on the living room coffee table. A hybrid woman, part shark, part doe.

The small hours of the morning find her sitting at the kitchen table. She catches herself wishing Micha were there; he would have considered the situation with the same equanimity he would display when faced with most of the vagaries and dramas of the world around him. His coolness sometimes annoyed Madeleine, but it had a soothing effect whenever panic came scratching at the door at about three in the morning. One night Joanna comes downstairs as if she has heard her host calling. She tiptoes in and sits down next to Madeleine.

"Insomnia or an early hike?" Madeleine inquires.

"A bit of both," her guest answers slowly, with her typical stress on the consonants. "Can't get back to sleep, so I'm going out."

Madeleine collects the crumbs of the last meal between her fingers and shapes them into a small nest bounded by one of the squares on the check tablecloth.

"And you? How are you doing?" Joanna asks.

Madeleine smiles, adding a few specks of bread to the mound.

"All right."

"Can I ask you something?"

"Yes."

"Do you remember?"

"What?"

"When you were separate?"

Madeleine shuts her eyes to better concentrate and tries to discern what she has striven so hard to imagine that it has already become a kind of memory: the pink of the uterine world, the aquatic motion, an amoebaean form dancing nearby, brushing her in the amniotic wave.

"No, we were too small."

"Pity. Just imagine if you could recall the sensation of merging with another human being. In a way, you experienced in the first moments of your existence what everyone spends their whole life desiring."

Madeleine sets down her cup with the camomile dregs floating at the bottom, stands up and, leaning over Joanna, kisses her on the cheek. Outside, the sun is coming up. The animals throughout the peninsula are chomping at the bit.

In the village the parade of compassion has resumed in the aisles of the grocery store. People stop to ask after Édouard in hopes of leaving with some clarifications, anecdotes, or an exclusive insight into the chimera.

"Do you eat more than a normal person?"

"When you're injured, does it hurt in only half of your body?"

"Do you believe you have two souls?"

Madeleine makes an effort to be patient, answers the strange questions as best she can and sidesteps the stupid ones. What takes place at the lighthouse museum's board meeting is hardly any better. In an attempt to forestall awkward questions from her colleagues, Madeleine picks up a report as bulky as a loaf of bread and tries to start her presentation as quickly as possible, but she has trouble breathing under the inquisitive eyes of her audience. The silence grows heavy; Madeleine is paralyzed by the many eyes fixed on her, by these colleagues who are not interested anymore in the number of visitors or the box-office takings at the lighthouse, but rather in the little museum of horrors that she incarnates. She looks at their notepads covered with doodles, their drained pens, the requisite cups of acidic coffee left hovering in front of their faces so they can scrutinize her on the sly while she parses the attendance graphs, until she finally breaks off.

"I'm not going to split in two, if that's what's troubling you. You can stop staring at me."

The administrators squirm uncomfortably in their office chairs.

"I insist," she adds, surprised by her own firmness.

There are bursts of laughter here and there, a few knowing glances cross the room. They expected this. This is why they are here. They came to see her lose it.

"I'm aware how small your world is, how much you need the monsters and miracles of others. But I am neither one nor the other. You all know how to read, so I leave you in good company. You can make do without me."

With the dazed board members looking on, Madeleine tosses the thick report onto the table, where it lands like a slumbering body, and then slams the door behind her. Once again she finds herself at the foot of the lighthouse and leans her back against it facing the sea spray. She inhales the infinite and the multitude of the ocean that is numberless—neither one, nor two, nor a hundred—a plural, incalculable world before which she wants to kneel down. In the distance, she sees Yun, both feet planted on the deck of a sailboat as slender as a spear, with a cabin strangely similar to a Chevrolet Monte Carlo.

As she is leaving, the watchman hobbles up to her. She ferrets in her bag looking for her keys. He lays his hand on her wrist to interrupt her frantic searching. He has never touched her this way.

"I have a present for you."

Poking around in his jacket pocket, he retrieves a stone whose blue and white colours are combined in a sort of mineral swirl.

"I picked it up on the beach a long time ago. I knew it had come from far away, from another world, and that it was there for someone. So I've kept it at the bottom of my pocket. It's yours. This stone is you."

"Do you find me so very cold?"

Monsieur le gardien smiles.

"I didn't say it was your heart. I said it was you. You're not alone, Madeleine. Remember that."

Madeleine's fingers gently caress the pebble's coolness as the watchman walks away with that slow gait of his filled with certainties. "For him," Madeleine mutters, "the whole world is strange and twisted. He expects nothing else." She takes the stone out of her pocket and presses it to her lips.

Paul's second pillow always has too many smells. In every fold of the pillowcase she finds a different aroma. Roses. Lavender. Some tobacco. It all makes her want to sneeze but, instead, she lets out a sigh.

"Are you bored?" Paul asks, stroking her temple.

"You make my head spin."

He gets up to part the curtains and let in the setting sun; then he goes out and comes back with two bottles of beer all beaded with drops of July. The first swallow awakens Madeleine's languid nerves, and she sits up, putting distance between her nose and the pillow.

"You know, I have no trouble believing there are two women inside you. You're as fickle as the wind, Madeleine Sicotte."

"I have no trouble believing it either, you know. The problem is that I think I've always listened to the same one. The other has been muzzled."

"What did she want?"

Madeleine shrugs. "Beer," she is thinking. "A cigarette."

"Something darker, I guess. Or grander."

A fly starts tapping stubbornly on the window, and Paul abruptly swings around, hoping to discover a bee. Disappointed, he turns back to Madeleine.

"Why don't you come live with me here?" he blurts out.

Madeleine twists the sheet around her forefinger. The cloth is riddled with holes from hot cigarette ashes.

"Because you fuck anything that walks," she tells him.

"What? That's not true."

"Yes, it is true. You even fuck my neighbours. I saw Violette Godin's locket on your night table a few weeks ago."

"Who can blame him?" she adds in her mind. Paul is the village's only decent bachelor. He is a good lover and a good cook. Madeleine has always put up with her lover's unfaithfulness without saying a word. But today she can't understand what has kept her from being forthright for so long.

"We all know it; none of us has any illusions about you. That's why no one wants to be your wife, Paul. You'll never have one if you try to have them all."

Lying there naked, Paul is unable to meet her gaze, and he keeps stroking the rabbit's foot that goes with him everywhere. Madeleine finds him handsome and is sorry to have shamed him yet at the same time she feels a huge weight has been lifted from her shoulders.

"You smell nice," she whispers as she kisses his ear.

"You know," he says as he draws away, "if you came to live with me, there wouldn't be any others. From then on, you'd be the only one. You're the one who belongs here. Anyway, you can't go on forever alone in that big house taking in one traveller after another. Especially once your son sails away on that boat."

Stepping toward her pile of clothes, Madeleine stops short.

"What are you talking about?"

"I think I heard someone say that he and his girlfriend plan to leave on a boat after his operation. That would be the right time for you to move here and settle in."

Madeleine dresses quickly.

"I will not settle in with you—that's out of the question! I don't want to settle anywhere."

"It's because of Micha? It's been years, Madeleine!"

"Be quiet! You don't know a thing about it!"

A few minutes later she is tearing along the dirt road toward the highway. Paul is still standing in his bedroom in his underwear with a stony look on his face. Madeleine hits the brakes to let a hare go by. Then starts away again.

"What's this business about a cruise?!"

She is shouting at the top of her lungs. A scream that she held in when she found the house full of her son's childhood friends and while she waited for them to leave, for Joanna to go out to do some shopping, for Yun to take a shower, and finally for Édouard to be alone in a room with no way out. Like someone who has just been struck in the stomach by a cannonball, he recoils.

"Uh, well, me and Yun have hunted up a cheap boat. We'll have to patch it up a little after I get my kidney… We'd like to see if it's possible to follow the route of Marquette and Jolliet: sail up the Saint Lawrence and then…"

"Are you insane?" Madeleine cuts in. "After the operation, you'll need to recuperate and wait several weeks in case your body rejects the transplant."

"I know, but after my convalescence I'll be on my way again. That's what I've always done."

"Well, enough is enough! I've had it!"

Édouard holds himself stiffly with his fists clenched behind his back.

"You almost die, you land up here and then as soon as you're able to take a few steps you shove off? Is that how it's always going to work? You come back to sleep and eat and then you bolt?"

"What more do you want? I'm an adult. I don't live here anymore."

"What I want? I want a son who comes to visit his mother, that's what I want. Not another vagrant who stops here just long enough to get his strength back so he can disappear the very next day."

"But that's what I do. I come to see you—what else?"

"Bullshit! We've barely had a real conversation since you arrived. And that was only because you're ill and they thought I wasn't your mother. As a rule, we say a word or two about the weather and that's all. But here you are waiting for a transplant and here I am with two people inside me, and it's as if nothing has changed! You spend your days glued to your girlfriend—don't get me wrong, I adore her—but you use her like a shield. Then afterwards you work things out so you can take off at the first opportunity, even though you'll still be in poor health and courting death at any moment in the middle of the Mississippi or Lake Ontario, without any help, without me."

"I don't need you!"

"Oh, I do realize that. And, you know, I don't need you either. But that doesn't mean we need to avoid having a relationship."

She punctuates this last statement with a hard punch against the wall. Madeleine is surprised by both her gesture and the flimsiness of the wall. Without thinking, she goes on pounding the wall with all her might, with her hands and feet, with the strength of the righteous and the stubbornness of the tender-hearted, with a sort of love that passes through her muscles. Slowly, the partition gives way, the panelling crumbles under the blows, and the familiar angles of the corridor become visible.

"You've completely lost your mind."

Her eyes are fixed on the gap; Madeleine is no longer looking at her son.

"I was hoping that at least all this shit—the illness, the DNA business—I was hoping it would bring us closer together. That you would learn to speak to me."

"And where would I have learned that? You never tell me anything. Nothing about your family, about your life with dad. I lost my father at seventeen and you never talk to me about him. It's as if he never existed. And you! People in town say you have a lover, that you take pictures on the seashore. I know nothing about any of it."

"You never asked me anything!"

"Neither did you."

On the other side of the hole, Yun's tear-streaked face appears.

"Anyway," Édouard mutters, "there may not be an 'after the transplant.'"

Right then, the beeper lying on his nightstand starts to vibrate. It's the hospital. They're expecting Édouard.

Sitting in the grey waiting room, grey like all the waiting rooms in the world, Madeleine thinks about Micha and his cancer, her sister and her psychotic episodes, her father and his cirrhosis. It seems that every ten years the flesh of someone close is demanded of her, as if a Minotaur were pacing along the maze of hospital corridors, lurking behind the respirators and MRI devices. "It's time for him to leave me something. It's time for me to leave here together with my loved ones," she decides while her son is subjected to a battery of tests.

Because, to be entitled to a kidney, he must pass a raft of examinations. The long road to Halifax was not the last stop. Nor will the transplant—assuming it actually happens—be the finishing line. Sixty days will be needed to be sure the body has not rejected it. Before the great event, it is imperative to verify that the recipient is perfectly healthy and completely free of viruses. With her fingers clutching her key ring, Madeleine makes one wish after another, laying claim to all the wishes that, for lack of inspiration, she did not make on her birthdays, and all the shooting stars she passed up on. In the space of a few hours she has turned into a superstitious freak.

After several hours of testing, Édouard is set free. He is tired; the clock struck twelve long ago. The operation has been scheduled for the next morning. While he is getting settled in a room that looks more like an alcove Madeleine can easily see that her son will not be sleeping.

"Would you like me to ask for a tranquillizer?"

Édouard's gesture means no. He seems to have forgotten their quarrel; his brow is dark but shows no sign of anger. On the other side of the curtain a man groans between nightmares. He is dreaming of a giant cigarette, Madeleine guesses from the whistling sound of his breathing; he is dreaming that he is wallowing in smoke. She can almost smell the aroma of tobacco drifting above his bed. She can recognize a true smoker with her eyes closed, the ones who wake during the night for a few puffs, the ones who are doomed. Micha slept just like that toward the end.

The noises in the corridor die down, but Édouard can't sleep. His eyelids grow heavy and suddenly start to flutter but then they pop open again. Madeleine places her fingers on her son's arm. Under the skin, his nerves are restless.

"Édouard, I'm convinced it will be just fine. You've got everything on your side: you're young, you're strong. And there's something about you that not many have. You accept everyone. I've never seen you judge someone or reject the company of another person."

Édouard's face is tense and he frowns. Madeleine elaborates:

"How could your body reject a kidney? If you'd known the donor you would surely have liked him. You would have bought him a beer and talked about Johnny Cash, Kerouac, baseball—right? It's written in your cells. Every fibre in you knows it."

The water wells up in Édouard's eyes. For many minutes he keeps silent. Then he gives Madeleine a look so desperate that she is obliged to lean closer.

"All that doesn't make the slightest difference. I'm going to die, Ma."

"Don't talk like that."

"No, I'm sure of it. This disease, it didn't just happen. It's punishment."

Madeleine straightens up and gazes at her son in bewilderment. He averts his eyes, and what he exudes is in fact shame, scuttling out of his pores like rats fleeing a ship. The palms of Madeleine's hands grow damp.

"Punishment for what?"

"For choosing to save my skin instead of saving a life. Two lives."

"What are you talking about?"

"A few months ago, in Savannah, I witnessed a horrible accident. Two little girls hit by a train. They tried to get away, but they weren't able. There was blood everywhere. I saw them. But instead of going to help them, I... I hopped on the train."

"You didn't alert the authorities?"

"I couldn't. I couldn't."

He pauses to push some air through the sobs that are choking him. Madeleine breathlessly kneads his arm.

"I'm a piece of shit. I let two children die. And now it's my turn to die."

Madeleine says nothing more. She can't find the words to tell him that is not how life works, to explain to her still very young son that the world is not a vast pair of scales where bad actions offset each other, where misdeeds are consistently sanctioned. The world is an unjust place where the good go bad from never being rewarded, where the truly wicked are very rarely punished and where most folk zigzag between the two extremes, neither saints nor demons, tacking between heartache and joy, their fingers crossed, knocking on wood. Every person split in two, each with a fault around which good and evil spin.

When the pale morning light comes through the curtain separating them from the sick smoker, she finally manages to utter a few burning words.

"You won't die. It's impossible. Because I love you."

She very gingerly gets up and gives up her seat. Yun is standing in the doorway wearing a purple dress that seems to herald a celebration, a healing, but in which Édouard will see the colour of grieving. In fifteen minutes, the anaesthetics will carry him off to the murky lands of his consciousness and a stranger's kidney will come to nestle in his back like a hazardous treasure.

"I wonder what the person was like," Yun says pensively.

"The donor?"

153

"Yes. We don't know anything about him—or her: age, sex, if he loved his kids or believed in God."

Madeleine nods. Already over the past two hours she has formed a very clear idea of the person she pictures as having left Édouard a kidney, so that she has a detailed image of the man in her mind. A father in his forties, a long-haul truck driver who died of a heart attack after discovering his wife was having an affair with their neighbour. His name is George, he likes bowling, barbecues, and Simon & Garfunkel. To make amends, his widow agreed to donate all the dead man's serviceable organs: the lungs, pancreas, kidneys, and eyes. She convinced herself that half a dozen lives saved would make up for a cuckold's death in the eyes of God.

"You know," Yun continues sheepishly, "if you don't approve of the sailing trip we've planned, we could always change our plans."

"It's not my place to approve. There's nothing wrong with the plan as such. Actually, it's a lovely idea. You're free, the two of you. Completely free."

"Yes. But Édouard's health comes first. His health and his family."

"We'll see. We'll see in sixty days."

Using her fingernail to whittle down the rim of a disposable cup, Yun adds in a low voice:

"He loves you more than you think."

Styrofoam particles pile up like a little snow bank at their feet. A muffled warmth stirs in Madeleine's belly and spreads to each of her limbs. She is filled with peace. Her son is safe and sound—now she is sure of it.

An hour later, the woman who performed the operation comes out to meet them and to confirm that the transplant was successful. Édouard is taken to the recovery room, and Madeleine and Yun spring up in unison, a modest honour guard for a patient they cherish with equal strength, from source to estuary.

The man in the photo appears to be some thirty years younger than Joanna. His teeth are so white one might suspect they glow in the dark. He smiles warmly on the arm of the bride. Both are dressed in white and surrounded by musicians with instruments as close to agriculture as they are to music, such is their resemblance to dried fruits and hollowed out vegetables.

"He is very handsome," Madeleine says.

"At his age, all men are handsome," Joanna adds.

Madeleine gives her an amused look. The evening settles in lazily; the scent of the sea is everywhere. Édouard is asleep. This is the first time since he was discharged that the household can catch its breath. His ten days in the hospital were exhausting for Madeleine and Yun, who took turns at his bedside. On returning from Halifax they had to rearrange the house, set up a bedroom on the ground floor, learn to manage the medication, accompany Édouard when he moved about, and clean the wound shaped like a half-moon. Joanna's help in carrying out these tasks proved invaluable. Given her high spirits and Yun's gentleness, Madeleine senses that the healing will go quickly. The kidney is holding up, and in the surgeon's opinion it's working as if it had always been a member of the family. Only the cat is showing signs of flagging, as it spends the greater part of its days sleeping under the armchairs.

Sitting on the front porch steps, the two women drink beer while Joanna recounts her adventures. Married to a young Cameroonian for the past five years, she displays such cheerful clear-sightedness that it is impossible for Madeleine to make the slightest judgment about this bizarre union. The couple spends scarcely a few weeks together once a year, after which they are "free as the air."

"Of course I'm aware of what people think: that in his eyes I'm just a wallet or a visa for Europe. What would a handsome young man be doing with a woman in her sixties? But he's a good man, and marrying him has made me happy."

Madeleine puts back the photograph while Joanna grabs one of Micha and her on their wedding day, a picture she agreed to take out of an album that she never opens anymore. She steals a glance at their earnest expressions, their hands locked together. That they were so madly in love early on seems odd to her today, as when you discover an old dress, now too small, and can't believe your body could ever have slipped into it. Joanna pores over the portrait trying to extract from it some vital element, to understand the couple and the times portrayed.

"Your husband had a hard life," she declares.

In the sky's fading light Madeleine makes out the pointed movement of a kite, probably a kilometre from her house but high enough to remain visible. Then, for the first time, she dares to share with someone what she held close to her chest for so many years, the secrets that Micha had confided to her on the eve of their wedding, saying, "Now you know everything; you're free to change your mind." The rape of his mother and sister before his eyes, the murder of his brothers, his own rebellion at the age of sixteen, when he left the tomb of his people and took up arms to kill and rape in his turn, to spit back at war what war had forced him to swallow. Madeleine had listened to the man pouring out his story, coldly, disappointedly, sadly, but unrepentantly, and she had chosen to disregard those revelations.

"I still don't know how I was able to go on loving him so, given everything he had done."

With the round hard edge of her fingernail, Joanna strokes the photographed faces of the young newlyweds, first one and then the other.

"You behaved like half the inhabitants of the planet. Not everyone has the luxury of growing up in peacetime. The conscience of most people who have lived through war is like your husband's. It's…"

The Dutch woman fumbles for words, sifting through her French to pinpoint a synonym that isn't there.

"It's a terrible conscience. Victims and executioners often coexist in the same person. Those who forgive them are the ones who enable the world to heal."

Madeleine takes back the photo in which her face and Micha's are slowly fading.

"I have never found a way of telling all this to Édouard."

"Now you have the time."

The two women finish their beers without speaking, while the wind gets caught in the red-tinted hair and the cotton skirts. The sky has darkened but Madeleine thinks she can still distinguish the kite, pulling on its leash like a dog, hoping, like every sail in the world, to be allowed at last to fly away for good.

Édouard's steps are surer, his movements sturdier. It isn't so much his gait as the fact he looks at the sky, the trees, and places his hands on tree stumps. As if he were coming out of himself after staying rolled up in a ball, a clenched fist, so that no energy whatsoever might escape. Madeleine is waiting for him beside a freshly dug hole. In an old shredded blanket lies Shabby the cat. He did not survive the heat wave or the commotion in the house or simply his eighteenth year in this world. Hugging the small, expired body one last time, Madeleine wept, but she could not help thinking that it had come at the right moment. Édouard gently lays the departed at the bottom of the hole and then, holding his shovel, straightens up.

"The first time I travelled by train, I couldn't sleep for the first three or four days. I couldn't get used to the rocking, the noise of the cars, the wind. And going through remote areas that were completely uninhabited, I had the sensation of being the first man ever to have set foot there, and the thought obsessed me, kept me from closing my eyes. After a few days, of course, my body gave out. I fell asleep somewhere near Reno. When I woke up it was dawn. I looked around and I thought the train was sliding over water. We were on the track that splits the Great Salt Lake exactly in two. Because of the railroad ballast, the lake is divided in half, and the composition of the water isn't the same in both halves. The northern side is full of wine-red algae, but on the southern side it's green. The clouds were perfectly mirrored on the surface and took on the colours of the lake. The train rolled along slowly. The air was warm and soft. There was no sound; it was as if the universe had come to a standstill. Right then, I had the feeling that I would never again be hungry or cold or in pain or afraid."

Édouard deftly throws a handful of earth on the cat's body.

"That's what I wish for him, for your Shabby. That's what I wished for Dad. That's what I wish for every one of us."

Copying her son, Madeleine pours a little earth on her pet, the earth he was so fond of. Édouard picks up the shovel and calmly fills the grave, with his braid keeping time on his lower back. Madeleine is impressed by the sureness of his movements. She thinks about the organ that continues to bond to him, generating day after day new connections with the body to which it now belongs; she thinks about this piece of another human being, which is keeping her son alive.

"Now we both have another being inside us."

"Let's hope there'll be no more," Édouard adds. "There's no room left."

Madeleine takes a deep breath of salt air. The summer wind carries the messages of migrating whales.

"Just one more month," she says.

Édouard sighs happily. In a month, the dangerous period will be over. The risk of rejection will become almost nil. And the boat that Yun has been slaving away at every day will be able to cast off. He squeezes Madeleine's hand.

"Are you certain?"

He repeats the question as a matter of form. The discussion was concluded days ago. Together they finish burying Shabby, Madeleine's interlocutor, guest, hot-water bottle, guardian, night-light for nearly a third of her life. She takes her son's arm, looks out over the acre of land that belongs to her, and considers the extent to which she never belonged to it, the extent to which her desire drew her far from the demands of the soil and its shoots, far from the roots that probe the soul. Far from a house that was never open enough. The two of them stop in front of the slowly swaying willow. Two grey stones have been added at the foot of the tree. Madeleine casts Édouard a questioning look.

"For the little girls," he explains.

Madeleine nods.

"These grounds are getting crowded with the dead."

She feels as though she is standing in the palm of a large, restless hand. She must readjust herself with every step and test the floor she is treading; the angle is constantly shifting, as are the forces changing it from moment to moment. She endeavours to walk without holding the guardrail, to trust only the rhythm of the rolling as she tries to learn its syncopations.

The luggage and equipment have all found a place in the boat. The berths have been clothed with clean sheets and thick blankets. The provisions are hanging in a net over the little galley. The camera and about fifty rolls of film are tucked away on the deck in the small cabin that in another life was an old-fashioned car. Outside, on the passenger side, Joanna's bicycle has been solidly secured. As for Édouard and Yun, they've settled down under the deck, amid the waves lapping against the hull.

On the pier a few people are waiting in the spindrift. Paul, looking melancholy, is worrying at his rabbit's foot, while the watchman waves a spotless handkerchief. A few of Édouard's friends who have gathered are trying to play him a farewell song, but their instruments are stifled by the wind rushing into them. Even the doctor has come, dressed in a fisherman's raincoat, clearly delighted at the chance to be by the seaside. Madeleine could swear that there, behind them, she has caught sight of Frank and Missy and all the other travellers who have passed through the village, leaving footprints and the indelible impressions of backsides in the sand. She gives them a joyous wave, while Joanna, like a star from the Fifties, smiles and blows them kisses. Édouard weighs anchor as Yun contemplates the shore with an earnest expression, trying to commit its shape to memory so she can include it in the map she is drawing in her mind. There is a bitter onshore wind blowing. Fall is approaching and the warmth of the South throbs on the horizon like a sack of gold at the foot of a rainbow.

They button up their raincoats and lower their hats down on their heads, as if this detail was the last thing that needed to be attended to. When the boat finally casts off, Madeleine has the sudden sensation her lungs have filled with twice as much air, and she hangs on to Joanna's arm for fear her feet will slip off the deck. The boat heads out clumsily toward the mainland, toward that immensity still unseen, though its mineral rumbling can already be detected. In a few days they will plunge into the maw of an immeasurable gulf that will slowly narrow and gulp them down into the interior, between cliffs bristling with life, reeking of history, shimmering with strength. They'll avoid the shoals and greet the pods of cetaceans, as they brush by a string of salt-corroded cargo ships and let themselves be guided by a thousand beacons into the heart of America, where they will cut across the Prairies or slide along the Appalachian crests, and there they'll catch the scent of the deltas and the lakes welling in prehistoric craters. And Madeleine, her fingers buried in her jacket sleeves, will no longer feel her as-yet-unsteady steps on the deck, will no longer hang on to stones and walls, and will stop counting, so that she may, finally, for the first time, be but one.

A Penny
(MONETTE AND ANGIE)

THE GRASS is so high that it stands a good head taller than Monette. This doesn't bother her, and using a branch she found where the trail begins, she knocks away the stalks that bar the path. She insisted on taking the lead; Angie is close at her heels, brushing the burrs off the little girl's pink T-shirt and scanning the bushes for snakes and venomous spiders. The cicada's song covers everything: the crunch of their steps, their thick breathing in the vegetable humidity, and the rustling of potential enemies on either side.

With her free hand, Monette still keeps a firm grasp on the molasses cookie, which she nibbles at parsimoniously. As far as Angie can see, a significant portion of the treat is crumbling its way out of the wrapper, but her sister is too absorbed by the walk to pay attention. Angie recalls the story of Hansel and Gretel and the bits of bread they strewed to be able to find their way again. She turns around several times to see if the birds are snapping up the cookie crumbs.

From time to time the girls must stride over a tiny watercourse gushing across the path toward the river. Monette invariably bends down to try to see some fish and asks:

"Brook or river?"

"Runoff from the rain," Angie explains.

As it hasn't rained for weeks, this answer does not sound entirely satisfactory, but Angie makes no attempt to elaborate. Such rivulets and the silty furrows they create are part of the terrain. Water is so abundant in these parts.

The vegetation grows thicker and with it the insects' song, the cries of the blue jays.

"Are we still in Georgia?" Monette inquires.

"Uh-huh," Angie softly answers.

The little girl gives her big sister a doubtful look. She asks this same question whenever she finds herself in a place without houses or pavement, as if the state were defined solely according to its degree of civilization, its signs of human engineering. As if such an untamed environment could have neither name, nor border, nor government.

A mockingbird passes overhead and draws Monette out of her questions. The smell of oil and tar filters in through the grass, and Angie guesses they are not very far. After about forty paces they reach a clearing streaked with train tracks, which lie behind a fence too rusted and broken to warrant that name. Pulling back a section of the chain-link mesh, Angie lets Monette through first and, once she herself has crossed, puts her hand on the diminutive crumb-littered chest to keep Monette still. There is a rumbling noise to the north.

"Don't move. The train's coming."

She can almost feel Monette's heart leap as she hops up and down. The spectacle of the train is an endless source of excitement for her.

"Let's put down a penny! Let's put down a penny!" she shouts.

Angie searches in her pocket for a one cent piece and nimbly rushes to the tracks to lay it down. When she comes back and takes hold of her sister's hand, Monette, to be heard above the approaching roar, yells in a high-pitched voice:

"Let's count, okay?!"

Angie agrees without taking her eyes off the railroad. Just before the train arrives, she thinks she has caught sight of something, a strange shape heaving on the other side of the tracks. Her pulse races and then the train saws the space in half. Monette launches into the arithmetic refrain that marks the rhythm of the passing cars.

"One! Two! Three! Four! Five!"

The freight cars speed past, covered with dust, graffiti, and rust stains, every one numbered, every one named. None will be forgotten.

She Is Not Burned
(ARIEL AND MARIE)

THERE IS something reassuring about the structure of the horizon here. Of course, a house or a man is completely exposed on the Prairies. But, on the other hand, anyone arriving can be seen a long way off. That is why each morning, even on cold days, Ariel goes out and walks around the house, scanning the vastness of the plains. He counts the foxes and the hares bearing their pale winter fur, and only when he has confirmed that the animals are their sole companions can he go back in to Marie and the aroma of coffee, which has remained unchanged from one existence to the next.

They do not own much furniture. They took what came with the house, which seems to have been abandoned by people fleeing from a sudden apocalypse. Now, weeks after they moved in, a cake with only two or three slices missing still sits majestically in the middle of the table, as neither Marie nor Ariel can bring themselves to throw out the dessert that bespeaks those interrupted lives. Once they had given some clothes found in the cupboards to charity, replaced the curtains and acquired a few dishes from a second-hand dealer in Rockfield, they considered themselves properly moved in.

Marie took the main bedroom, and Ariel, the adjacent room, where he shoved a twin bed with a sagging mattress against the wall. This slender barrier is all that separates them when they go to sleep. Each presses a hand against the wall to wish the other goodnight. Sometimes they wake up at dawn in a state of confusion, failing to recognize the unfamiliar shadows licking at the abstract furniture, their hearts still pounding in fear of what lies in wait outside, of what is lodged in their marrow. Then they remember. The moving, the prairies, the neighbourless house. Everything has already exploded; the world has already been annihilated. That is the advantage of surviving the apocalypse: there is nothing left to either protect or fear.

A family of raccoons has taken up residence in the attic, and, out of respect, neither Ariel nor Marie goes visiting. In the spring, the constant squealing signals the birth of a litter. Marie spends a long time imagining the blind, toothless offspring whiffing the dusty air under the eaves in search of their mother's milk, and then she places her hand on her breast, which will grow old but never heavy. Like the land where they have come to live, Ariel and she have become sterile, two celibates scraping by on nothing, a worn-out hide salvaged from their past that day after day they manage to stretch enough to make it resonate. A beat of the drum to confirm they are still alive.

The party's cops were the first to arrive after the disaster. Impelled by an indignation that was amplified by their thirst for revenge, they forced the door of the little house after nightfall. As they no doubt expected denials from Ariel and Marie, they sat them down in separate rooms for questioning. They soon realized their interrogation was futile. He and she immediately admitted the truth, even offering to supply the adoption agency's documents in support of their statements and as proof that they were unaware of being siblings when the elections took place. Thrown off balance by the confessions, the cops proceeded to the next stage of their plan and ordered Ariel to resign immediately. They drafted a speech for him, which in no way resembled what he would have liked to say, but he came to terms with endorsing it. He readily consented to shut himself away for the following weeks and to refrain from any contact with the media. The reporters, constantly stationed in front of the house, shivered like animals that would rather freeze to death than starve to death.

The next day Marc succeeded in elbowing his way through to them. There were only a few hours left before the press conference, which had been put off long enough for an interim leader to be found whose curriculum vitae did not include incest, procuring, polygamy, or bestiality.

"How?" is all Marc managed to articulate.

"You're the only one I shared this with," Ariel replied.

"And you, Marie?"

"My sister found out, but she didn't tell anyone else about it."

Marc looks at her in disbelief.

"Everyone knows the Leclerc clan are all hard core independentists. Do you truly believe your sister could have kept something as explosive as this to herself?"

"Yes I do. My sister sets great store on family."

"There's no point in playing the blame game," Ariel decides. "It's too late."

It was indeed too late. The global media had latched onto the scandal. Forgetting their fight against modern science, the evangelists were marching in the streets now to demand not just that Ariel step down, but that the marriage be dissolved, that the twins be imprisoned, and that they be subjected to all manner of physical retribution involving fire and white-hot metal instruments. The Left's reaction was hardly better, as it responded to the attacks by sparing no effort to downplay the situation, arguing that family ties are "a matter of biography and not biology," and that, since Marie and Ariel had not grown up together, their kinship meant nothing. The party was floundering and the country's instability had never been greater.

Marie watched Ariel's resignation alone, dry-eyed and glued to the screen of her laptop. She could never compare their situation to the sexual scandals that shook the world of politics with clockwork regularity. Still, hearing the contrition in her husband's voice, seeing his wan complexion and his shoulders drooping in mortification, she had to admit he resembled the hundreds of men before him who had seen their careers disintegrate and slip through their fingers as they stood behind a plain lectern, sometimes flanked by a spouse, who clenched her teeth to hold down the bitter pill she was being made to swallow. Such people, no matter their misdeeds, were all to some extent the same; they had been forced, one way or another, to disclose facts that by their very nature should have remained secret. Sex, though socially acceptable, is not supposed to be described in public, detailed, analyzed, dissected. These defeated human beings mourned, not the end of their aspirations, but the fact that a space of intimacy had been forever altered, that a pleasure, wiped out by an avowal, was as dead as a wish uttered out loud. She came to pity all the infidels, closet homosexuals, Sunday nudists and other outsiders, even the most perverted, of which she now was one. Yet she envied them. Once the scandal had blown over, they could go back to a semblance of normality. For her and Ariel no such thing could ever exist again.

At night the northern lights wave like flags and shake the sky with supernatural vibrancy. Still, it's hard to forgive this firmament, where everything seems to be written, and those distant constellations, which, even before the invention of fire, were recounting their misfortune. Ariel and Marie spend a great deal of time watching the stars, questioning Castor and Pollux.

They might have chosen Patagonia, the Kamtchatka Peninsula, or the Kerguelen Islands, but Ariel refused to leave the country. Unable to persuade him to go into exile, Marc resigned himself to helping them find an adequately remote community, and to weave a discreet security net around them. All that was left for them to do was to fashion new identities for themselves.

Ariel is now known as Albert Morsehead, and Marie has become Anne Leblanc. Marc provided them with false papers, new fingerprints, artificial irises, and other necessary biometric devices. But because their faces had been plastered across the screens of North America for weeks, they had to attend to their more superficial physical attributes. Marie underwent a minor nose reconstruction as well as a reshaping of her eyebrows. With her hair dyed blond and cut short, she was unrecognizable. Ariel's case was somewhat more complicated. In spite of major plastic surgery, a beard, eyeglasses, and a different accent, something of the former prime minister persisted.

Marie was the one who suggested he put on fifteen kilos. This simple idea was the missing piece of the camouflage. Ariel was nowhere to be seen in the new, bulkier body, as if he were concealed in his own flesh. In any event, in this region of vast distances, where neighbours are recognized by virtue of their cars more than their faces, no one studies them up close. The inhabitants of central Saskatchewan have become so scarce they hardly look at each other and are identified from a sideways glance at their hairdos, their voices, the unique vibration of their presence, always perfectly distinct from someone else's.

The town of Rockfield is a place where one quickly feels at home but to which one never belongs. "Too windy, too flat," Ariel notes. Very soon the cashiers in the stores recognize Marie (or, rather, Anne) and call her by her alias, and the waiter at the café remembers that Ariel takes two sugars in his coffee. Both of them find this fabricated life deeply comforting. Here, no one will photograph them surreptitiously, no one will cover their house with graffiti. No one will shoot at them.

Marc, who still has friends in the army, helped Ariel find a job on the military base located in the vicinity. It involves introducing recruits to international politics and law. The young soldiers put him in mind of tight shells that crack open upon discovering the complexity of the world, the magnitude of the underflow that shapes its movements and tremors. The job, chosen by default, has grown on him. He likes giving these men, barely out of adolescence and the insulated world of rural traditions, a horizon, however condensed, and enabling them for a brief moment to enjoy an informed view of the countries where they will soon serve as cannon fodder.

As for Marie, she teaches French to kids who are completely untouched by the notion of the founding peoples and the bilingual imperative, now virtually obsolete in a province long ago swallowed up by the majority. Fortunately, they are also too young to understand their parents' disdainful remarks about the "lazy people's language," and they have no reservations about singing the old-fashioned songs that Marie teaches them: *Il était un petit navire*, *À la claire fontaine*, *Alouette*, and so on. She takes pleasure in watching them recite the confused syllables with open mouths or lean over the coloured keyboards, typing away with wondrous dexterity, their pudgy fingers hopping effortlessly from key to key like ignorant, agile little birds.

Sometimes Ariel comes to meet her at the end of the day and stations himself near the classroom door to watch her, pale and eager in front of her captive audience. Then he contemplates his own reflection in the glass door—fat, bearded, disappointing—and once again realizes she is worth all the failures, all the humiliations, all the relinquishments. Marie, his half of the world.

Ariel's mother could not stop crying and his father clenched his teeth so hard that a fine snow might have appeared

between his lips had he not pressed them together so tena-
ciously. The Leclercs, for their part, paced up and down and
shuddered—the outward expression of their ineffable distress.
In both cases it was not easy to know whether their families
were reacting to the drama itself—the unmentionable word
incest—or something else. Marie suspected her parents were
no less horrified by their circle having learned their daughter
was adopted, a fact that contradicted the notion of a blood-
line as strong and pure as the water of the last glaciers. As for
the Goldsteins, Ariel wondered if they were in fact mourning the fall of their angel, the end of their dreams of glory.
One night on his way to the bathroom he even overheard his
mother whispering, "None of this would have happened if he
had become a dentist."

"You're going to divorce," Martial declared in a tone that
was more imperative than interrogative.

"We have no choice; the law obliges us to dissolve the
marriage."

"But you are still living together?"

"Until the dust settles and we've sold the house," Marie
replied half-heartedly.

The truth was they had no wish to separate. There was
no one anymore who could look at them in a way that was
unmarred by disgust. They were their only refuge.

In the meantime, Marc investigated, slowly but deter-
minedly retracing the steps of the scandal to its source.
The Canada of shining tomorrows was dead and a culprit
had to be found, a traitor to be crucified in the history
books or, at the very least, a name to be placed on a list of
enemies and slipped into the inside pocket of a jacket, over
the heart.

In March the snow does not melt so much as evaporates, leaving the fields dry and dirty. Then in June the pitiful wisps of

grass that remain catch fire here and there, speckling the plain with orange-coloured nests of desire. In August the temperature drops inexplicably and the ground freezes, imprisoning thirsty spiders and snails in the frost. In October, the rain awaited since the spring equinox finally decides to fall, trapping the houses in a turbid lake.

Luckily the place is equipped with a canoe, wisely stored on the upper floor, this sort of deluge having become a common occurrence on the Prairies. For a week Ariel and Marie move about by paddling, with no definite destination, for the simple pleasure of exploring the region without submitting to the dictates of roads and territorial boundaries. They come across a few frantic deer, several soggy cows, and a handful of neighbours searching for dry patches. They are looking for earth or sand banks to fill some bags and keep the water from flooding their basements. As if that were possible.

At night, the darkness is so opaque that Ariel and Marie feel as though they are floating in a submarine. The big diseased trees, whose bark has begun to give off a rotten stench, turn into giant algae surrounded by whirling swarms of bats and gnats. Occasionally, persistent glimmers appear in an atmosphere too damp to belong to the ground, and Marie and Ariel move closer, plunging into the private lives of neighbours of whom they know the names but not the faces, the number of children but not the joys and woes. Besieged by the flood, the inhabitants take shelter in front of their screens, where they find comfort in news from abroad a hundred times worse than their personal calamities; they crowd around meals based on canned foods that had been stored in deep larders in expectation of this sort of climatic glitch. Occasionally a naked couple brushes by a window they had not bothered to cover, certain of being alone in the ruined vastness of the Prairies. Two bodies sizing each other up, consoling each other, revelling in one another.

"Do you miss it?" Marie asks.

In the darkness Ariel stays mute. Of course he misses it, and Marie knows it. He wishes they had never had sex or that it were transformed into a superior act, a sort of communion that could not be associated with anything and to which no horrid labels could be attached. He wished he were living in one of those courtly poems where love is elaborated in extended metaphors and prolonged hand-kissing, and had never looked at his twin sister with the carnivorous eyes of men when they are something akin to animals. But it seems to him now that sex can no longer be extracted from the equation. Marie drops her paddle in the canoe and moves toward him.

"It doesn't have to be sordid, you know. We're the ones who determine the meaning of our acts."

She presses her cheek against his, her breast against his shoulder. She waits. Ariel dares not budge, but each of his atoms becomes electrically charged and hurtles toward Marie.

"It's all a question of designation," she continues. "Here, we're just a couple like any other."

While keeping a firm grip on his paddle, Ariel's hands tremble; he averts his gaze from Marie's temple, and from the window where the light still falls on two bodies entwined.

"Ariel, I love you. You belong to me."

Someone in the house turns off a lamp; everything goes completely dark, except for Marie's increasingly naked skin, which is clad in a luminescent whiteness. Then she vanishes, concealed beneath a body that has swooped down on her— Ariel, at last relieved, damned for all time.

After Ariel's resignation the universe went quiet around them, and they believed it was over. For a few days they lived in a sort of sensory void where the hours flashed by filled with nothing at all. Suspended moments. Then daily life started up again. Ariel was called back to the capital to help with the transfer of dossiers, and Marie went on a trip. Saying good-bye, they chastely kissed each other on the forehead, their hearts balanced on an invisible rope.

The drive south cannot be made non-stop, Marie was told, but she ignored the advice. For more than twenty hours she travelled down the hurricane-ravaged coast, through cities once bustling with summer vacationers and fishermen but now abandoned by inhabitants worn down by the struggle against an ever more merciless climate. Only the aged and the insane stayed behind; only the seabirds thrived there.

At dawn, her heart pounding, she ventured down a road full of potholes. Trees on either side were bent down like beaten men. On a scrap of paper stuck between her hand and the steering wheel an address written in ink was staining the palm of her hand. The last known address of Eva Volant. When she pulled up in front of the house—a cracked, dilapidated building—she burst out sobbing, unable to do what she had come to do: step out of the car, walk up to the door, ring and wait for someone to answer, speak the words: I'm looking for my mother.

With her head buried in her hands, she did not see that someone was coming toward her. The knocking on the car window made her jump.

"Can I help you?" said a quavering voice.

Marie looked up, rolled down the window and contemplated the old man standing before her. Everything about him seemed washed out. His brown eyes, his flannel clothes, his skin that must have been naturally swarthy but was now as dull as poorly steeped tea. She got out of the car, her legs still rubbery from the long road. The air was dusty and lacked cicadas.

"It's very quiet here," she noted.

"Oh, not all that much. There are the airplanes. At all hours, day and night. Going to the war, you see."

She nodded. The old man stared at her.

"You've got my address on your face."

This brought Marie up short. She looked at herself in the side mirror. From paper to hand, from hand to face, the directions for finding her mother's house had ended up smack in the centre of her left cheek. Rubbing her skin, she turned back to the old man.

"I'm looking for a woman, Mrs. Volant. Does she live here?"

"No, there's just me here, dear lady."

"Does it ring a bell, even vaguely? Eva Volant?"

"Doesn't sound familiar. I've known Julias, Christinas, Franciscas, but no Evas."

Because the information about her mother was not quite up to date, his answer was unsurprising and did not have the demoralizing effect she had feared. Searching her heart, Marie found nothing but relief. What would she have done with a mother, now that her whole life was falling apart because of this woman? The slimmer the chance of finding her became, the more Marie realized that what she was pursuing since she had set out on this journey was a place rather than a person.

"May I go in? I'd like to take a look inside."

The old man stiffened.

"I tell you I'm alone here—have been for at least ten years. You don't believe me?"

"I do believe you. But I'd like to go inside just the same. I was born in this house. I'd like to visit. Five minutes, that's all, and then I'm gone."

"You were born here? You should have said so right away! This is your home."

He bowed and left the way open for Marie; she stopped at the doorway as if to say a silent prayer. The interior smelled of tobacco and mildew.

"Please don't mind the mess. You see, I wasn't expecting visitors."

The house was not large but it let in the light so as to create an impression of open space, of continuity with the world outside. One could easily imagine its first inhabitants being happy here, just as it was obvious that those who had followed had known all manner of misery. The old man showed Marie the kitchen, with its clutter of frozen dinner wrappings and its warped linoleum floor. He took her to the tiny bathroom, peppered with brown patches, and then the living room, which contained an unmade bed.

"I put my bed here. I prefer to sleep by the TV, you see."

"And the bedroom?"

"That's for my souvenirs."

Marie stepped into a room that was darker and tidier than the rest of the house. Everywhere, the man had hung photographs of what looked like the streets of Mexico at the turn of the century. There were boxes stacked against a wall, and an old rocking chair had pride of place in a corner. Marie took a deep breath and felt as though a tree was trying to grow inside her chest. She moved to the centre of the room. It was here, under this sloped roof, that Ariel and she had come into the world a few minutes apart. She began to weep. Here is where they had taken their first breaths and together let out their first cries. They had been washed, swaddled, and no doubt laid down side by side a few hours before Marie was taken away, thereby pulling on an invisible string, an elastic waiting only for the right moment to stretch tight and hurl the twins toward one another in a movement as inevitable as the orbiting of the planets. For the first time Marie realized that their reunion, however fateful, constituted an immense consolation for that primordial sundering. The fact of having known the bliss of childhood for just a few wretched moments before being abandoned was made bearable only by the thought of having found Ariel again, no matter the circumstances and the consequences. A sort of return to the zero point of her existence, an obliteration of all those years of isolation and sadness.

Behind her she heard the noise of the television. It was time to leave. Had it been possible, she would have cut out the little bedroom and taken it with her so she might find refuge in it once Ariel went away, once the reporters began to swarm around her again, once another Jackson Pollock picture came to attack her. She fiercely clenched her fists, trying to engrave inside her every angle of the room and to imprint her own silhouette on the place that had witnessed the first hours of her existence.

"Have you found your memories among mine?"

"You might say that," she answered, drying her eyes.

The old man walked her back to the car. At the last moment, she sensed that he would have liked for her to prolong her stay, that he had already grown accustomed to another person's presence in his home, undoing in a few minutes years of training in solitude.

"Thank you, sir."

"Roberto. My friends call me Roberto."

"Thank you, Roberto."

Her car churned up a cloud of dust and as she drove off a strident roar could be heard overhead. A warplane sliced through the sky, crossing Marie's trajectory so as to form an X with it. Never-ending wars. So many things to fight against, and Marie was so very tired.

Far away from the major cities, the noise of the news reaches them somewhat blurred; the distance lends an unreal sheen to events. Politics has taken on the shape of a masquerade for them, and human-interest items seem like sordid tales drawn from mythology. They are not shocked by the Alaskan man accused of killing and eating his four sons, because he does not really exist. The Newfoundland cult that tried to crossbreed dogs and humans is just a joke. Nor are they even surprised when the woman receiving handsome payments in exchange for getting struck by lightning turns out to be a robot. As far as the planet's decline is concerned, they have let go. They are ordinary spectators of a world grown so warped as to beggar belief.

As for word from their families, it is as rare as sprouts in the ground here. Marc is the only remaining link between them and their former existence, allowing Marie and Ariel to send their close relations the occasional letter, the content of which is always so insubstantial that even the cleverest spies could not determine its point of origin. The information travelling in the opposite direction is hardly more specific. Ariel's parents, having also yielded to the appeal of exile, have entered into old age on what is left of the Yucatan Peninsula and confine their messages to the weather and sometimes their health. Meanwhile, morality has gained the upper hand at the Leclercs', who have refused to communicate with their daughter ever since it became clear she had no plans to leave Ariel. Marie has registered this loss without dramatizing it, like one more thing gone down in the ocean of all she has had to give up. Only Rachel, equanimous with regard to her sister's choices, continues to correspond with her. As for the information passed on by Marc—the tribulations of the cops, the rebuilding of the Party—Ariel does his best to ignore it, just as he refrains from broaching with Marc the subject of his divorce from Emmanuelle. The less he knows about it, the better. An island with too many bridges is no longer an island.

In any case, it is not hard to turn a deaf ear on the plain, where silence is stronger than all else. Ariel and Marie give themselves up to this landscape, with its smooth horizons, its regular surfaces devoid of hills or fjords or the rectangular woods of the cities. Their self-sufficiency is more than ever necessary. They are friends, family, lovers; they share all the loves that go into a life, and all the solitude this entails.

When Marie returned to Montreal ready to describe to Ariel her journey in search of Eva Volant, she found him on the street, red-faced and stupidly rooted in a puddle of melted snow. The fire seemed to float weightlessly like a will-o'-the-wisp, a paper airplane ignited through spontaneous combustion. It took Marie a few seconds to grasp that it was their house.

No criminal investigation was needed for them to understand that the blaze was the work of an arsonist. During his stay in the capital, Ariel had been informed that a slew of letters had flooded his office in recent weeks. He had opened a few of them at random. One of them depicted its author as a sexual libertarian and offered Marie and Ariel a "haven of peace and tolerance where they could live their forbidden love and share it with a community of like-minded people." Most of the others saw themselves as agents of divine wrath and condemnation to the fires of hell. It was hard to guess which of the fallen prime minister's thousand foes might have burned down his house.

The day after the fire, Ariel and Marie treaded around the smoking ruins of their home trying to recognize its wrecked forms, to identify the living room, the staircase, the kitchen wall, the remains of what had been no more than a temporary structure, an ephemeral order they had believed in for so long. A few blackened objects peeked out here and there like little corpses rising to the surface of dark waters after being submerged in the depths: a toothbrush, a juicer, a Montblanc pen, a flashlight. The cat's body could not be found. Unseen since the scandal had erupted, the animal had no doubt been dematerialized just like the rest of their world.

They had been circling around their former life for what seemed like hours when Marc arrived out of breath.

"Thank God you're safe and sound!"

He paused beside them to contemplate the black pit where a fine snow was doing its best to settle.

"Witch," he hissed between his teeth.

Ariel and Marie looked up at the former military man.

"Emmanuelle. It's all her fault," Marc explained.

Just as the house was going up in flames, Marc—by tugging on the many lines he had cast—learned that the person responsible for the leak was his own wife. Emmanuelle, rooting through her husband's affairs, had found out. She was the one who had sent the journalists the anonymous message, which Marc's men eventually traced back to her.

"She left even before I could confront her. I can't believe she did this to us."

The snowflakes covered their coats and their hair turned frizzy by a night without hope, but expired in contact with the seething rubble of the house. Nothing of this broken life could ever be washed clean again. Marie turned to Marc with a glazed look in her eyes.

"We want to disappear. Together. Can you help us?"

In Marie's class a few children stand out, colourful faces in a room too often black-and-white. Little Marco with his second generation Italian accent, who curls the few French words he learned with an altogether Latin theatricality. His mother comes to fetch him every night and sometimes presents Marie with arancinis, murmuring, "For my boy's favourite teacher." Then there's Sophia, with ponytails that defy gravity, law, and order, who keeps her hand permanently raised, even when she does not know the answer or has nothing to say. And, finally, Angel, whose classmates are all at least a head taller than her; her gaze is piercing and her French pronunciation perfect. Every Friday Angel tearfully presses Marie's hand before running off to the weather-beaten yellow bus.

At the end of the fall term, Marie takes advantage of the parent-teacher meeting to apprise Angel's mother of these incidents.

"My husband is in the army," the mother explains. "We've changed cities four times since Angel was born. Even though we think we'll be here for some time, she's constantly afraid of moving again. Whenever she says goodbye to people she's fond of, she has the feeling it's the last time."

"I see. Your husband works on a military base?"

"Yes, he gives combat training to recruits."

"Mine teaches them politics."

"Oh, Albert Morsehead! Richard often talks about him. They get along well, I think. You should come over for a meal!"

After accepting the invitation Marie asks about Angel's remarkable aptitude for French. The mother smiles.

"I don't know who she takes after. Certainly not me, and her father even less. In the neighbourhood where I was born in Savannah, French was as rare and exotic as Pakistani is here."

"You're from Georgia? How did you end up here?"

"When you grow up near a military base you fall in love with soldiers. When I met Richard he was in training near where I lived. I was smitten."

When she returns home, Marie recounts her meeting to Ariel.

"Richard Vernon? Yes, I know him. He's a bruiser. Gives the recruits a rough time."

"His wife invited us for dinner."

"Well, find a way to beg off. He's the last person I'd want to socialize with."

Looking out over the empty plain that surrounds them, Marie sighs. Their life seems so spare. There's no room even for friendship. Ariel gently squeezes her shoulder.

"That's not true," he says. "It just takes longer when you start from scratch."

As Ariel expected, he found Emmanuelle in a vast loft perched on the top floor of an abandoned factory, the kind of place that bolstered the image of the impoverished artist but which only the wealthy could afford. Despite the large windows, the room appeared dim. Pewter mobiles floated a few metres above the floor like swords. Curled up in a red leather armchair, Emmanuelle was dreamily contemplating her works of art. She started when Ariel walked in.

"They've burnt down our house."

Stretching her legs, she turned toward him, the defiance already showing in her eyes.

"Fire is cathartic."

"It was all we had left, Emmanuelle."

She stood up, walked over to a table littered with empty glasses, and poured herself a purple liquid.

"Antioxidant?" she offered.

Ariel shook his head. Her lips moistened with purple juice made her look like a vampire.

"We're leaving tomorrow, Marie and I. Oddly enough, you're the only person I wanted to see before going."

"I'm flattered."

"Don't jump to conclusions. I've come to call you to account."

Swinging her endless mane of hair, Emmanuelle turned her back to Ariel and stepped toward a window. Hochelaga—the livid reptile, the many-headed snake—uncoiled at her feet.

Montreal had already begun to fade in Ariel's mind, like the world of Peter Pan, its outline dissolving as one stops believing in it. Emmanuelle kept silent; Ariel pressed the point.

"You couldn't stand having to share Marc? To see him devote himself to a cause bigger than you?"

"You all think I'm so jealous and possessive. You just don't get it."

Setting her glass down on an empty pedestal, she approached Ariel with measured steps.

"It was an artistic gesture, Ariel. That's all. When I learned you were brother and sister, I immediately grasped the beauty of your story. The grace of loving striving to reconstitute itself by any means, like water cutting a path through solid rock."

"How poetic. Couldn't you have just kept your metaphors to yourself?"

"I wanted to create an event. Today's art resides precisely in such performances. Reality and the actions that disfigure it. To place one's finger on an object teetering on the edge of the abyss. Delivering that message was so easy, a flick of the finger, really. And the face of the country was changed."

"For the worse."

"It's inappropriate to assign a moral label to this work."

Ariel exploded.

"Stop talking about it like a piece of art," he bellowed. "You've ruined our lives!"

He would have liked to slap her, to point the mouth of a giant canon at her skinny body and blast a hole through it, and then blow up her appalling sculptures one by one. Unimpressed by Ariel's rage, Emmanuelle gave him a smug half-smile.

"No, your lives were already ruined. I gave you a chance to live as you choose. If the secret had stayed hidden, you would have spent the rest of your miserable existence loving each other secretly, repressing that love. But now you are going away together. What will you do? Disappear? Change your identities? You'll grow old side by side. It's more than you could have dreamed of if you had hung on to your position as prime minister."

An ominous grating sound went out from the far end of the loft, and as if by magic one of the more substantial mobiles overhanging the loft came loose. It twisted in mid-air before crashing down on the cement floor in a metallic clang and a shower of sparks. Emmanuelle took a few steps toward the mobile and stopped short, perplexed, as though wondering what was left of her piece. When she turned to come back to Ariel he was already gone.

No agriculture worthy of the name has existed on the plains for the past ten years. People still sow seeds and keep little kitchen gardens as a matter of form, but autumn usually yields just a few shrivelled potatoes, peas as hard as gravel, and ghosts of tomatoes. The proudest—or richest—farmers equipped their operations with complex irrigation systems only to throw in the towel a few years later, as exhausted as their fields. These days, the towns just barely scrape by with populations that skim over the topography more than they inhabit it. The places where ancient traditions connected people to the land have become transient landscapes that remind Ariel of American desert towns where nothing ever seems to put down roots.

This means stores with boarded-up windows. Hospitals shut down and doctors you need to drive for hours to see. Families that leave without bothering to sell their now worthless properties. People without work, and dreams either crushed or forgotten in a corner. Only the military base keeps on providing employment and sustenance to a part of the town, which nevertheless continues to empty as steadily as an hourglass.

One winter morning, the daily routine on the plain is upset by a rumour. While people are prepping for another year of exasperating extremes, the word goes out that a biomass conversion plant may be built in Rockfield. This fast-growing industry is apparently looking for a central location where it could process all of the province's waste.

Though impossible to confirm, the rumour races through the military base, the school, the shopping mall and the church—the cardinal points of the town's social life.

This is the moment when something that was slumbering in Ariel awakes. His sense of community, his instinct for crowds. His urge to hold the reins. The electronic devices in the house gradually come to life again; the news rings out every hour in the kitchen, research files linger on the computer. Ariel comes back into the world.

Together with two other residents, he organizes a public meeting to which he invites industry spokespeople. Taking on the impromptu role of moderator, he welcomes them on behalf of the people of Rockfield, gives them an overview of the community, and questions them. Then, after getting hold of documents specifying the conditions that need to be met for the plant to be built, he sets up a citizens committee to ensure that the city fulfills every condition. Locations must be proposed, road repairs demanded, water drainage problems solved. The town's elected officers, delighted by this unhoped-for help, encourage these initiatives. Soon, volunteer work is being organized on a colossal scale in an atmosphere of contagious enthusiasm. A handful of townspeople travel to Regina to petition for their cause and ask for investments. After a few weeks, the entire town is mobilizing around a single objective: to revive a moribund region.

From day to day, Ariel grows more effervescent, more radiant. His best efforts to preserve the extra weight that serves as his disguise are unsuccessful. The excitement melts away the kilos. His voice regains its previous timbre. He is vibrant. And increasingly recognizable despite his altered face. With every passing day his beard looks more and more like a ridiculous postiche on the face of the man who seduced the nation; Marie is afraid to see him unmasked yet cannot bring herself to clip his wings. She would prefer to start her life over again a hundred times rather than confine the man she loves to the desolate trance of exile. There is no taking the Ariel out of Ariel. No matter how many pseudonyms are affixed to him, he remains the one who leads. He will always find a mission, even in the midst of nothing.

Little by little the house fills up. Meetings are held there, neighbours stop by to leave cookies or a spray of flowers, borrow books or just chat. Out of shyness and a wish to protect the little privacy that belonged to her, Marie had jealously kept the doors of their former home shut, thus depriving herself of the joys she is now discovering—a kitchen full of friends, loud voices, shoes heaped up in the hallway, and the kind of solidarity that people at the top are not entitled to. Children roll around in the cruddy snow of their yard. A neighbour shares the fish she caught under the ice. The local lush comes to drain their bottles and spin a few yarns. Quite unexpectedly, life is rekindled.

Oddly enough, Ariel has trouble sleeping not when he is distraught but when he feels hopeful again. His intense involvement in the community not only mitigates his grief at having lost his place among the governing elite, but also brings him solace for his political disillusionment. His new project keeps him up late into the night; it is a vital hub foiling his regrets. As the long wakeful hours tick past, he misses his cat Wretch. He pores over the international magazines and watches the daily news reports to the point of nausea. When his head is too full of the noise of the world, he turns to more rustic occupations.

He reads novels, discovers old records abandoned by the former residents, cleans the attic, does a few bodybuilding exercises. Then, in the depths of the night, he drifts toward Marie.

He stands in front of her room to listen to her breathing. The breath humans produce when they sleep is prodigious. It dives into the deepest reaches of their being and, upon exhalation, raises the treasures and monsters buried under accumulated crusts of civilization. Dense, troubled, insightful, Marie's breathing is a masterpiece. To come nearer to it is the only moment of purity available to Ariel from now on. Their physical proximity is always steeped in pain; every surge of desire is accompanied by disgust. Rare and difficult, sex has become the site of a self-loathing equal to their mutual love. But when he looks at her silky arms lying on the sheet, discerning her breast and pubis under the muslin, he is unable to feel regret about anything. One life would not be enough for him to turn Marie into simply a sister.

On other nights he just sits down at his wife's desk. He holds the pencils between his fingers, leafs through her books, most of them textbooks, a few of them collections of poetry in a dying language; he whiffs the pages that her pointed forefinger has ranged over. Then he rests his cheek on the back of the chair that welcomes Marie's thoughts day after day. This is how he likes to love her—in her absence, in the imprint that her existence leaves on the night.

In the course of one of these little rituals, he discovers a file folder bearing an accursed name: Eva Volant. For several minutes, Ariel remains stock-still, unable to contain his anger. He was too devastated by the events to say anything when Marie went on her trip to the southern United States. But he continues to disapprove of all efforts aimed at finding their mother. For him, surviving means keeping her out of the picture. How could their so very fragile daily life overcome this strident reminder of their biology? It is already dangerous enough to maintain their love without which they would both be lost; chasing after Eva Volant amounts to juggling with knives.

In the end, he opens the folder and pulls out a sheaf of documents whose cloying smell puts him in mind of the fall floods. He finds the adoption papers, the fateful lines that overturned their lives an eternity ago, it seems to him. Then there are letters and forms testifying to Marie's investigation, all dated before their move to the Prairies. A considerable sum of work, Ariel sadly acknowledges. Marie was truly determined to resolve the question of their origins.

Under the forms he stumbles on a sheaf of blackened sheets of paper. He brushes his hand over them, leaving his fingers stained with fine soot. Portraits—all different but all alike—in which he recognizes here Marie's mouth, there her chin, both their eyes, the hair of one of them, the cheekbone of the other, their nose, their forehead, a sharp wrinkle that he might recognize reluctantly, an earlobe suggesting a familiar texture. With small, uncertain touches or broad, desperate strokes, Marie has tried to reconstitute their mother's face, conjugating all possible combinations. Ariel cannot help thinking that this visual genealogy lacks one essential component: the face of the father. But the thought is too dizzying and he drives it away just as Marie must have with a stroke of charcoal.

He silently returns the papers to their original place in the folder, but not without first pilfering one of the sketches, the simplest one, the one in which Marie dared to put a smile on Eva's face, an embarrassed smile or possibly the sneer of those who dice with destiny. He folds the portrait and unthinkingly slips it into his wallet, then he picks up his guitar and plays a tune so old it might be telling their story, their mother's story, the story of all who one day doubted their humanity.

They go to church. It's impossible to avoid this monument to consensus built during the reform period and therefore afflicted with an architectural style at once unbridled and conventional, somewhere between a temple and a shopping mall—the mandatory style of contemporary believers. They would have preferred to stay neutral with respect to religion, but Marc advised them to swell the Christian ranks and not turn up their noses. In small Prairie communities, suspicion starts with impiety.

They therefore show up each Sunday at the church square and join the assembly of neighbours and colleagues, young soldiers eager for absolution, students and their stubby-nosed, thick-legged parents. Ariel and Marie sit in the back like dunces. The church is the only place where they once again have the feeling they are making an exhibition of themselves. True, they are constantly playing a part, but the part is confined to an alias and a disguise. The rest is far from being as scripted as their life in Montreal and Ottawa. Only in church do they still act in ways that remind them of politics. The right answer at the right moment, standing up and sitting down at the same time as the others, nodding one's head, giving the appropriate look. As she plays the game and sees Ariel making an effort to remember how to cross himself properly, Marie realizes how intolerable it was for her to play the Prime Minister's wife.

Fortunately, the pastor is a moderate and his attitude rubs off on his flock. He preaches tolerance, mutual support, modesty. The congregation is not afraid of him, so the nave is suffused with a certain degree of warmth. As a result, Marie and Ariel can manage a few seconds of contemplation, while sharp-angled forms rain down on them like wedges, the slanting shadows of stained glass windows where stylized Jesuses walk on the water and sink for the third time.

The topic of the exercise: "what my name means." After questioning their family on the subject, the pupils must present, in French, the origin of their given name and surname.

With her little feet firmly planted in front of the class, Sophia says that her given name means "wisdom." Marco talks about his Venetian ancestors and the explorer Marco Polo. Junior admits he was astounded to learn that his first name refers to his father's, a fact of which he was unaware for the first seven years of his life because during that time he was just called *junior*. Lastly, Angel explains that she was baptized in honour of an aunt who had met with a serious accident.

Stepping closer to congratulate her for her presentation, Marie notices some oddly shaped black-and-blue marks on Angel's forearm. In addition, the little girl's chin is scraped, a wound that Marie had ascribed to an ordinary childhood mishap. During the written exercises, she discreetly tries to get a glimpse of Angel's knees under her yellow skirt. There, too, the skin appears to be rubbed raw, and Marie suddenly gets the impression Angel's small chocolate-coloured body is covered with scars. Recalling Ariel's remarks about Angel's father, Marie spends two days looking for a way to broach the question with her. She finally decides on the direct approach.

"Angel, sweetheart, you certainly have a lot of bruises!"

Quite unexpectedly, the child breaks into a grin, rolls up her sleeves, and displays her marks as if they were trophies.

"I got them during training! It's not for wimps!"

"I see! What sport do you play?"

"It's not a sport. They're exercises my dad makes me do. To be stronger."

"Like… like a soldier?"

"Yes. You know, Mrs. Leblanc, we've got to be ready for war."

Marie solemnly nods her head and lets the little girl scamper away. Waiting for Angel outside is Monette Vernon, who lifts her off the ground to kiss her. Under a grey sky, the school buses stir like exhausted dinosaurs; the kids' small feet stamp on the indifferent ground. Watching the mother and daughter as they move away, Marie slowly brings a piece of chalk to her mouth and bites into it. "And what does *my* name mean?"

The rain is coming down in small, grey, icy packets when the news hits Rockfield: the company that was expected to build the biomass processing plant has dropped the project. Despite months of effort, of transformations and investments on the local level, the managers have decided to defer the plan indefinitely.

This is more than enough to demoralize the townspeople. After decades of disappointment, this new failure seems to partake of the natural order of existence. Now it's back to vacant afternoons, empty bank accounts, boredom, and the bleak sound of trucks rolling by without stopping anymore. Ariel is the only one who refuses to be discouraged by the decision. And the only one convinced that he alone can change the course of events. Rather than daunting him, the bad news has spurred his ambitions even further.

Within a week he succeeds in contacting a record number of townspeople and convincing them to carry on the campaign among their friends and relations. Yoked to his mobile phone, he creates a virtual movement that grows into a groundswell within a few days. At first Marie balks at getting involved, but she eventually gets swept up by the rising tide and endeavours to rally the other teachers and the students' parents. Sunday night sees hundreds of people crowding into the school gym. Adolescents desert the abandoned quarry that is their secret meeting place; the elderly leave their too-cozy armchairs. Even the military personnel, ordinarily standoffish about civilian matters, have let themselves be carried along by their colleagues' idealism. Marie spots Richard Vernon among them, with Monette on his arm looking twice as small beside her giant of a husband. Marie's heart clenches as she imagines the father forcing his daughter to do a series of exercises meant for elite soldiers and pictures the little girl crawling through mud or striding over fences to make him happy.

"My friends," Ariel says to get the assembly underway, "whether we've been lied to or whether they simply changed their minds doesn't really matter. What matters is that over the past number of months we've learned to pool our energies. What matters is what we decide to do with them now."

His tone of voice and the applause that greets these introductory remarks remind Marie so much of his electoral speeches that her head starts to spin. It's as though she can once again see the cameras flashing, smell the sour odour of calculated stress, the sweat of the strategists and image-makers. Ariel remains oblivious to this apparent revisiting of the past. Standing before the crowd alive to his optimism, he is aglow.

He asks the townspeople: What do you want to do? How do you think you can improve your situation? What are your dreams? Terms like "cooperative" and "public project" ring out; Ariel's new collaborators take notes to keep track of the increasingly excited conversations. At midnight, an hour that most of Rockfield's inhabitants haven't seen in years, the enthusiastic assembly disperses, creating a human fireworks in the parking lot. Ariel is in the doorway, thanking every participant and wishing them all goodnight. Richard Vernon walks past and completely ignores him.

"Your colleague—what's eating him?" Marie asks.

"Who knows? I'm amazed he showed up in the first place. It's not his style."

Once the hall has emptied, Ariel's associates join him to go over the most interesting suggestions. One is to build a large collective greenhouse that could provide the community with food security and give jobs back to idle farmers. Another involves self-financing a private wind farm and selling the energy to the state, an idea that has already proven very lucrative a little farther west. Ariel sees the dreams he had as prime minister slowly taking shape again, nourished by a spirit of solidarity and a sense of initiative that he had never witnessed in all his years in the Labour Party. So it's true: revolutions are all about small-scale actions.

Spring has returned with, in tow, all the vagaries of weather gone awry. They spend long hours on their porch watching the rolling clouds and the patterns that the wind etches on the tender grasses. The heat rises in whorls on the horizon. What Ariel sees there are white sails, or Marie. For her, the asphalt seems to be littered with gold nuggets, or there is Ariel soaring before her eyes. The world has become a collection of signs through which their love manifests itself, a distant respiration where they can safely love each other. Marie caresses all that is yellow; Ariel embraces the mist that forms on a glass filled with a cold liquid. She plunges her hands into a bag of almonds; he blows softly on the skeletons of dandelions. Their symbols are manifold and so intricate as to render any inventory difficult to compile. The secret code of twins who chose one another; the litany that reiterates the only possible bond.

As May tips over into June the northern lights jockey for space and stretch out their bare legs in the premature heat. In the fields Marie and Ariel perceive the manes of yawning lions and the horns of emaciated zebus. It's said that one truly belongs to the plains the day one catches sight of animals that have never lived there. After two summers in this northern savannah, a complex menagerie appears before them, circling in the vicinity of their house when the sun sets or when it reaches its arms out toward morning. Hand in hand, keeping watch day after day, Ariel and Marie discover that surviving has again become living; their hearts at ease, they are poised in a fine equilibrium, finally at home in this fenceless landscape.

On the first morning of the summer holiday, Marie is up at dawn so she can be the first to arrive at the farmers' market in the neighbouring town. After a number of fruitless attempts she has learned that the early bird gets the well-ripened cherry and the unblemished tomato. Holding her shopping bag, she pokes her head into the bedroom for a wordless goodbye. Ariel is still asleep; in the half-light of the shuttered room, a small flame seems to be playing over his ribs. But it's only a sunbeam that has slipped in between the wooden slats. Marie kisses her fingertips and blows the kiss toward Ariel. She turns away too quickly to glimpse the tremor in his sleep, his hand limply gesturing toward his lips.

At the market she finds the first heads of lettuce already shedding their youth like some girls who, barely out of adolescence, already walk with a stoop. She sifts through the pale strawberries and brushes away the insects hovering over a basket of figs come from afar. A wasp reacts to this provocation by stinging her. She cries out and lifts her hand to her mouth. She misses the bees.

On the way home she bumps into several colleagues and greets them with a nod of the head. Back in downtown Rockfield, she spots Monette's car. Sitting in the back, Angel casts a worried look at the main street and its boarded-up windows. When Marie waves hello Monette stops her car in the middle of the road and dashes over to Marie.

"Anne, thank God! I've been trying to reach you for the last hour."

"I was at the market. Is everything okay?"

"No! Your husband is in danger!"

Unable to say any more, the woman breaks down in tears and her head seems to retreat into her plump torso. Marie opens the passenger door and motions for her to sit down. To their left, drivers honk and steer their way past the car parked at the intersection. Monette doesn't appear to mind this, or the fact her daughter is stuck inside the vehicle.

"It's Richard. He found out your husband's identity. He knows he's the former prime minister. He rushed out of the house saying you were his sister and the two of you were in an incestuous relationship that's an affront to God."

Marie feels all the blood draining out of her body through one of the thousand invisible doorways through which life comes and goes; without thinking, she squeezes Monette's hand.

"I'm so sorry. I was the one who recognized him the night of the meeting. I should never have said anything to Richard. Anne, he took his gun. He's heading toward your house."

The straight road between the centre of town and their house is a fifteen-minute drive. Marie covers the distance in nine minutes that seem an eternity to her. The asphalt sticks to the wheels, the false flatness turns into a steep mountain. Her head is swimming, her skin itches as if a nestful of wasps were planting their stings in it at once. When she arrives there's a van parked in front of the soundless dwelling. Darting from room to room, she shouts Ariel's name. There is no sign of Vernon either.

Only when she reaches the porch does she catch sight of him in the distance, to the west, where the plain lies. She runs toward him for a few seconds then slows down, unable to go any farther. Richard Vernon is walking toward her with a pistol in his hand and reeking of turpentine. His strides are slow but he is moving at superhuman speed. He soon reaches Marie, who can do nothing but lift her hand to her throat as if to protect herself from the fatal gunshot, from a lack of air. But he does not raise either his fist or his weapon. His look transfixes her, a look damning her for the rest of her days.

Then he disappears from her field of vision. All that's left is a small fire in the distance, its heat distorting the horizon and the threshold of reality. Marie treads toward the flames like a zombie.

They say the smoke produced by a burning man is black if he was bad and white if he was good. Ariel emits no smoke at all. Only the golden birds escaping from his chest, his skin already almost completely consumed, his boiling organs, his bones devoured by the fire. Kneeling beside him, Marie tries to take hold of whatever is left of him, the incandescent limbs of which she has licked every square centimetre, the heart that seems to be still beating inside the flames, and the head she has loved with an epileptic rage. She thrusts her fingers into the fire and she is not burned.

Rat's Tail
(MONETTE AND ANGIE)

A FINAL gust sprays the two little girls' faces with fine soot, and all at once the horizon becomes visible again.

"Thirty-nine! Thirty-nine wagons!" Monette exclaims in a voice whose enthusiasm never waned as the train rolled by.

Angie does not respond. She was not counting. She was preparing to confront whatever she thought she had seen through the fleeting gaps between the wagons. She diverts Monette's attention to the flutter of butterflies the train has stirred up and discovers what the train was hiding from her. A few metres away, two half-naked people are rubbing against each other. The man is tall and tanned except for his buttocks, which move back and forth while he presses the girl against a tree. A long, thin braid whips his dirty T-shirt with every movement. A rat's tail, Mam would say in disgust.

He appears not to have noticed Angie and Monette and grunts, "Lie down, I'm getting tired." The girl obediently stretches out on the grass, which Angie guesses is strewn with rocks and traps. Her body, slender and very fair, is a weave of delicate ovals. Only when she turns her inscrutable face toward the two girls does Angie recognize her. It's Eva Volant, a ninth grader who lives near them. Their eyes meet and Eva looks like she's received an electric shock. She murmurs something in the man's ear.

This has the effect of a detonation. The man jumps to his feet and into his pants. Angie grabs Monette by the arm and yanks her onto the train tracks.

"We didn't pick up the penny!"

"It doesn't matter. Hurry up!"

Behind them she hears Eva.

"Don't worry, I know them! They won't say anything!"

Monette hops from one tie to the next holding a daisy. The sun has planted itself directly overhead. The scent of lunch reaches them from the little houses backed on the railroad. Angie quickens the pace. Behind them Eva begs the man not to leave. Angie does not turn around.

The wind picks up as they come to the bridge. The pong of seaweed and fish skeletons prickles their noses. Thirty metres below, the river has carved a ravine.

"It's dangerous!" Monette protests.

"Nah, the train just went by. Come on, hurry."

Monette grasps her big sister's hand as they set foot on the dizzying structure that straddles the precipice. Everything happening below is visible through the tracks: the flow of muddy water, the circling of bees gone astray, the snake skins scattered on the rocks. With her eyes glued to the void beneath her feet, the little girl walks on bravely. Angie can't hear Eva or the man with the rat's tail anymore.

Halfway across the bridge she realizes her mistake. The wind had covered the rumbling, and the impulse to run away had kept her from thinking. She excluded the possibility of two trains coming through within fifteen minutes of each other as if this were mathematically impossible. A serious error of judgment. She turns around. The locomotive has not yet rounded the bend. But if the vibrations rising from the tracks to her legs are any indication, it's a matter of mere seconds.

"Monette, we have to run."

Looking squarely at her big sister, the little girl's eyes fill with terror. She has never been given such an absurd order. Run? Now? When they are perched over an abyss? It's impossible—Angie sees this in her sister's face. Already, the train whistle is blaring out behind them. Monette is paralyzed. Without a moment's hesitation, Angie lifts her off the ground and begins to stride awkwardly over the ties, powerless to pick up the pace as she would like. Calculating the risks at breakneck speed, she entertains the notion of jumping into the river with Monette but is immediately dissuaded by the rocks poking out of the water. Hanging onto the guardrail is too much to ask of the little girl, and it's too late now to consider reaching the far end of the bridge in time. The train is so close she can feel its breath on her back. She keeps running as best she can amid the shriek of the whistle and the awful screech of the engine bearing down. Tears spring up in the corners of Angie's eyes. They are going to die.

Then the solution comes into view. Ahead of them is a niche set into the guardrail, a sort of balcony whose floor consists of a beam just large enough for a man to stand on. In a few nimble movements, the final grace of her child's body, Angie leaps toward the niche and shoves Monette at arm's length against the railing, tumbling forward on the beam in the process, still firmly grasping her little sister's trunk to prevent her from tipping over. Monette screams as if one of her limbs has been slashed away. Only when she sees the blood spewing over the pastel clothes and chubby face does Angie grasp that tons of steel are rolling across her legs. A surge of heat bellows through her body.

The Laughter of Archimedes
(SIMON AND CARMEN)

THE ICY wind, the chapped skin, the crusts of blood freezing in her shoes, the frost stuck to every fibre, every strand of hair—all of it is lost in the chalky cadence of her steps in the snow. For the past forty-eight hours Carmen has been running in a world of shadows where night and day have become indistinguishable, and she still has some ten hours to go before the finish line. But she has stopped counting. She has stopped thinking. The all-powerful beat of her running, her regular strides striking the ground—this is the only order, the only law, the only statement in this sharp-edged land.

The first day, her awareness still kept pace with her. Carmen let herself take in the landscape, the taiga and its thorns, the earth smothered beneath the snow, the stigmata of petroleum leaking from a pipeline. She still had the luxury of being attentive to trifles like the torn skin of her heels, her toe turned blue, and the burning sensation that had overwhelmed her lungs during the first hours. At kilometre forty-two, the distance of a marathon, she began to regret not having chosen the 565-kilometre run rather than the 160-kilometre run. At kilometre fifty-four she wondered what sort of mental illness had prompted her—who had never experienced real winter weather—to enter this insane race in the middle of February in the heart of the Yukon. At the next rest stop she was told there was only one woman ahead of her, which spurred her into returning to the trail as soon as she'd had her portion of stew. Four kilometres later she collapsed and a patroller had to help her put her tent up for the night.

Now she is soaring. The race no longer matters and her thoughts wander as in the moments before dreaming, that minute just before one tumbles toward sleep. Her mind is filled not with her worries, her projects, the peaks and troughs of her personal life, but with insignificant fragments of her daily existence: the broken window pane in the dining room, the sumac sucker that she'll have to burn when she gets back, the flock of small birds of prey on the hills around the house. Snapshots that remind her she is human and has a life, before she dives back into the great white emptiness of the race.

Although she had signed up months before Frannie's death, the fact of taking part in an event dubbed the "Death Race" hardly seems trivial. As she packed her bags, scarcely a week after the burial, she recalled Simon's terse remark the day of the funeral: "We're next." She had brushed this off with a joke before heading off to mythical Whitehorse, ready to run as long as necessary to ascertain that she was very much alive and Frannie would not be coming back from the dead.

Just fifty kilometres left, a distance she has covered hundreds of times, sometimes without giving it any thought, occasionally in utter pain. A distance long enough to reawaken interior struggles, especially after two days of contending with arctic temperatures. Night falls. Running at a steady pace, Carmen hauls her gear without feeling the weight of the sled or the icy cramps gnawing at her muscles. In the fading light she passes the last heated rest stop but the thought of pausing there does not cross her mind. She leaves the open stretch and plunges once more into the forest, determined to run through the night, to stop only after crossing a finish line, something intelligible in the wild arctic winter.

A name. Now he's got his hands on a name, unspoken at first, written down in Frannie's arthritic script and then his own clearer, more regular handwriting, a name he has copied dozens of time. Roberto Aurellano. It took three days before he could bring himself to say it out loud. As soon as he felt up to it, he burned the letter, hoping to break the spell cast the night of Frannie's death by her innocent messenger, whose only means of defence was a cat's tail and the two copies of the letter. He wonders if Carmen has kept hers.

So Frannie had no intention of leaving this world without enlightening her children as to their origins. She simply wanted them to learn the truth without her. Which is why she went to the trouble of drafting her explanations in a tone as dry as her life had been and then of entrusting them to the young student who did double duty as her nurse and her maid.

While it is practically impossible to get over the death of your mother, no matter how irresponsible she may have been, Frannie's death is nothing compared to what she hid from them. During that night of tremors and departures, Simon lost more than his mother; his sister was taken away from him. He had always envisioned undertaking the quest for the father alongside Carmen, and now he was left on his own. Still today, ensconced in the driver's seat of the patrol car washed by the downpour, the clamour of that solitude continues to deafen him, to trumpet the great turning point of his existence.

His partner scurries back to the car balancing a tray of coffee and muffins on one hand. The other hand holds a bouquet of balloons, which he unceremoniously stuffs in the rear of the car, where there should be one or two sinister-looking criminals. A green balloon bursts, giving Simon a start.

"It's my daughter's birthday. Six years old," the policeman explains sitting down beside Simon.

"Which leaves you seven more years of happiness. Enjoy them," Simon grumbles as he grabs a coffee.

The rain drives the vagrants out of the streets, making it easy to carry out today's orders, which are to keep them far away from the hotel where some dignitaries are gathering. The fog rolls in from the Pacific and envelopes the hall in a bluish filter that snags the thoughts of the few passersby.

During the funeral, a ceremony infused with a flamboyant Catholicism that Frannie had never been seen practising in the past, Simon scanned the crowd. Any strangers over the age of sixty-five were subjected to his discreet scrutiny. To prevent any potential fathers from slipping out he came up behind them and whispered, "Roberto?" None of the five men ambushed in this way answered to the name. If his father was still alive he had not bothered to come say farewell to the woman who had borne his son. As the coffin was being wheeled out of the church, Simon's heart almost stopped: he could have sworn he'd heard someone knocking inside the casket. He slowed his pace for a few instants to regain his composure and then continued on through a shower of religious hymns.

Carmen wept a little after the mass, when a few rare individuals still attached to Frannie gathered around a tasteless buffet, and for the first time Simon felt distant from her distress. Claire and Alan were showing signs of impatience, unaffected by the death of a woman they had not appreciated when she was alive, while Jessica tried to conceal the enormous camera with which she was photographing the event—inconspicuously, she believed—as though it was a county fair. Exasperated by his family's behaviour, Simon left the lunch without saying goodbye to the guests.

Ever since then something has been brewing inside him. When he quarrels with Claire she ascribes everything to a midlife crisis, a vague and stupid notion far removed from what he is actually going through. Simon has no wish to seduce other women or buy a convertible or Botox the frown lines on his forehead. What he wants is to find a cave, seclude himself in it, and huddle far away from the light of day and shouting voices. He wants to taste the magmatic solitude of geological faults. His crisis has nothing to do with life's high noon; it is a Cyclops, a yeti, a cave painting.

The receiver sputters the report of a hold-up a few blocks from the intersection where Simon and his partner are wolfing down their muffins. They switch on the siren, utter some numbered codes for the dispatcher, and the car pulls out cutting through some giant puddles. But not even speeding up hills or running red lights can stir Simon's blood anymore. As he presses down on the gas pedal, all he can think of is burying himself in rock and chewing on stones. A way to be completely alone.

During all those years Carmen never once touched that orange coat, still abundant but transformed by the absence of life. The pliant fur lets itself be stroked without reacting, without standing on end or secreting the invisible oils animals drape themselves in to neutralize human petting. It is nonetheless a pleasant, even soothing gesture, and Carmen has come to understand what for so long she took to be a compulsion of Frannie's.

For three days now she has been looking for an appropriate spot for Bastard the cat, which she has inherited along with a pile of knickknacks. When she came home from the Yukon she found in her hallway three boxes containing what was apparently her share of Frannie's things. Simon no doubt deposited them there after his wife had retrieved from the deceased's apartment the few rare items of any value. Carmen wonders who bothered to reattach the stuffed cat's head after it had been separated. Simon, maybe, out of a sense of guilt for having dashed it against the hospital wall? The question is added to the list of things she would like to ask him, which she patiently enumerates in his voicemail in the hope of getting an answer, now more and more belated.

Meanwhile she has tried everything: the living-room coffee table, the bookshelf lined with detective novels whose edges have been chewed up by bathtub readings, the window sill, among the lush green plants... It turns out to be terribly difficult to fit a stuffed cat into one's decor, especially when it was loved to the point where parts of its coat have been worn thin by petting.

The remainder of the boxes' contents leaves her just as baffled. What is she supposed to do with a hair-straightener from the sixties, a collection of dried out lipstick and hardened blush, a guitar-shaped cookie box adorned with rust spots, and a rabbit's foot dyed pink? The dead woman left behind a strange hodgepodge of objects, the absurdity of things that have survived but which, taken together, never account for the life lived.

When she finally reaches the bottom of the last box she discovers a collection of poems by Pablo Neruda. She grasps it in disbelief; she never saw Frannie read anything but the TV guide. The book bears its original Spanish title: *Odas elementales*. Inside, in the top right corner of the first page, is an inscription in black ink: *Magenta, 1963*. A shiver takes hold of Carmen and she forces herself to lay the volume down on the floor.

An hour later the sunlight strikes the hills. Carmen grabs a dust frame with a picture of her when she was twenty taken after her first marathon. It was during that race that Carmen first encountered "the wall," the stage of paralyzing exhaustion that sometimes occurs at the midpoint of the race. Inexperienced and stubborn, she reacted by stepping up her pace, with the result that she was forced to walk the last

THE LAUGHTER OF ARCHIMEDES

stretch. In the picture, her smile cannot hide the humiliation she had felt at having to cross the finish line walking.

After dusting the frame she carefully places it on the mantelshelf next to her trophies and medals. Among all these testimonies to her resilience, she places Bastard the cat. Satisfied, she steps back to contemplate her work steeped in the light of the setting sun. Then, on an impulse, she buries her hand in the earth of a ficus and closes her fist. She would so much like to grasp something—a root or mislaid pirates' gold.

The angst that has Simon in its grip has grown to such proportions that it now seems hard for him to move about the house, as if the air has been thickened with invisible plaster. Claire's evenings are increasingly devoted to so-called yoga lessons, Alan lives in his room, and Jessica comes back to the nest only to sleep and shower. The infrequent family gatherings are so fraught with tension that Simon has accepted a night shift to avoid them.

The term "graveyard shift" is perfectly apt: the darkness and silence of a cemetery always mask a ghostly existence, the invisible dramas of the dead and their mourners. He patrols solo from midnight to eight in the morning. The hour of knives and black stones, the hour when parties explode in a huge viscous uproar, and wrecks rise to the surface again. It's in such moments that Simon truly feels he is keeping watch over the city, when he gets out of his car and listens to a vagrant wheezing in his sleep, or when he observes from a distance a young woman finding her way back home on foot, torn between fear and intoxication.

At six o'clock he buys a last cup of coffee to wash away the sand from behind his eyelids. For a brief quarter hour he shuts off the dispatcher's gravelly voice and lights a cigarette. He restricts himself to just one a day, and it must be mooched from a stranger. A drunk, a bouncer, a jaded hooker, a bewildered teenager—any Joe Blow will do, so long as Simon doesn't know him.

One night, as he is about to light the unfiltered cigarette given him by a French tourist, the dispatcher's weary voice jingles out on the radio. Some passersby noticed suspicious goings-on at the Sutro Baths on the seashore. Nothing but ruins are left of the old swimming pool complex, whose heyday had passed in the early twentieth century, but the place continues to attract curious visitors and carousers. Simon puts away his cigarette and heads off toward the ocean.

As soon as he meets the scent of iodine and stale water, it comes back to him. This is where he and Claire ended up on their first date, walking among the half-empty pools and contemplating the remnants of an opulence that still made its presence felt between tides. They kissed inside a small tunnel in the rocky cliffs, and Simon did not dare touch the breasts of this woman too beautiful, too smart for him. Pulling over at some distance from the baths, he takes a swig of cold coffee to flush out the chalky taste that has spread over his tongue.

He leaves his headlights off for about ten minutes, long enough to see what is happening. Very quickly he concludes there is more going on here than a mere teenagers' party. Torches placed at regular intervals are lighting a gathering, which even from afar appears calmer and more orderly than the groups that usually take over the beaches at this time of day. Here and there he can make out bodies diving headfirst into the abandoned pools.

The first glow of dawn will appear in less than a quarter hour. Not much time left to take advantage of the element of surprise; he radioes in a request for the backup of two more patrol cars. The move is motivated not so much by the urgency of the situation as by Simon's curiosity. While waiting for reinforcements, he sneaks closer.

There must be about thirty of them. Those who aren't wearing bathing suits are dressed in period costumes: long white dresses, top hats, tailcoats. Some are sipping luminescent drinks from wide-mouth cups, while others wave fans in front of their faces. From the pool, the bathers call out to the strollers and laugh as they splash them. Simon finds it hard to understand why anyone would willingly dive into the muddy and probably icy water. But the swimmers' demeanour appears absolutely natural, as if this were a Sunday like any other in 1906.

Hypnotized by the *faux flâneurs* strolling up and down, Simon forgets the officers he has called for, just as he forgot to ask them to be unobtrusive. When the wailing sirens disrupt the oceanic silence, the bathers react more quickly than he does. In no time, the pools empty out and the crowd disperses. Simon collects his wits, flicks on his flashlight, and runs after the delinquents. Soon joined by his colleagues, he signals to them to intercept the suspects who have fled along the road while he pursues those going down the beach. He knows it's too late but he does what cowboys do. Chase after the Indians.

His flashlight sweeps the ground in time with his strides. The tracks of the runaways show the shape of their toes, the impact of their heels on the ground, and their feet seem too tiny for this sort of sprint. Simon gradually closes in on the silhouettes scattered over the damp sand. A few metres ahead of him a man in a jacket and a woman in a bathrobe are running hand in hand. "Stop! Police!" Simon orders. In response to his shouting the woman briefly turns her head without breaking stride. Simon stops dead. In spite of the half-light he recognized his daughter.

The raid is poorly organized and not very successful. Only two people are arrested and a few objects are collected around the pools. A team from the day shift has been dispatched to comb the beach. The mandatory report will run to many pages. A huge task, it seems, for such a frivolous misdemeanour, and the officers give Simon dirty looks. The lieutenant, on the other hand, is delighted: the reporters are going to love this weird story and he'll be able to spin the incident so as to make his unit shine. Walking out of the police station, Simon pauses on the sidewalk and fingers his telephone, itching to hear Carmen's voice. His hands fumble in his pocket and he pulls out the cigarette he stashed away there a few hours earlier. The lighter snaps, the cigarette starts to burn, and Simon takes a long, salty drag. He puts the phone back in its case. The night is over.

Nothing breathes in a columbarium. The boxes are insultingly small and appear altogether unsuited to holding an entire being, albeit in the form of ashes. Their volume is barely enough for a rosebud, a letter, or a square of silk. The layout of the wall adds to the atmosphere of coldness; one might just as well be in a bank vault lined with safety deposit boxes. Except that here, the boxes will never be opened; these bodies reduced to dust will never again experience the open air and its untameable winds, nor will they be able to transform into something, to blend with the earth and nourish wild flowers and ideas. How can anyone choose to spend eternity here, Carmen wonders as she walks through the hushed aisles looking for the number marked on the back of her hand.

She is in no hurry to find the niche of Magenta Lopez. In her pocket the sloppily folded piece of paper makes a deafening noise as it crinkles with each of her steps. It is from this document that she learned the truth: her mother was not Frannie. Of course there is no gentle way to impart this sort of news. The way Frannie had chosen was the most brutal: a letter in two copies that looked more like a shopping list than the confession of a lifetime. Each line contained a piece of their family puzzle. First line: Roberto Aurellano, the name of Simon's father. Second line: Magenta Lopez, the name of Carmen's birth mother. A quick inquiry among relatives revealed that she was a cousin of Frannie's who had died when Carmen was still an infant. Frannie, who was already pregnant, agreed to take care of her. In Carmen's eyes this act of generosity was the most baffling part of the story. She came to the conclusion the family had paid Frannie to adopt the child; nothing else could account for this decision, made by a woman with just enough maternal instinct to take care of an alley cat.

Whereas Simon was entitled to a complete name by way of a father, all Carmen had to chew on was the word "Hector." A nearly senile aunt told her that not much was known about the man who had "put Magenta in the family way," except that he was a not very "respectable" person, who was coerced into marrying her and absconded immediately after the wedding night. While her brother began a nation-wide search for Roberto Aurellano, Carmen gave up all hope of finding either one of her biological parents alive. Curiously, however, she was none the worse for it. Having refused from a very young age to define herself as Frannie's daughter, she had abandoned the idea of having parents. That they were dead or gone missing for good made little difference to her; she was done with grieving, and it was only out of some automatic compulsion that she had decided to visit the ashes of Magenta Lopez.

Treading up and down the uniform aisles of fake gold and sculpted glass, she thinks about Simon far more than all the parents who deserted her. It's been a month since the funeral, and still no news from him. Her messages and emails have remained unanswered, and when she does manage to catch him at home he stays distant, like a vague acquaintance bumped into at the supermarket who just mouths a few tired greetings while eyeing the frozen products. What the posthumous letter changed has nothing to do with Carmen's origins and everything to do with her brother.

She finally comes to Magenta's niche. It gleams; there are no fingerprints marring its polished gold surface. This absence of life saddens Carmen, and she promptly brushes her thumb over it to spread a little dirt, a trace of smog, of humidity, of the salt air and the bustle of the outside world. The inscription on the urn is *Magenta Lopez, 1943–1966*.

Without warning, a thick lump rises from her chest to her throat, a warm, invasive surge. The tears take her unawares; until a few seconds ago nothing in this whole affair had managed to move her. But now, those two dates—1943–1966—tell her something she had not contemplated: Magenta died at the age of twenty-three. "I'm older than my mother," she murmurs, with her reflection rippling on the glossy surfaces in front of her. She cannot explain why, but she is shaken by this realization. Her mother was just a young woman when she died. Now Carmen meets her and she is almost twice her mother's age. There is something unbearable about this role reversal.

As she tries to regain her composure, Carmen searches in her pocket and pulls out a sheet of paper. She rolls it up like a miniature parchment and affixes it to Magenta's niche. The last page of Neruda's *Odas elementales*. How else could she pay tribute to a woman she knows only through a deceased poet?

For the last few minutes she has not been alone in this aisle of the columbarium. Behind her, someone else is weeping in short bursts of muffled sobs. Gradually, this sound, so very alive, draws her away from the dead. She turns around and finds herself facing a man in his early sixties, hair turning white, proffering a tissue as though he had been just waiting for the opportunity.

"Paying a visit to one of your relatives?"

Carmen nods.

"Me, it's my children," the man says pointing to two urns graced by faded colour photographs and fresh flowers.

"They died young," Carmen remarks.

"Yes, seven and nine. It seems like only yesterday."

Unable to cut short the conversation, Carmen positions herself in front of the pictures and studies the round faces of the two kids, one on a blue bicycle, the other holding on to a swing. The odour of incense comes out of nowhere and, as is the case whenever she smells it, Carmen feels an invisible foot treading on her chest.

"I'm Marcus," the man says.

"That's funny. I met a Marcus once in similar circumstances."

Not knowing why, she starts to cry again, and, like a giant sweeping over acres of land, Marcus places his hand on her back. The columbarium comes alive, as if thousands of urns were suddenly spreading their dove-like wings.

The telephone rings at around 4 p.m.; he is in the depths of sleep and his formless, aimless dreams coil around him like a boa constrictor. He grunts a little by way of answering, hangs up, and staggers over to his daughter's bedroom. She is out but her things are there. The blinds, as always, are down and he gropes around nervously in the dark. In her backpack is a binder, a Bret Easton Ellis novel, and an astonishing number of pencil drawings haphazardly jammed into the pocket. No sign of his daughter's wallet.

His colleague called after the investigation unit had shared its leads with the city's precincts; nine wallets were found amid a pile of clothes at the Sutro Baths. Their owners are to be summoned to the police station for fingerprinting. The prints will be compared to those collected at similar gatherings, because the nighttime bathers are suspected of belonging to a group that entered the prison at Alcatraz as well as a military bunker and a few other off-limits locations. While this appears to be a minor offence, the media focus on these characters' stunts may give rise to exemplary penalties.

Growing more and more anxious, Simon hunts so frantically through every unwashed article of clothing, ever piece of paper in the hope of digging up Jessica's wallet, that he doesn't hear her come in. She clears her throat to interrupt his search.

In her left hand she waves a tiny red purse.

"I still have it, don't worry."

"How did you know what I was looking for?"

"Nine of my friends have just been arrested. News travels fast."

She gracefully flicks on the ceiling light and begins to sort out the mess caused by Simon's digging. She is beautiful and he is nearly taken aback by this realization. He so seldom looks at her.

"Why did you do that? Why did it bother you so much that we spent the night at the baths?"

"It was dangerous. The pools are unsanitary."

"Oh, bullshit!"

Simon sits down on the single bed populated with intertwined unicorns. For some reason, Jessica never expressed the wish to get rid of her childhood sheets, even though she in many ways leads an adult life, with all the attendant furtiveness.

"I'm quite willing to discuss it, but you have to enlighten me about the group you belong to."

"Are you going to talk to Mom about it?"

He thinks about this briefly.

"It didn't cross my mind. Why?"

"Because she's too dumb to understand."

Simon's cheeks flush and he averts his gaze so his daughter won't detect the petty pleasure he derives from her statement.

Jessica sits down in an armchair shaped like a huge open hand, and mechanically grabs a pen to scribble with. Keeping her eyes down, she explains:

"We revive the past. The idea is to occupy deserted or misused historical sites and bring them back to life."

"Why go to all that trouble?"

"Why do hundreds of morons get together each year at Gettysburg to recreate the same battle? History shouldn't be confined to books; it has to live, breathe. Bleed."

While Jessica's pen produces oddly shaped figures, Simon stares at his feet. He feels ashamed. His daughter finally lifts her head toward him.

"What about you? What's your excuse?"

"I was doing my job."

"No, not for the other night. For why you stay with mom even though you know very well she's cheating on you."

Simon winces, averts his eyes again, and refrains from asking her how she knows this. He realizes how alike they are. Taciturn but observant. Through the wall from the adjoining room come volleys of Japanese speech. Alan has come back from school and resumed his never-ending marathon of anime, to which Jessica is wholly impervious. The mutual indifference manifested by his son and daughter never ceases to amaze him.

"Is that why you brought out the heavy artillery at the Sutro Baths? That's where you went on your first date, Mom and you. You were angry?"

Once again Simon finds nothing to say. Jessica's perceptiveness is hard to bear, but knowing she watches him so closely warms his heart.

The next morning when he comes home from work he discovers an envelope under his pillow. *I found this in grandma's apartment. Your turn to make the past come alive.* Inside is a photo of a handsome, dark-complexioned man standing in front of a small house painted green. Written on the back in faded ink are an address and the name of a Mexican city. And the inscription, *la casa de Roberto*. Simon shakes his head in disbelief; the outlines of the picture seem to quiver. As if his father was waving to him from the last millennium.

It's impossible this morning to tell the sky and mountains apart. The clouds perfectly imitate the hazy crest of the Sierra Nevada so that everything is confused. Were they pioneers worried about getting to the cordillera before nightfall, Carmen muses, they would find it hard to estimate the remaining distance to the foothills. She has always tended instinctively to see her country's geography through the eyes of the first ones to have crossed it, whether on foot or horseback, in heroic circumstances.

Beside her, Marcus is snoozing, as he does each time he sits down in the passenger seat. When a bluish snoring fills the car, Carmen turns down the piano filtering out through the speakers. Her companion's purring guides her through the hairpin turns that lead to Yosemite Park.

Since they first met at the columbarium, they have frequently gotten together. If she had to explain this new friendship to someone, she wouldn't know how. As luck would have it, she is enough of a loner to be spared that task. Marcus invites her to the restaurant, she suggests outdoor expeditions, they stop for lunch in cafés so out of the way that no chain has managed yet to hang its logo on them. With Marcus, everything seems to belong to another world, another period, where the wheels turn more slowly, the floors creak, and the dust settles in swirls that the cleverest folks decipher the way others read tea leaves. His hands tremble constantly and behind the thick, foggy lenses of his glasses he seems to scan the landscape as though looking for the key to it, the vanishing point.

Though generally reserved, Carmen turns into a bona fide motormouth in Marcus's company. First she holds forth on neutral topics: the importance of fire for the reproduction of sequoias, gardening in a Mediterranean environment, the training of marathon runners, the life of John Muir, in whose honour the trail running along the crest of the mountain range was named. But soon she finds herself baring her soul to him as she has rarely done, even with her lovers. Only Simon knows as much about her, because he alone has witnessed everything.

And so she confides to her new friend the truth about her ill-fated love affairs, and the story of the other Marcus, Marcus Wilson, the father that Frannie concocted for them. She relates Frannie's death, the discovery of her birth mother's identity, Pablo Neruda, and Simon's silence, since he apparently decided he is no longer her brother. Like a hollow tree trunk into which one's secrets are whispered, Marcus gently receives these confidences. He, on the other hand, is not forthcoming with the details of his own life. Nevertheless, Carmen manages to establish a timeline, one that was shattered at its midpoint. From the bits of information provided by Marcus she has gathered that he lost his wife and two children in a brutal accident. His career in computer engineering nosedived in the aftermath and never entirely recovered. Marcus then went from job to job, drained and worn out, under the orders of contractors who would meet him on the roadside with a handful of labourers, hence his smattering of Spanish. That is why he can make sense of Neruda's poems, which he reads aloud with a tolerable accent. No one has ever recited poems to Carmen. The old-fashioned romanticism of the gesture is not lost on her. Nothing, however, in the old man's behaviour suggests anything beyond innocent affection, beyond the joy of still being able, at the age of despair, to find a soul mate.

Yosemite Valley gradually unfolds with the twists and turns in the road, starting with its prow, El Capitan, the majestic granite rock formation that dozens of climbers grapple with every day. As they round the peak, Carmen sniffs the air, convinced as she has been from a very young age that she can detect the unique scent of the stone and of the thousands of hands that have bequeathed their sweat and blood to it, suspended halfway between the sky and death. Marcus rouses, his eyes blinking in the shadow of the cliffs. Carmen parks the car near the perfectly round mouth of a trail wreathed in dense foliage. She shoulders the heaviest knapsack, the one with water and the compressed biscuits that Marcus had her buy "for survival," and they set out.

The road ascends in tight loops; Marcus keeps up despite his raspy breathing, about which he never complains. From time to time, the splash of falling water and his hard breathing overlap. The forest teems with hidden microcosms. When they reach a promontory with a lookout the old man points to the far side of the valley: a rock shoulder spiked with fragile conifers, its summit like a hat with a massive brim.

"When I was young we would go up there on a small road—it doesn't exist anymore—that ran along the scarp. When we reached the top we waited until nightfall, then we lit fires. Once there were enough embers, we would pitch the burning chunks of wood into the air and whack them with a baseball bat. The embers would explode into a thousand pieces and tumble all the way to the bottom of the valley. Below, the campers would watch the show. We called it 'making shooting stars.'"

Carmen peers at the rocky crest and imagines the hot brands plunging a thousand metres, an incandescent snowfall attesting to the mighty strength of boys who still have their whole lives ahead of them. Each time Marcus harks back to his youth she is engulfed by a nostalgia that does not belong to her, a vision of what a man is before life dismantles him, of what remains of him afterwards.

They reach the upper limit of the trail at dusk, and like all mountain climbers who go up to those bald, windswept heights, they sit down and peel off layer by layer the weariness that the climb has deposited on them.

"I've always enjoyed getting to the end of a road at nightfall," Carmen says. "Finding myself in the remotest place just as the shift happens, when one world tips over into the other."

Biting into one of his energy bars, Marcus agrees. The light sighs among the trees, ready to give birth to all manner of magical creatures, to raise the invisible worlds left behind millions of years ago by the glacier that split the mountain in half. As their vision loses its purchase on things, the sounds that come to relieve the watch are such that neither of them knows for certain which are real and which not. After almost half an hour of hovering like this between their imagination and the landscape, they perceive a stocky silhouette on the flat stretch of granite a dozen paces away from them. Marcus is the first to stand up.

"A bear?" Carmen asks.

"No."

The animal is small but sturdy looking, its sides and head streaked with white, the rest dark, almost black in colour. It is observing them with its mouth open and partially exposing fangs that illuminate the night. When its odour reaches them, powerful and pungent, Carmen understands.

"A wolverine," she mutters.

"Creator of the world," Marcus adds.

Even the most hideous animal becomes magnificent when you realize it can kill you. With a swipe of its paw, a snap of its teeth, the beast could satiate its ravenous hunger with one of them, and there is nothing they can do to stop it. To her own surprise, Carmen feels an urge to retreat behind her companion, but she holds back. Marcus, meanwhile, takes a step forward.

The wolverine shudders, lifts its head to scent the wind's messages, swings its bushy tail. The night is too thick now for her to be certain, but Carmen could swear the animal has shot them each a cutting grin. Then it turns around and moves off toward the trees, where the forest is unmarked and the trails wield no authority. As soon as it has joined its fellow predators in invisibility, Marcus's legs buckle and he drops to his knees on the stone. Carmen comes and lays her hand on his shoulder.

"It's okay, he's gone. He won't be coming back."

With his face screwed up, Marcus continues to peer into the darkness.

"I wish he had eaten my heart."

Simon has forgotten the most important thing about Mexico: the noise. Amid the Victorian tranquility of San Francisco and its milky winds, the possibility of such a clamour is easily erased, especially when one lives with a woman like Claire. Here, even the most faraway villages are alive with the shouts of vendors, untamed motors, hammers, saws, indignant dogs, and music. The horns of some cars carry on for nearly a minute at a time, blaring out the tunes of popular songs. Even the dozing siesta sleepers raise a hellish racket, as each breath, striving to out-whistle and out-snort the previous one, escapes through the open windows into the street. The other thing Simon has forgotten is how much easier it is to think among this profusion of sounds.

Since Frannie's death he has followed dozens of trails leading to dozens of Roberto Aurellanos, each of which turned out to be a dead end. He was about to call it quits when his daughter handed him the photograph. This trip is his last chance. Yet as soon as he got to Valle de las Palmas, he was struck by the absurdity of the whole undertaking. He had travelled to a godforsaken *pueblo* on the sole basis of the picture of someone who could just as well not be his father and of an address that kept him wondering why Roberto would have sent it to Frannie. To start with, he sits down for a meal at a *taqueria* counter. It's been a long ride and on account of the hot weather he forgot to eat. As he scoffs his tacos, he puts a few questions to the old woman chopping a heap of tomatoes swarming with flies. She is uncooperative and confines herself to shaking her head at the mention of the name "Roberto Aurellano."

After his meal, Simon goes out to tour the few streets of Las Palmas. Tijuana is only about ten kilometres away, but nothing about the little town suggests how close it is to the vice-ridden city. Peaceful and populated with half-deaf old folks and agile youngsters, it's the sort of place a visitor may tell himself he could spend the rest of his life in, and then move on. Possibly the sort of place where runaway fathers put an end to running.

The street marked on the back of the photograph no longer exists, Simon soon learns. There are no more than a dozen avenues in Las Palmas, and Calle Azul is not one of them. He questions four different passersby before finally getting a guarded response: "Calle Mayor." Without questioning the rationale behind this change of name, Simon sets out in the direction indicated to him. The street is the longest one in the village and he finds this encouraging. The number 15 is scribbled on the back of the picture; Simon puts his hope in this because he would otherwise be put off by the similarity of the little sunbaked houses, all painted more or less the same colour, all surrounded by concrete walls topped with shards of bottles to keep intruders at bay.

When he reaches number 11 his heart begins to thump. At number 13 his hands go from damp to dripping wet. At number 17 he walks back and forth a few times before acknowledging the facts: the addresses jump from 13 to 17, skipping

221

over 15. And yet on the other side of the street, 16 follows 14, which comes obediently after 12. In disbelief, Simon walks up and down in front of the houses searching for an explanation.

In the front yard of number 13 an old woman has been watching him for some time while stirring what could be either laundry or food in a basin. Simon approaches her and inquires about the absence of number 15.

"15 doesn't exist," the lady replies.

"Why?"

She shrugs:

"Because we were in a hurry to get to 17."

Annoyed by the townspeople's penchant for the oracular, Simon feels around in his pocket and pulls out the photo.

"I'm looking for this man. He used to live here. Roberto Aurellano. Do you know him?"

One look is enough for the old lady to conclude, "Your father."

"How did you know?"

"Because of the resemblance. But I've never seen him, and I've lived in this town for seventy years."

Refusing to be discouraged by this verdict, Simon spends another hour interrogating the neighbours, waving the photo to prove he is not insane. At first indifferent, the townspeople gradually take an interest in his story, put forward theories, take him to the adjacent streets in search of number 15. Each time, Simon meets with the same disappointing results. The whole town seems to have banished "15" from its buildings.

Toward four o'clock, tired and thirsty, he begins to accept the truth. His father never lived here. No one knows his name or recognizes his face. On the other hand, many have noticed the family resemblance—a sliver of certitude in the mist of his story. Catching sight of a shop, Simon goes in to buy a soda and enjoy the imperfect but still welcome air conditioning. The cashier is scratching a lottery ticket with a frown on his

THE LAUGHTER OF ARCHIMEDES

face, and Simon wonders whether he is looking for number 15. Outside, a tall man as dry-looking as a piece of deadwood is walking in circles while casting inquisitive glances inside.

As soon as Simon steps out again into the swelter of the valley, the stranger accosts him:

"The man you're looking for—I know where he's gone."

On the way back, Carmen dared not ask Marcus about his reaction to the wolverine. In fact, even though they spent half the trip reviewing their three hikes in the valley, at no time did they make any mention of their encounter with the beast. Marcus appears calm as they approach the Bay, but Carmen is reluctant to drop him off at his house as planned. At the very last minute she suggests he come along to her place.

They end up squatting in the garden gathering up eggplants and cucumbers, tomatoes and lettuce. The soil is warm and soft and wafts enticing fragrances in their direction, distracting Marcus from his chore while Carmen persists in picking the slugs off the young shoots one by one.

"The trick is to trap them with beer," Marcus advises.

Carmen shakes her head. She has tried everything: beer, coffee grounds, egg shells. West Coast invertebrates are endowed with a vitality inherited from the settlers who, ever since the Conquista, have vied relentlessly for its land, and it takes more than a few table scraps to intimidate them.

"It's slower by hand, but more effective."

"You're quite fond of long-term projects, aren't you?"

Carmen smiles.

Coming from a girlfriend this kind of remark would have annoyed her; she would have seen it as an attempt to label her, to foist a theme on her personality. Which is what most people who enter into a relationship do after reaching a certain age. Put people in boxes. She has often told herself that this was the reason she was incapable anymore of such a commitment: she has reached the stage where women her age no longer believe it possible to be surprised, thereby destroying a form of freedom that Carmen refuses to give up. Coming from Marcus, however, the comment sounds rather charming.

"Yes. That's why I take you hiking," she retorts.

With a flick of her finger she sends the last slug flying into the pail, which she then sets down on the other side of a brook cutting through her property. Marcus waits for her in the middle of the garden with an armload of vegetables, gazing at the hills.

"You're lucky. Living here isn't cheap."

Given her modest income as a park patroller, Carmen never considered herself privileged. It was when she dropped Marcus off in front of his run-down building that she was forced to face facts: she lives in one of the fanciest counties in California. For a split second she considers asking him to move in with her.

"I owe it to my brief carrier as a star athlete. I received a sponsorship that enabled me to live here," she explains while leading her guest toward the house.

While they putter around the kitchen, Marcus takes a deep breath and then raises the issue that Carmen cannot elude.

"Why did you throw everything away at the Atlanta games?"

Carmen sighs. Coming from Marcus the question does not vex her as much as usual, and she decides to take the trouble to answer for once. She sits down on a stool and pours herself some ice coffee.

"The day of the race I'd already won my medal for the 10K and I felt more confident than ever. The starter's pistol rang out. I worked my way up through the pack focussing on my strides and my breathing. Then, after about 1500 metres… it's hard to explain, but something inside me whispered that that's not what I was running for, that I wasn't there to cross finish lines, to beat records, to pit myself against other people. I tried to keep on but couldn't manage it. My heart wasn't in it. And in long-distance running it's the heart that decides. Always. At the first intersection, almost without thinking, I turned left. But I didn't stop. I kept running, it didn't matter where, on the sidewalks, along expressways… I must have chalked up sixty kilometres that day. But they weren't the right ones."

"I still remember it. It touched me to see this girl, in the middle of the most important race of her life, decide to head off somewhere else. To free herself from her fate, you might say."

"Not everyone found it moving. My trainer ditched me the very same night, and my sponsors all pulled the plug. When I got back here I was a pariah."

"No regrets?"

Carmen douses the eggplant with olive oil.

"None. I'm a hundred times happier trotting over the trails of Muir Woods than training like an animal. And whenever I have run in a race it was for the right reasons."

"And what might those good reasons be?"

"I don't know. Feeling the ground under my feet. Not having to think. Not having to count. Just listening to the rhythm of my strides, the vibration of each impact. Letting the soles of my shoes give something back to the earth."

Marcus nods with a suddenly solemn expression. Carmen would like to talk about the wolverine, still convinced that episode conceals an important truth, but all she does is invite him to take a seat. They eat without speaking and, enfolded by the fragrances rising from the earth, from the honeysuckle opening its flowers to the night birds, they watch the sun sink behind the hills and the phantoms come up from the ocean. Although they drink nothing but spring water, at the end of the meal Carmen feels drunk. She offers to put Marcus up for the night; he declines. Too exhausted to make the trip to Oakland, she calls a taxi and insists on paying the fare. Waiting for the cab, both of them rock from one foot to the other in the cool onshore wind, all at once silent and chilled to bone. When the taxi honks from the road, Carmen, seized by an inexplicable urge, steps up to her friend and, closing her eyes, gently kisses his worn lips. She keeps her eyes shut as he moves off toward the car and in that interval sees herself again fifteen years earlier leaving behind the throng of runners and the chance of a lifetime, to roam the streets of a city in thrall to sports. An impulse that did not change the face of Olympism, but which reshuffled the order of her existence like a providential earthquake.

The tall, thin man sits beside him impassively. Simon has been a policeman long enough to know this kind of situation can be the starting point of the ugliest incidents, especially since the cartels have changed the roads of northern Mexico into veritable cutthroat zones: murders and kidnappings are commonplace, and some of the victims are not even connected to the drug trade. Still, from the moment the man spoke to him in the doorway of the grocery store, he had just one thought in mind: leave with him and drive until the truth was laid at his feet. With a loaded pistol concealed under his shirt, Simon invited the stranger to take a seat in his car.

"My name is Pablo," he says, looking out the window at a gaggle of kids chasing a puppy.

"What do you want from me, Pablo?" Simon asks.

"Nothing. I don't want money. I just want to tell you one or two things." Pablo points north and Simon is not bothered by the vagueness of the signal. The car starts away in a cloud of heat that blurs the horizon behind it. The air conditioning is mercilessly lacking. Simon punches the dashboard a few times in the vain hope of reviving the faulty system.

"You were born up there?" Pablo asks.

Up there: a term used by some to refer to the state located literally above theirs on the map; a phrase that sometimes seems to denote an elusive beyond. Simon nods, surprised as ever by how easily Mexicans can spot those who have never experienced life in Mexico. It's not a matter of accent or appearance so much as a way of being—this is how it's been explained to him. It galls him, this inability to blend in with those whose complexion he shares, after all, while it is enough to mark him out as an outsider in the eyes of all Americans.

"And you're a cop?" the passenger adds.

Once again, Simon nods without asking how he guessed his profession. Cops, for some people, are even easier to recognize than second-generation immigrants.

"How do you come to know my father?"

"I don't know him personally. But I know where he's gone."

They drive for almost an hour on the road to Tijuana, where white students daring to venture south of their usual playground cross paths with workers going to work their shifts in the city's bars, discothèques, and brothels. Pablo asks Simon to turn off toward a suburb and takes him down an almost deserted dirty road. Exactly the sort of place where hundreds of people have met their deaths. Simon squeezes his arm against his side to feel the weapon tucked over his ribs.

The heat thickens like a garment saturated with dirt, and even the wind rushing in through the open windows is insufficient to cool them off. And yet the passenger is not sweating at all. "Maybe he's a ghost," Simon muses, giddy from the sun.

After half an hour, a hazy structure finally appears on the horizon, giving the lie to the theory that has been growing steadily in Simon's mind, to the effect that the car would soon reach the end of the world and drop into the void. Little by little, the building comes into focus, an immense, uniform shape, a factory or possibly a prison. The frontage is topped with barbed wire.

Gradually, however, the breadth of the building negates all such suppositions. As the car draws nearer, the building's extremities retreat beyond what can be grasped, vanishing beyond the limits of what can be seen. A wall.

"The wall," the passenger confirms.

Simon parks the car about thirty metres away and both of them get out. Although he has often seen it on TV and had enough time to be outraged and then to put it out of his mind, Simon has to admit the structure is impressive.

"And my father?"

Pablo looks at him sternly.

"Each year, millions of people try to climb over this wall. They're caught on the other side by civilian patrols, self-appointed protectors of America, or they're hunted down in the desert by coyotes—that's if the psychopaths that hang out on either side of the border don't eat them alive first. You think your father was an exception to the rule? If he had a kid in the United States it's certain he tried to cross over."

"I'm not sure he was so intent on finding me."

Pablo obstinately shakes his head.

"I'm telling you. The people who leave something behind on the other side are the worst. They spend their whole lives trying to go back. Like deranged pigeons."

Feeling bitter and frustrated, Simon does not have the strength to explain to his companion that his father never showed any interest in the family, which he had engendered probably by accident. He places his hand on the wall, the way that pilgrims and travellers at the end of their rope do.

"What about you? You don't go across?" he asks.

"Me, I cross whenever I like," Pablo replies. "I go through walls."

An unimaginable fatigue settles on Simon's shoulders. Suddenly there is only one thing he yearns for: the coolness of San Francisco summers, and the sea breeze. He walks back to the car.

"Where can I drop you off?"

Eyeing the barbed wire glinting at the top of the wall, Pablo declines with a wave of his hand.

"You go on alone. I think I'll stay here for a while."

Simon gets back into the car, which reeks of overheated plastic. He turns on the ignition, giving the silence a slap, and does a U-turn on the powdery road used only by clandestine migrants. The man soon becomes a threadlike detail in his rear-view mirror, a burning mirage. Simon's right hand presses against his left side where the pistol is cradled against his skin, the ultra-smooth metal and the bullets nested in the barrel like so many possible deaths. At sunset he stops at the beach in Tijuana, the most northerly in Mexico, where, in close proximity to the bathers and sand castle builders, the wall stretches into the sea. A barrier five metres high, which at this time of day casts an even longer shadow, and yet could readily be skirted by a good swimmer or a sufficiently cunning sea monster.

It wasn't what she was looking for. The article came out of almost nowhere while she was searching the Internet for Marcus's date of birth. He had declined to tell her the exact day, but knowing his Zodiac sign was Cancer, she had seen an opportunity to surprise him. Then a series of links popped up about a dramatic event going back some fifteen years but still alive in the strands of the web, where nothing is forgotten.

Contrary to what Marcus had led her to believe, his family did not die in an accident. While Marcus was away on a business trip his wife killed their two children before taking her own life. According to newspaper reports at the time, she had found out her husband was cheating on her. Carmen immediately thinks of Simon. She can't shake off the urge to call him, to leave yet another message in his voice mail and hear the chemical silence at the other end.

When he learned of the death of the three people he cherished most in the world Marcus tried to end his own life in the hospital but was thwarted by a male nurse. The follow-up articles recount the father's descent into hell, his struggle with alcoholism, his confinement to a psychiatric hospital, and so on. Choking back her sobs, Carmen charges out of her house and sets off on a run that takes her into the night. When she returns, the computer has shut down and the house is dark. She keeps the lights off and goes to bed with her clothes on and her eyes open, as if the ceiling had just disappeared and she were looking directly at the sky.

The next day, holding an armload of daffodils, she knocks on Marcus's door at the same time as the rising sun. True to his habit each time she comes to visit, Marcus questions her before opening. He always needs a few moments to acknowledge the possibility of her presence.

"Who's there?" he asks.

"It's me, Carmen."

"Carmen who?"

"Lopez."

Nothing can be heard on the other side of the door. Marcus is weighing the chances that this is really and truly she. Carmen considers the door and thinks how easily a simple peephole could alleviate her friend's fears. Unable to wait for him to make up his mind, she speaks up.

"Marcus, I've come to tell you something important. I've found out how your children died. I learned this by chance, I'm sorry, I wasn't trying to dig up your secret, I just stumbled on it. Yesterday I ran fifty kilometres for them."

There is still no sound from inside Marcus's apartment. Not even a slight cough.

"Marcus? Are you there?"

She can feel something vibrating against the door panel. It takes her a few seconds to realized it's Marcus's trembling body. Then she hears his voice, so dry one might think he had swallowed sand.

"I gave everything away, afterward. It's what they would have wanted, even her. It's my one consolation. A part of them goes on living in a dozen bodies spread around the world. Their flawless little hearts. My daughter's beautiful green eyes. My boy's lungs—the kid could run like the wind! And her, even her. Her kidneys saved some poor slob some-where. Someone who has no idea he owes his life to a mon-ster. It's the best thing anyone could get out of her."

Carmen has sunk down on the doorstep, dropping her flow-ers, leaning her head back against the door. Her legs are numb. Marcus is still shaking on the other side. The day is breaking.

Two rooms in the shadow of the hills—that is all Simon has from now on. In their relationship, it was Claire who earned the most money. Given the rents in San Francisco, his police-man's salary is enough for no more than a dim, two-room apartment a few paces from a cable car that makes the dishes dance whenever a train passes by.

Considering his wife's barely disguised dalliances, Simon could have tried to squeeze every last cent out of her, but he did nothing of the sort. On returning from Mexico, rasped by the sun and worn out, his mind was already made up. In a matter of days, his lease was signed and his boxes packed. When Claire saw he was leaving she barely batted an eyelid. He didn't think long explanations would serve any purpose, so he restricted himself to a terse, "We hate each other," something she could not deny.

When Alan heard the news he was hardly more forthcom-ing with his feelings and confined himself to muttering, "So, every second weekend?" As for Jessica, contrary to Simon's expectations, she expressed no wish to live with him. A few weeks after he had moved out she announced she would be spending the summer in Europe. Claire made a scene; Simon, no longer bound by his wife's demands, gave his daughter the money for her airfare. After twenty years of family life, all he was left with was this vague alliance with an adolescent girl who was already far away.

Living alone calms him. He works the night shift, gets back before dawn, draws the blinds, sinks into his sofa, and stares at the shadows flitting on the wall without trying to interpret them. He speaks to only a few people and the telephone has stopped ringing. He is scarcely aware of world events, the royal wedding, the death of Bin Laden, the Dodgers' victory. Roberto's picture, Frannie's letter and all the other elements of his investigation have been stored in a cardboard box marked with an X. His trip to Las Palmas, in addition to dispelling any desire to go on living with Claire, drained him of his last drop of hope. He resigned himself to remaining an orphan.

He eats frozen meals, drinks cheap tea, and dozes off just anywhere, sometimes even on the threadbare carpet, like a dog suddenly overwhelmed by fatigue. The sounds of the street and the neighbouring apartments come to him muted and he soon learns to ignore them, to live in a chosen silence, a blinding solitude. He has finally found his lair and discovered what sort of creature he is. An animal that thrives in the midst of scarcity and austerity. In the evening, when his clock sends out its shrill alarm, he finds the wall covered with rough patches, like granular stone. He blinks his eyes three times and the room regains its cubic shape, its civilized texture. He stretches his back, counts his vertebrae and once again dons the uniform of an ordinary man.

The runners are divided into categories that are fenced off in specific enclosures: marathon, semi-marathon, ten kilometres, etc. In the family paddock, a handful of parents are warming up behind strollers and some eager kids are itching to tackle the thousand metres allotted to them. The adjacent section is for the handicapped, who will follow a special route that avoids the city's most treacherous hills. San Francisco is a place of inclusion and its marathon aims to embody this spirit of tolerance, which doesn't preclude classifying people in a manner worthy of the heyday of segregation.

Carmen is warming up. It won't be her best race—she can already sense this in the pit of her lungs, in the jut of her ankles. She slept badly and the humidity weighs on her. She is busy tying on the number 132 that has been assigned to her, when a familiar voice reaches her ears.

"Mrs. Lopez! Carmen!"

On the other side of the fence Carmen recognizes the young woman who took care of Frannie during her last months. She is grinning from ear to ear.

"Angie! You're doing the marathon? I didn't know you were a runner!"

"It's recent. Actually, it's you who inspired me! I've been training for three months; I even got these legs, specially designed for impact sports."

She shows the prostheses attached to her knees. Carmen knew she was handicapped, but this is the first time she has seen her artificial legs, which look both highly sophisticated and strangely organic.

"I hope you don't find this too nosy of me, but I never knew how you lost your legs."

"You're not being nosy. It changed my whole life, so I don't mind talking about it. I was run over by a train when I was nine."

"My God! I'm so sorry."

"There's no need. I wouldn't have lived the way I have if it hadn't been for that brush with death when I was young."

The two women continue their conversation as their respective enclosures fill up. Carmen relates how the stuffed cat recovered its bygone dignity; Angie tells her she has won a scholarship that will allow her to pursue post-graduate studies in Berkeley. Then she asks about Simon.

"To be perfectly honest, I haven't spoken to him in a long while."

Angie nods with a knowing expression on her face.

"It was that letter that upset him, wasn't it? I hesitated for a long time before handing you those papers."

"Why is that?"

Looking ill at ease, the girl examines at the tips of her soles.

"Your mother wrote those letters one day when... well, I believe she'd been drinking. She asked me to give them to you after she died. She was doing okay at the time so I put them away and forgot about them. But not too long before her heart attack—I guess she was beginning to sense the end was near—she pulled them out again and ordered me to burn them. I have to admit, I read them. I told her I'd destroy them but I couldn't do that. I thought it would be better to let you have them. Maybe I was wrong."

"Not at all! We had to find out the truth at some point. My only regret is that Simon took it all so literally. From one day to the next he stopped being my brother."

"You know, even blood relations can become estranged like that. Siblings don't make up an indestructible organ. Not many things do, actually."

Carmen gives her a sad nod of agreement. Now a whistle sounds to rally the runners. Carmen squeezes Angie's hand through the steel mesh.

"Any last minute advice?" the young woman asks.

"Do a proper warm-up. And when you get to the point where you think you're about to croak, keep going. There's always life left, even when you can't see it."

A few minutes later the starter's pistol goes off and Carmen bursts out of the enclosure jostling against hundreds of runners who are about to do violence to their bodies to prove to themselves they have the stuff of winners, of survivors, to forget their shortcomings and faults, to stop thinking altogether, or to lose themselves in the essence of absolute effort. The throng on either side of the road cheers them on. Despite the massive number of spectators, Carmen immediately spots Marcus's face. Overjoyed, she veers away from her path to slap his open hand. When she gets closer she sees he is holding a daffodil petal out for her. She slows down to snatch it and puts it against her lips. Marcus kisses her fingertips as she picks up the pace again, her strides diligent, her ambition discreet, running at the speed of those the pack never catches up with but who don't overtake the frontrunners. Those who run for the sake of running and nothing else.

Simon wakes up and checks his alarm clock: 3:20 p.m. He mechanically turns on the TV. A glowing female announcer declares the weather will be dry with a gentle breeze. He lets her gush while he puts the water on to boil, and then he comes back and settles into the sofa with a pale cup of tea and some porridge. The weather report gives way to the news; the local news begins with a shot of the always majestic Golden Gate. Below the bridge the Coast Guard is hoisting a body out of the water. The man threw himself into the Bay at sunrise. Before jumping he apparently chalked a message on the pavement: *Freed from my fate*.

"Poor guy," Simon mutters.

He hears the sound of knocking and believes at first that it's coming from the TV. But when the sound grows more insistent, Simon goes to the door in disbelief. No one has knocked on his door since he moved in here. He slips the door chain without giving it any thought.

When after months of separation you see a person with whom you previously had spent a great deal of time, there is always something peculiar about her appearance. Carmen has not changed, but her hair tied in a ponytail seems longer and drier than ever. Her chin looks pointier, her muscles harder. Her lean chest now appears to have a hollow, a concave space where someone might plant his cheek, or fist. There are tears streaming down her face.

Without asking permission she walks in and collapses on the couch. Her sobbing rises when she sees the images of the events below the bridge. Simon does not wonder at how easy it is for him to sit down beside her, to wrap his right arm around her, to hold his sister in face of the winds working to uproot her from the clear, measurable world that she has always dealt with equably. Without speaking, they return to the original magma of their story, the wound that made them into steadfast allies.

After a few minutes Carmen finally opens her mouth.

"It's Marcus. He's the one who jumped off the bridge. It's my fault."

It doesn't even occur to Simon to ask who Marcus is or what in the world Carmen might have done to drive him to suicide. He sighs and gently strokes her hair.

"If only we still had the cat."

Carmen lifts her bloodshot eyes toward him.

"He's at my house, on the mantel. I don't know what I'd do without him."

He chose the Sutro Baths, as if this place explains everything. At least it has helped to loosen his tongue for the first time in months. Carmen listens in amazement to Simon's account of his divorce, his daughter's double life, and his search for Roberto Aurellano. While he talks, Simon mechanically thrusts his finger into the holes dug by the crabs. When he was small,

Carmen had him believe that under the sand was a crab-controlled warren of tunnels and galleries, which could cause the ground to collapse. The boy would walk on tiptoes and fling every crustacean he managed to get hold of into the surf.

Carmen in turn relates her experiences of the past few of months: the Death Race, Magenta Lopez's urn, meeting Marcus. Simon tries to reassure his sister, who is convinced she reopened her friend's wounds by bringing up his family drama.

"He lived with that suffering on a permanent basis. It's the kind of thing that haunts a man, and he can't forget it even for a second. Whatever you told him had no bearing on his decision."

A thin smile finally forms on Carmen's lips.

"I'm so happy to have found you again, brother of mine."

Simon gazes out to sea and squeezes his sister's hand.

"Me too. I'm sorry, Carmen."

Carmen sweeps the air with her hand to brush away her brother's remorse. As the light starts to wane they find a spot on the beach and set about surrounding themselves with sand walls. As children they made this their ritual: as soon as they set foot on the beach they would build a canoe around them and play at braving the incoming tide and the seagulls with their imaginary paddles. This time, however, they make no attempt to row. It is enough just to drift.

"I guess we'll never really understand where we come from."

Carmen doesn't take her eyes off the pointed prow to which she is putting the finishing touches.

"Is it really so important, Simon? You spent more than forty years next to your birth mother. You know more about your true origins than I ever will."

Simon turns around, as if to make certain no ghosts in tailcoats are hanging around the baths.

"That's the point. I was hoping to be something other than Frannie's son."

The light goes down in the prodigious riot of colour exclusive to the Pacific Ocean, its heat, its monsters, its vortex of plastic waste, and its untamed islands soon to be swamped. With the sun now just a golden rib, the brother and sister scan the horizon looking for the famous green flash that appears just as the day star slips away to present a new morning to another continent. Carmen thinks about the pioneers who discovered this spectacle, about the sensation of standing at the world's edge that must have overwhelmed them; it would never leave them again but would cling to their thoughts in prayer, in toil, even in their last resting place. As for Simon, for the first time in months he imagines himself embracing a woman, here, at the mercy of the wind that would add the taste of salt to their kiss. He opens his hands to the air laden with mist and microscopic algae.

The crash of the breakers on the shoreline grows stronger and the roar makes their outstretched legs tingle at the bottom of the sand canoe. The day moves off into the distance, and Carmen and Simon start speaking Spanish, and German, the language they learned in school so Frannie would not understand them, and then various dialects, invented codes, creoles of sad children, until they are repeating themselves, unsaying what they have said, re-Christening themselves. The scent of the nearby woods arrives on the offshore breeze and is accompanied by the noise from the road, the whoosh of passing cars blending with the murmur of the waves in an elusive refrain. On top of this comes a rumble like a deep explosion.

The fierceness of the elements makes it impossible for them to quickly grasp what is happening. Only when their canoe comes alive do they realize the ground is shaking. Suddenly they are shooting down rapids, they are riding a sand storm. Everything is in flux and they have no paddles.

For the first minute they stay calm. But as the quake gains in amplitude and persists, fear wells up inside them. Something enormous is shifting under their feet. The continental beast is turning in its sleep; one tectonic twin is shoving away the other. Simon moves closer to Carmen and presses her hand. Night has fallen; it's hard to see anything but silhouettes. Already, the landscape appears to have changed, with new ruins added to the old, but they cannot be sure of this.

The tremor lasts almost five minutes. When the ground stops moving, the brother and sister have formed into a compact ball that refuses to be undone. The noise of the waves seems twice as loud as before, and a furious commotion has latched onto the air. In the distance they can hear sirens and voices screaming, but around them, no one, no movement of living things. Clasping each other in the wet sand, they are incapable of standing up, of taking stock of the damage, of deciding to head back to the city to help those who are left and to mourn the others. Tonight the fault has spoken, perhaps once and for all. Perhaps the coast has slid into the Pacific never to emerge again; perhaps an entire civilization with its myths, its excesses, its violence, and its poetry has just been engulfed. It already doesn't matter. Carmen and Simon, their eyes fixed on the sea, are waiting for the wave. If part of the world has fallen into the ocean, out of it will surge an equal part of water. Archimedes' laughter reaches them while, far away, oceanic shadows bare their teeth, the grin of those that will subdue everything.

The Sisters in the Walls
(MONETTE AND ANGIE)

AMID THE TUMULT of sirens and tourniquets, Angie sees nothing. Not the movement of the stretcher, not the comings and goings of the paramedics, not the great absence below her knees. She does not hear Monette sobbing in the arms of a policeman, or the neighbour saying how to get in touch with their mother, or the birds that don't care and keep on keening because it's hot, because the tree barks are alive with larvae. The only things Angie manages to recognize are the silhouettes of two little girls. The only thing she hears is Mam's voice telling them that story before putting them to bed. The story of the little girls in the walls.

In a crooked old house, two inseparable sisters had parents who were mean and stupid and would beat them morning and night and shut them in a closet, sometimes for days. The little girls stayed there and made no attempt to escape because even though they did not like to be locked up in the dark, they had far more to fear on the outside.

One day they discovered a secret passageway from the closet to the space between the walls, which allowed them to move throughout the house. Since the place was in a bad state of repair, they could look through the cracks into the rooms. Keeping quiet, they knew what their parents were up to at any given moment and could be back in the closet when it was time to be let out.

Protected in this way and enjoying the advantages of spying, the two sisters began to be less afraid of their father and mother. Pretty soon they came to see them as mere scarecrows whose bellies were stuffed with straw. Speaking in whispers, the girls learned to make fun of their parents, to laugh at their cruelty and foolishness.

Then they hit on the idea of never leaving the walls. What was the point, they said to each other, of obediently going back into the closet only to be beaten anew? The elder sister stole nails, while the younger, a hammer. Then, after patiently waiting for their parents to go shopping, they slipped through the passageway and sealed it for good. When their father came home he could not find them anywhere. Their mother went to the window and started shouting their names. Inside the opposite wall, the two children laughed to themselves.

The parents looked for them everywhere and wept at having lost them, but the sisters never wavered. At night before going to sleep, one of the girls would slip her arm through a hole in the pantry and take cookies, potatoes, raw eggs. They slept back to back and spent their days making up silent songs or pantomimes in which fairies danced with show dogs, and they learned to write by etching letters into the panelling.

After a few months, their parents gave up all hope of finding them again, and they were declared dead. From time to time they would amuse themselves by scratching or whistling between the planks to frighten their erstwhile tormentors, who would go out to the garden in the middle of the night, believing the house was haunted. When, out of exhaustion, the parents decided to move to a faraway city, the two little girls chose not to leave the labyrinth. They stayed between the walls, their bodies growing flatter and wider, their thoughts and joys flattened out, their days unfolding horizontally. Still today, when visitors come to explore the abandoned house, they knock on the partitions, and those with keen ears can hear smothered laughter, an eggshell cracking, the rustle of a skirt, and a hand turning a page as large as a wall.

ABOUT THE CHARACTERS

THE SITUATION of Ariel and Marie is based on the one of a British couple whose marriage was annulled in 2011 after the truth about their origins came to light. Their respective parents had never told them they were adopted. Hence, on the day they pronounced their wedding vows they were unaware of having a twin sibling. Their identity has never been revealed, and my characters, as well as their occupations, family circumstances, temperaments, and decisions are entirely the fruits of my imagination.

The Angie character was inspired by Anaiah Rucker, who, at the age of nine, saved her younger sister's life by pushing her out of the way of a truck. She lost a leg in the accident. That she hails from Georgia is, as far as I know, the only feature she shares with little Angie and her sister.

Madeleine's story draws on the life of Karen Keegan, one of the very rare natural "chimeras" identified by science. But while the sequence of events in the fictional narrative—kidney disease, compatibility tests, absence of genetic filiation, and then the discovery of two distinct DNAs in the same woman—coincides with that of the lived experience, Madeleine Sicotte and those close to her are in no way similar to Ms. Keegan and her family and intimates.

As for Joanna, she is modelled on someone I met during a trip to Asia several years ago. I have changed very little except for the traveller's name, and her presence in my story should be seen as a humble tribute to that larger-than-life woman.

Aside from this one outright debt to reality, I have taken nothing from the other stories but their framework, to which I have added several layers of fiction, so that my characters should not be regarded as copies of actual persons. If any of them should by chance—something I have learned to be wary of—read this novel, I respectfully thank them for lending an impetus to my work through the extraordinary paths they have followed and their no doubt equally remarkable courage.

ABOUT THE AUTHOR

CATHERINE LEROUX was born in suburban Montreal in 1979. She studied philosophy at Université de Montréal, and worked at a wide variety of jobs in Quebec, Ontario, the United States, and Europe. She later became a journalist and was the Toronto correspondent for Radio-Canada. Her first novel, *La marche en forêt*, was nominated for the 2012 Quebec Booksellers' Prize. *The Party Wall*, her second novel, was a finalist for the 2013 Grand Prix du Livre de Montréal and won the prestigious Prix France-Québec in 2014. Both novels were published in France. Her most recent book, the story sequence *Madame Victoria*, appeared in 2015.

Catherine Leroux lives in Montreal, where she is a full-time writer and translator.

ABOUT THE TRANSLATOR

LAZER LEDERHENDLER is a full-time translator specializing in contemporary Québécois fiction and nonfiction. His translations have earned him many distinctions, including the Governor General's Literary Award and the Cole Prize for Translation of the Quebec Writers' Federation. His work has helped acquaint English-language readers with a new cohort of talented, innovative writers, such as Nicolas Dickner, Alain Farah, Perrine Leblanc, and Catherine Leroux.